ROGUE AGENDA

by
KEVIN PAUL TRACY

Published By
Daydream Industries, Inc.
http://www.DaydreamIndustries.com

ROGUE AGENDA

ISBN-13: 978-0615857855
ISBN-10: 061585785X

Cover Art by Donna Murillo.

For Cecil.

ACKNOWLEDGEMENTS

Thanks to John Turley, Mario Acevedo, Jeff Shelby, Jeanne Stein, the Tuesday night Southwest Critique Group, and Rocky Mountain Fiction Writers (http://www.RMFW.org.)

Additional thanks to Mom, Jimma, Sheryl, Sue, and Lisa.

CHAPTER 1

Lainie Parker rolled her eyes as her phone rang. She turned the TV off with the remote and picked up the receiver. Only one kind of call would be coming in at 2 AM.

"Hello, Kim."

"Hi, Lainie. You're next up on the roster."

"Cool," Lainie said. "Thanks."

She hung up. Making herself comfortable on the recliner, she picked up the small laptop computer from the end table next to the phone and balanced it on her knees. Opening her browser, she entered the URL for the website of Capri Entertainment, Inc. and entered the staff area. Answering with her ID and password, she was rewarded with her call screen. The man's name lurked at the top.

When a customer called he got a Screener, like Kim, who took down his credit card information and telephone number. All Lainie could see was his first name and telephone number, so she could call him back through the web site, and any notes about his preferences or prior calls.

Putting on her headset and adjusting the microphone so that it hung suspended on its armature in front of her lips, she pressed the call button. She wasn't entirely sure how the call went through over the Internet, something Orin the

1

technician called *VOIP*, but he promised her that there was no way anyone could trace the call back to her. She was safe from psychos.

"Hello," came the man's voice over the line. The screen said his name was Michael and he was thirty years old...just four years older than Lainie.

"Hi, Michael," Lainie said in her sultriest voice. "This is Samantha."

"Hi, Samantha." He sounded sort of nervous and uncertain, like a newby, not all familiar and creepy like a regular.

As the call timer churned away at the top of the screen, steadily chewing chunks out of his credit card, Lainie sighed, long and sensuously. "I'm, bored, Michael. What are you doing tonight? Would you like to entertain me?"

Her job, according to Mitch, her boss, was to keep that timer rolling as long as possible.

"I...um...could you just...start...y'know?"

It was a delicate balance.

"Of course, sweetie," she said.

Draw out the titillation too far and the caller got frustrated and was likely to hang up, but let things get too hot too fast and he was liable to finish early, same result. Newbies popped quickly, just like in real life, but if you can somehow hook them enough to call back, it usually took progressively longer the next few times.

Lainie turned the TV back on, muted, and activated the closed captioning. *Notorious*, starring Cary Grant and Ingrid Bergman, a black and white Hitchcock classic.

The screen said Michael liked it straight, no kink. Thank God for that, at least. "First of all, I'm there right now. Can you see me, standing by your bed? I'm five-ten, long blond hair, jade eyes, in a nightie. A red one. My legs are long and tanned. As I slip one strap off, you..."

"No."

"Pardon?"

"No sex," Michael said. "Just...just be nice to me.

Okay?" His voice cracked on *okay*.

"Well, I...um...okay. I sit on the edge of the bed beside you. I stroke your arm. I've never met a man as handsome and strong as you."

She heard him sigh, not with pleasure, but with impatience.

"No," she amended, "I mean, you are kind, and a little funny, you make me laugh. That's what makes you attractive to me, whether others see it or not."

This time the sigh was no less exasperated. "This is stupid," Michael said.

"What is?" she asked.

"You don't even know me."

"Sort of the point," she said.

"It's like sending flowers to yourself on Valentine's Day, only even more...pathetic."

"Stop it," Lainie said. "That's not fair." She turned off the TV again and sat up in the chair. "Look, you sound lonely. Nothing's wrong with that."

He didn't answer.

"It's better than slitting your wrists, isn't it?"

No answer.

"Michael?"

"I gotta go."

"Wait, Michael, you're not thinking of doing something like that, are you?"

"No."

"Really?"

"Now I'm really sorry I called," he said. His voice got hard, ugly. "I had to get the one phone-sex girl with a heart of gold."

"Fuck you," she moved the mouse pointer to the *hang-up* button, but when he didn't respond immediately, she hesitated.

"Samantha?"

"What?"

"Don't hang up."

"Why? Are you done being an asshole?"

He sighed. "I shouldn't have called. It was selfish of me to burden you with my angst. For talking to you like that. For everything."

"Are you a writer?" she asked.

"Um, no. Why?"

"Angst. No one says that these days." His laugh sounded hollow. "I'm a fact finder."

"A what?"

"You ever watch the news? Ever see the newscasters compare this snowfall with the one back in 1864, or those election results with the ones in Nowhere, Kentucky in aught-six, or reminisce about the price of rice husks in Romania back in the fifteenth century? That's me. I find those facts for them."

"You must be smart."

"Just know where to find facts, that's all. You sound young. You in college, Samantha?"

"Graduate school," she said, "last leg."

"What's your major?"

"Doctorate in education, with a focus on special ed."

"Handicapped kids?"

"Excuse me," she said in mock disdain, "we prefer challenged to handicapped."

"Sorry. So you must do sign language, read Braille, all that stuff."

"Yup, all that stuff."

"Smart yourself."

"Thanks." She found herself smiling.

"So you do this to pay your way?"

"Uhuh. Friend got me into it. Lots of girls do. It doesn't pay as much as porn, but it's safer."

"And cleaner."

"And less embarrassing."

"How so?"

"You can't see all my cellulite."

"Oh."

"And there won't be videos of me circulating around for years to come to bite me in the ass, no pun intended, during an interview with Barbara Walters down the road."

"There's that."

"It could happen."

"Sure. Samantha?"

"Yes, Michael."

"Are you really wearing a red nightie?"

"Truthfully?"

"Yes."

"No. I'm wearing sweatpants and an oversized T-shirt with two pigs doing it and the slogan 'Makin' Bacon' on it."

He laughed, more naturally this time. "And the cellulite?"

"Tight as a drum, Baby," she said, not entirely truthfully.

"I'll have to take your word on that."

She realized that once again this call had turned into more of a therapy session than phone sex. It intrigued her how often this happened. Assured of her complete anonymity, Lainie never balked at talking on a personal level with her clients like this. She was careful not to give any identifying information like her real name or the city she was calling from.

"It's good talking to you," he said. "I feel better."

"I'm glad. No more talk of suicide?"

"I didn't talk about suicide, you did. I'm not suicidal. Maybe at one time, maybe not too long ago, but not now. Haven't you ever thought about it, though, even knowing you never would?"

"No."

"Never been depressed?"

"Well, yeah, but..."

"You're depressingly well adjusted, Samantha," he said.

"No I'm not," she said.

"No? Tell me one of your deep, dark secrets."

"No."

"C'mon."

"Well..."

"What?"

"I chew my toenails."

"No."

"I do. When I'm watching TV. I sometimes pull my foot up to my mouth and bite my toenails off."

"Setting aside how suggestive such flexibility is, why do you do that?"

"I don't know. Habit." She was embarrassed now, vaguely defensive.

"Well as deep dark secrets go, that one's not really very provocative. Creepy, just a little. Definitely worth a call to Guinness. But not really Earth-shattering."

"Fine, tell me one of yours."

He was silent.

"Michael?"

"I have to go."

"Oh no," she laughed. "You made me tell you one of my deep dark secrets. Now you have to tell me one of yours. You hang up on me and I'll put a thousand dollars worth of charges on your card."

"Samantha...I can't." His voice had gone all dark again.

"Why not?"

"I..."

"Look," she said, "this blind thing works both ways. The service doesn't give you my real name, and they don't give me any information about you except your first name and telephone number. Who am I going to tell? Come on. Dish."

He was quiet for a long time.

"I killed my first man at the age of twelve."

"Yeah, right," Lainie laughed. "Seriously, now."

He laughed, but it sounded forced, false. "Okay, seriously. I love the smell of expended ordinance...burnt gunpowder."

Lainie thought she should laugh again, but somehow, it didn't come. She just sat, her smile fading.

"I gotta go, Samantha."

She didn't say anything.

"Samantha?"

"Huh?"

"I just wanted to say thanks. You're a real peach. You have a nice..."

The gunshot was so loud in the headset that Lainie jumped, her laptop rebounding off the coffee table and crashing to the floor.

CHAPTER 2

She heard wet, raspy breathing. Michael's? Then there was a rattling sound as someone picked up the phone on that end from where it had fallen.

"Who's this?" A man's voice. Low. Not Michael's. Menacing.

"Who's this?" she asked.

"What's your name?"

"L...Samantha. Who are you?"

"Samantha what?"

"Samantha fucking-your-mother's-ass. Who's this?"

"Where are you right now, Samantha?"

"Fuck you. Where's Michael?"

"Who's Michael?"

"What have you done to him?"

"Never mind," he said, his voice dripping with venomous evil. "I'll find you. I always win."

The line went dead.

"Michael," Samantha screamed. "Michael."

She scooped up her laptop. A corner of the LCD screen was shattered, splattering the screen in the liquid rainbow colors of erupted imaging technology. But enough of the screen still showed the image of the website that she could see the red flashing word, "Disconnected."

CHAPTER 3

Her phone rang.

"Mitch?"

"What's up, Lainie?"

"Mitch, tell Kim she has to call the cops. I've been trying to get her to call the cops and she won't."

"I know," Mitch said. "It's policy."

"Policy? Policy. A man is dead and you're talking about policy?"

"We don't know if he's dead."

"I heard the gunshot. And then another man got on and he..."

"A man? Your John?"

She hated the way Mitch called them Johns, like she and the others really were no better than streetwalkers.

"No, another guy. This one was creepy."

"Yes, and that makes him different than all of the other callers we get in this business how?"

"It wasn't Michael. This guy shot Michael."

"Lainie, calm down, okay? Let me tell you a little story. One of my girls, she had a regular. Guy fell in love with her, okay, just from the sound of her voice. She wasn't a looker like you. She was three-hundred pounds, acne like the surface of the moon. When she wouldn't meet him, go out with him, he threatened suicide. Finally, he just stopped talking. That's all it took, just left the line open and stopped talking and she got convinced he'd done himself in. So against policy we went ahead and called the cops, and bet your ass when they busted in he was sittin' on the phone listening to her cry and whacking off.

"Lainie, these guys, the ones who call, well most of them are fat, zit-faced, mamma's-boy, can't-get-a-date losers to begin with. They'll do anything to get a rise out of you. Well, we just don't play their games any more. Strict policy, Lainie, we don't get involved."

"Mitch," Lainie tried to calm her voice, "I've been doing this for five years, long enough to tell the freaks from the straights. This wasn't your typical attention-grabber. This guy was different."

"They're all different," Mitch said, "that's what I just spent five minutes trying to tell you. Five minutes of my life I'll never get back, by the way. Go to bed. You're off duty for the night."

He hung up.

*   *   *

"Detective Gillis," Lainie heard after an eternity on hold.

"I need to report a murder."

His voice perked up, "Your name and address?"

"Lainie Parker. Twenty-three-twenty-two Flatbush Way, apartment C."

"Okay, we'll be right there."

"Wait. The murder didn't happen here."

"Oh? Why did you leave the scene?"

"I didn't. I was never there."

She explained it to him.

"You called 911?"

"Yes, but they couldn't do anything without an address to send someone to."

"Thought so. So you called me direct. Lady, your boss is most likely right. This guy's just yankin' your chain."

"And what if he isn't?"

"Well, I'm not sure it's in our jurisdiction. We'd have to trace the number, maybe get access to your company's records to cross-check and make sure it's the same guy, which could mean waking up a judge to get a warrant...hold on a second."

On hold again.

Notorious was over. They were showing an old *M.A.S.H.* rerun. Lainie saw the ending credits before Gillis came back on the line.

"I was right, Ms. Parker. Out of our J. You need the FBI because the incident happened over a phone line routed through the Internet. That's interstate commerce. That's federal."

"Well do you have their number?"

*   *   *

The eastern San Francisco skyline was lightening, splayed fingers of crimson outlined in tangerine reaching westward out to a still-dark sea, when the FBI guy showed up at her door. He was about six feet tall with brown hair receding and wire-rim glasses. He wore a navy suit and red tie and he looked tired.

"Ms. Parker? Agent Peck."

Lainie studied the proffered ID, shook the offered hand, and stepped aside to let him enter. She had dressed in jeans and a halter when he had called to tell her he'd be over, her black hair tossed negligently up in a butterfly clip.

"Do you have coffee?" he asked.

"No," she said. "How about a coke?"

They retired to her breakfast nook, he with the bright red can in front of him, before he seemed ready to tell her anything.

"First, that business about interstate commerce and all? Mostly a marginal call at best. Detective just didn't want to

11

get off his fat ass. However, turns out after we traced the number you gave us that the guy was calling from Commerce City, Colorado, so probably would have ended up in our laps, anyway."

"So did you find him? Was he..."

"Motel off State Highway 2. Sent a guy from the Denver office to check it out. Room was clean. Not so much as an eyelash. Checked the books and the gentleman hadn't checked out when he left, but that's not unusual."

"Did you fingerprint the place?"

Agent Peck leveled his gaze at her. "Let me get this straight. Guy calls you for phone sex, you hear what you think may have been a gunshot. I don't get it. What's your percentage in all this?"

"How about finding out whether a man is dead and who killed him?"

"No," Peck shook his head. "That's my line. What's yours?"

In the face of his cynicism how could she explain the way her heart stopped when she heard the gunshot? Or the intuition that never let her down before and told her now that the second voice, the voice of the killer, wasn't Michael putting on a false tone and accent?

"Look," she said, "maybe Mitch is right. Maybe Detective Gillis is right. Maybe the guy faked it all to get attention, and maybe that's the most logical explanation. What do I know? But I feel like I should at least put in the minimum effort to find out for sure, don't you? I mean it is your job after all."

"Fair enough," Peck said.

Lainie shrugged. "What's next?"

"Unfortunately, nothing," he said. "Nothing more to go on."

"A man might have been murdered."

"Ma'am," he said, "we have no evidence. We have no way to even identify who may have been on the phone with you last night."

She frowned at him. "Then why come all the way to my apartment, just to tell me this?"

He didn't answer.

"You came to check me out," she said, "see what kind of a crackpot I am."

He just met her eyes without blinking.

"Fine," she said, "it doesn't matter, whatever got you out here. How about the company's records? They have his credit card number, and to charge against that they had to have his name. His *real* name. The detective said something about subpoenaing those records..."

"Ms. Parker, we only have your word on what went on last night, what you heard. Maybe I believe you. But it isn't enough to open a case book. Chances are your boss was right about this guy just wanting your attention. Don't you think he's gotten enough of that? And frankly, I can't justify spending more time on this case without more to go on."

She nodded. "I understand."

"I'm sorry," Peck said, placing his card on the table between them and standing to leave.

Lainie wished there was a way that he could hear what she heard in Michael's voice last night, experience those little neck-hairs bristle at the sound of the killer's voice like she did.

Peck almost made it to the door when Lainie galvanized.

"Recording."

"Pardon me, Ma'am?" Peck turned back to her.

"Recording," she said again. "The company records the calls, keeps them on file for, I don't know, six months or so. For legal reasons, in case a minor steals his father's credit card, or a wife discovers the charge on her husband's card and he tries to claim fraud or something. At least go there, ask them to listen to it. You'll hear for yourself."

"Okay," Peck nodded indulgently.

"Please."

"Okay, Ma'am," he said again and saw himself out.

*   *   *

Lainie spent the Sunday catching up on mundane errands. She had papers to grade for the 600 level Psychology class she was assisting, but she couldn't concentrate on that right now. She needed something to occupy her time while she waited for Peck to check out the recording of the call and call her back.

The tech service guy at the computer store where she'd bought her laptop told her that, odd as it sounded, replacing the LCD screen of her computer was going to cost her more than the machine itself was worth and introduced her to a newer, sleeker, faster model with more memory and disk space. Luckily he'd be able to transfer everything from her old hard drive to the new one intact and have it ready for her to pick up by Monday afternoon.

She dropped off some dry cleaning and picked up some theater tickets. She got her fifteen-year-old Chevy Blazer washed and mailed some bills. She had lunch at a deli called Ruben's and an Italian ice at a place called Giaguardi's. Finally, she picked up some printer paper and a few small items at the grocery store.

By 5:00 she was home and had put everything away. She sat at her desk in the living room looking at a stack of Psychology papers that demanded her attention and fumed. Agent Peck hadn't called. He hadn't taken her seriously. He hadn't gone by Capri Entertainment, Inc. and requested the recording of Michael's phone call.

His card still rested on the table next to the half-empty can of Coke. She dialed his number, asked for him and got put on hold. The longer she was made to wait, the angrier and more determined she became. After almost twenty minutes he came on the line.

"Agent Peck, whose this?"

"You know good goddamn well who this is, Peck. You left me on hold so long because you hoped I'd just give up."

"Ms. Parker, how good of you to call."

"I want to know why you didn't call me back. Did you

even listen to the recording like I said?"

"You didn't tell us he threatened to commit suicide."
He had listened to it.

"What does that have to do with anything? Do suicides usually shoot themselves in mid sentence on a long-distance telephone call?"

"He didn't shoot himself."

"That's what I've been saying."

"Because if he had, we'd have found his corpse in the motel room, and a real mess for housecleaning, to boot. But the suicide threat does support your boss's interpretation of events more than it does yours."

He was right, it did. She felt her heart sink in embarrassment.

"Tell me, Ms. Parker," Peck's voice took on that particular brand of condescension reserved by cops for lunatics and children. "Do you have a boyfriend?"

"What does that have to do with anything?"

"Might have everything to do with why you want to believe this guy's stunt so badly. Might be you need to believe it."

"I'm not making this up just to get attention, Agent Peck."

"Okay. Was there anything else the FBI can do for you Ms. Parker?"

"Is there anything else that can be done to find out what happened to this guy?"

"Nope," he said cheerily. "Not unless you have more for us to go on."

"Do you understand what I'm asking? I want to be sure."

"How often do we get to be sure," he asked, "about anything?"

She hung up, hating Agent Peck for being right.

*　　　*　　　*

She clawed up out of her sheets, which seemed to

constrict around her like the cold wet tendrils of a giant octopus. She was drenched, not with water but with a thick film of slimy sweat stinking of fear. Her heart was beating so fast it throbbed in her ears like terror drumming to get out. She trembled, not shaken with the cold sweat but with a chill that went into her bones and made her teeth rattle.

She got up and rushed into the dark bathroom, ran a hot shower and stood under it, hands pressed against the hard, real tile as she turned her head this way and that, letting the water warm her and center her.

In her dream faceless men were lined up in front of her, kneeling, blindfolded, facing away from her, their hands bound behind them. She was similarly bound but not blindfolded. Someone wanted something from her and every time she begged them to believe she didn't know what it was, a hand came into view from behind her holding a huge black gun that smelled like rotting flesh and put a bullet into the head of another one of the men. The bullets flung each man forward into a tumble and blood spattered her face like spittle. By the time she woke up she'd been screaming in the dream and sobbing, begging the assailant to shoot her instead.

Even as the dream faded, washed down the drain with the water that brought her solidly back to reality, Lainie reflected that the gunshot on the phone shook her more than she realized. It was real, she hadn't imagined it, and the voice of the killer was just too sinister and threatening to be faked. Wasn't it?

Real or not, she knew she wasn't done. Not yet. She needed to be as sure as Mitch, Detective Gillis, and Agent Peck. She knew the nightmare wouldn't leave her alone until she found out for sure.

CHAPTER 4

There were two kinds of receptionists at Capri Entertainment, Inc. There were several switchboard receptionists who screened callers and paired them up with the talent, the girls like Lainie who would talk them through whatever fantasy would bring them the release they sought. Then there was a flamboyant boy of nineteen named Louis who manned the front desk. As Lainie walked in Monday morning he looked at her as if he didn't recognize her. Why should he? Working from home, she'd only been to the offices two or three times.

"Can I help you," Louis said, and then without waiting for her answer pointed with his pen over his shoulder, "auditions in the back."

"Lainie Parker," she said. "I work here. Talent."

"Ah," he said, beaming. "Are you here to pick up a check?"

"No," she said. Her wages were direct-deposited in her bank account and the company mailed her pay stub to her. "But I'd like to talk to Orin."

"Sure," he said. "Do you know where his office is? Then go on back."

Lainie rounded the big reception desk and headed along one of the corridors leading back. The offices of Capri

Entertainment were elegant and professional, not overly decorated or cluttered. Lined with doors into single offices, the hallway was well lit and clean, not dim and murky and lined with posters of centerfolds as one might expect.

Orin's office was almost as far back as the phone bank where Kim and the other screeners worked, and it was on the opposite side of the suite from Mitch's office. Chances of running afoul of either Kim or Mitch were slim, but Lainie remained alert anyway. If Mitch or Kim spotted Lainie in the office they'd most likely suspect why she was here and roust her.

Orin hit on her every time she came to the office and every time she called for troubleshooting help when the website wasn't responding, but then he probably did that with all of the girls. She hoped he remembered her.

"Lainie." Orin was an emaciated man with a black, oily comb-over and dandruff on his shoulders, who might be attractive if he worked out some and went outside more often, got a little color to that pasty flesh. His office was cluttered with four computers of different styles and designs, a dizzying array of peripherals, and stacks of programming and coding books.

"Don't get up, Orin," she said. "I just wanted to ask you something. I'm getting a new computer and I thought I might look into one of those digital music players everyone's been talking about. I wondered if you could help me understand what to look for."

"Sure," he said, jolly and sliding his guest chair toward her.

She sat.

"They're called MP3 players, even the iPod which technically plays audio at MP4 compression, and they're really something nifty," he said, sneaking a breath mint. "They hook up to your computer and you can copy CD's right onto them. There are no disks, no moving parts at all, which means no skipping while you're jogging or working out, and the sound is CD quality."

"Okay, now what if I have a recording on my computer and I want to copy it to a standard tape, like this one?" She handed him a blank audio tape.

"Analog?" he asked, curling his lip. "Why would you want to do that?"

Lainie shrugged. "Because I still have an old cassette tape player I like to use."

"Well, whatever, it's easy, just hook up your tape recorder to your computer's headphone jack, hit record and play the file."

"Could you show me?"

"Sure," he said.

She watched as he rummaged for an old dusty cassette tape recorder deep under the workbench along one wall of his office, fumbled with cords, and explained every step that he did.

"Now, what would you like me to put on the tape to show you?"

"Oh I don't know," she said, hoping she didn't sound too casual. "Let's just pick something at random. How about my last call on service? Let's record that."

"Sure," he said, and typed wildly on his computer. "I'm actually not supposed to have the password to these archives, but since I set the system up, of course..."

Lainie's imagination flashed on an unsavory image of Orin listening to these recordings in the privacy of his dank, dark cave here and suppressed a shudder.

Orin operated the record button on the tape deck and clicked his mouse.

Kim: "Hello, Capri Entertainment?"

Michael: "Um...hi..."

Kim: "Hi, sweetie. Would you like to talk to one of my girlfriends?"

Michael: "Um, sure. How do we do this?"

Kim: "Well, Hun, you give me your credit card number and some other information, and then I have a girl who fit's your preferences call you back in just a few minutes. Okay?"

Michael: "Guess so."

"Orin, can you turn that down a sec," Lainie said.

He did, to a low murmur they could barely hear.

"So," Lainie said to keep him talking, "tell me how this whole digital thing works. Why is the sound quality so much better?"

Orin waxed technological as the progress bar on his computer advanced slowly on and the tape in the recorder spun silently. Lainie endured this dry, tedious diatribe stoically, nodding and smiling in encouragement at just the right places, one eye on the advance of the digital playback. As soon as it reached it's end...

"Well, Orin, I'm sorry, but this is all just a little too, y'know, over my head. I'll just have to take your word for it. Thanks for the help though. I think I know what I'm looking for now." Then, as if it were an afterthought, "Oh, can I have my tape back?"

"But," Orin protested, taking the tape out of the recorder and handing it to Lainie. "We haven't discussed brands and memory expansion cards and..."

"Well, I have class, so I'll call you, okay?"

"'Kay," he said meekly.

CHAPTER 5

Lainie was anxious to listen to the tape as soon as she got home, but she hadn't been lying to Orin about having a class to assist-teach, Ecological Sociology, and then she needed to go pick up her new computer from the shop. By the time she got home it was nearly 5:00 again.

She had a digital music player, of course, but the tape was the best way she could think of to get Orin to copy the call without implicating him in her breach of protocol. Popping the tape into the deck in her stereo that hadn't seen use in years, Lainie jotted down the name Michael gave - Gaston - and his American Express number. Kim hadn't requested his mailing address, all she'd needed was his zip code to authorize the card, and Lainie wrote this down, too.

Turning on her computer she looked up zip codes on the Internet and found that the one he'd given, 92014, was Del Mar, California near San Diego, 500 miles south of San Francisco. She was looking up a Michael Gaston in Del Mar, California and wondering why the cops couldn't have done even this minimum effort in investigating, when her phone rang.

"Hello."

"Lainie?"

"Mitch." Her heart stopped.

"Heard you came by the office."

"Well..."

"Keep the tape, Kiddo," he said. "But you're fired. Okay?"

"'Kay," she said in much the same tone Orin had hours ago.

"So's Orin."

"But, Mitch, I..."

Mitch hung up.

They couldn't file theft charges against her because Orin, as a company employee with access, had given her the tape freely, so they'd fired him, too. Lainie felt two inches tall.

According to the online yellow pages, Michael and Adrian Gaston lived at 1450 S. Gramercy Circle, no apartment number. He was married. She jotted down the address and the telephone number given, then dialed the phone.

Not even sleaze-ball wife-cheaters deserved to be shot down in a motel room in Colorado.

"Hello." Man's voice.

Michael's?

She couldn't be sure. He'd have had time to fly back from Colorado in the thirty-six hours since she'd spoken to him on the phone. It sort of sounded like him and it sort of didn't.

She hung up.

She needed a better plan.

Her phone rang. The caller ID screen said it was Michael Gaston calling from Del Mar, California. At first she didn't pick it up, then realizing that would only pique his curiosity, she snatched at the handset.

"Did you just call here?" he asked.

"Yes," she said. "But when you answered I realized I had a wrong number."

"Who were you calling."

"Shaky's Pizza."

"Gee, there hasn't been a Shaky's Pizza in Del Mar since...well I don't know how long. Mother and I have lived here for nigh on forty year and I don't know if I ever recall a Shaky's Pizza."

"Thanks," Lainie said and hung up.

Now that she heard it at length, the voice wasn't even remotely like Michael's. Very possibly the man she spoke to via the website two nights ago, whoever he was, stole the identity and the credit card number given to Capri, a common enough occurrence.

Now, at last, Lainie lay to rest her instinct that the shooting she overheard was authentic. All evidence seemed to confirm Mitch's interpretation of things. She lost her job and, worse, got creepy but harmless little Orin fired for nothing.

Feeling stupid, Lainie tried to cheer herself up by treating herself to dinner out and a movie, finally graded those Psychology papers, and went to bed at 11:00 as humiliated as ever.

*　　　*　　　*

Shortly after 2:00 her phone rang.

"Hello?"

"Okay, I made my point." Mitch. "Care for a second chance?"

"Sure," Lainie said. "Wait, Orin too?"

"Huh?"

"Does Orin still have his job, too?"

"Oh shit. Fine. Whatever. But don't fuck up again, okay?"

Mitch transferred the call to Kim.

"Lainie? Mitch was so mad. Wonder what made him change his mind?"

"Don't know," Lainie said.

"Well, we have one here who has asked for you by name."

"That's why."

"What?"

"Why Mitch changed his mind. Money. It's always about money with Mitch."

"You're probably right." Kim didn't seem comfortable discussing their employer in this way.

"Okay, I'm on it, Kim. Thanks."

Lainie was booting her computer as she hung up, taking the warm-up time as an opportunity to go to the fridge and get herself a coke and to wipe sleep-sand out of the corners of her eyes.

According to her profile screen his name was Michael.

The possibility that it was the very same man who called her and faked his own shooting filled Lainie with a cold rage. She nearly called Kim back and told her to tell the caller to go fuck himself, but then she decided she wanted the pleasure herself and clicked on the *connect* button. Michael was a common enough name, and the number was different, she didn't recognize the area code, so she decided to remain cordial at first.

Ringing.

"Hello?" he said.

"You sick, selfish, twisted fuck. Where do you get off?"

Well, so much for cordial.

"Temper, temper, *Samantha*," the voice said, oily and sticky. It wasn't Michael.

It was the man who'd picked up the phone after he shot Michael. He said her stage name in a mocking tone, as if he knew it was fake.

Lainie's blood went icy in her veins.

"Remember me?" he said.

"Where's Michael?"

"There's a dog food manufactory in Denver, did you know that?"

"I don't believe you."

"FBI went snooping around the motel. That your doing?"

"No. They wouldn't believe me."

"Liar."

"They will when I play them this recording."

"They'll never hear it," he said. The sound of glass breaking. "Because I'm going to torch the place."

"What place?"

"Just a second. Let's see, where would I put a switchboard if I was the manager of a sleazy phone sex company? Aha."

"Who are you?" A woman's voice from his end.

"Kim," Lainie yelled, recognizing the voice.

A scream.

A gunshot.

"Better call the cops," he said. There was a moment of silence, then, "And Samantha? I always win." Then the line went dead.

CHAPTER 6

Call the cops she did.

They were there when she arrived, along with about four fire trucks of various size and function. One of three ambulances peeled away with lights flashing but no siren, which was ominous to her. The night was lit-up like dawn by spotlights from the cruisers and fire trucks. She parked at the Denny's across the street and ran toward the barricades. The entire fourth floor of the ten-story structure was smoldering and cascading with water. Firefighters with hoses sprayed water up from the ground. The fire had scorched and blown out the windows, especially at the southeast corner, where much of the walls were gone as well. Debris littered the street.

"Whoah there," a cop said, stopping her from sidling between two orange-striped sawhorses with bold black lettering: DO NOT CROSS. "And who are you?"

"Lainie Parker. I work there...worked there. I was on the phone when he shot her."

"Whoah, what? Who? Shot who?"

"A man. He called. Said he was going to torch the place. He shot Kim. I heard him do it."

"Okay just calm down. Let me take you over to the detectives and let you talk to them."

He let her past the barricade and walked her, hand on

her arm, to a cluster of men gathered around talking in tense, subdued tones. "Detective Gillis, this is Lainie Parker. She says..."

"Parker?" Gillis said, turning. He was one of those men that are slender but still gave off the aura of a fat, rumpled, unhealthy one. His breath smelled of nicotine gum and he had one of those beard-shadows that the closest shave would never completely obliterate.

"Gillis?" Lainie said almost in unison with him.

"Good of you to come to us. Save us the trouble of coming to question you."

"That's her." Louis, the receptionist, stood not far off, shaken and pointing at Lainie.

"Louis?" Lainie said. "What are you doing here?" He was still dressed in his pajamas.

"My loft is just up the street," he said in a quavering voice. "When I heard the blast I was as curious as everyone else."

"We understand you were fired today," Gillis said to Lainie.

"And rehired," Lainie said.

Gillis looked at Louis.

"Mitch didn't say anything about that to me," Louis said. "Last I heard, she was not to be permitted on the premises."

"It was earlier this morning, after hours, after you would have gone home."

Gillis nodded and made notes on a pad, but his sneer was wry and sarcastic.

"Look, I got a call," Lainie said. "It was the guy on the phone. The second one I told you about, Gillis. He said he was going to do this. I heard Kim scream. I heard a shot. Is she dead?"

Gillis was studying Lainie through slitted eyes. "Wasn't she the one who refused to call the cops for you that night?"

Lainie couldn't figure the connection. "Yes. So?"

"So she won't call the cops, and your boss, Mitchell

York, fires you."

"Yes," she said impatiently, "And then he called after midnight to give me another chance because a customer asked for me by name. It turned out to be the guy I told you about who got on the phone after shooting the first guy on the phone. I told you all this before." She felt like she wasn't making any sense, but was trembling too hard to try to slow down and be clearer.

"The two people," he went on relentlessly, "who refused to play into your little delusion and they're both dead, bullets in the head, nearly burned beyond recognition."

Lainie swallowed back bile.

"They and one other employee," Gillis added, "an unfortunate eye witness, who was also disposed of."

"You can't seriously think I..."

"Do you have proof of the call you got tonight, telling you he was going to blow the place?"

"Well no, but the company records all..."

"Conveniently for you," Gillis said, "the firebomb was set in the computer room. The servers got the worst of the blast. No piece in there bigger than a space bar key. Which means, no recording."

Lainie glowered at the detective. "The one piece of evidence that would corroborate my story gets blown up. How is that convenient for me, Detective?"

"Because now you can claim it existed with no proof that it didn't."

"How does that make sense?" She knew she was bellowing and couldn't stop herself.

Gillis just continued to observe her like a cat watches a goldfish in a bowl. The other men present, detectives and fire inspectors, watched her speculatively as well.

"Am I under arrest?"

Gillis took time answering.

"No physical evidence yet, so no. But we'll be watching you. Probably ought to stay in town for a while. Just so you don't spark our imaginations any further, you understand, make us think you're trying to escape justice. Might want to get yourself a lawyer, too."

CHAPTER 7

Lainie fumed and gripped the steering wheel so tightly that her knuckles were white. She couldn't settle on any one of the vast array of emotions coursing through her right now. Grief for Kim's death, and yes even Mitch's, and for the unnamed third victim. Probably Joslyn, the other graveyard-shift switchboard receptionist. The only three in the office at this hour, thank God.

Rage at Gillis' implication of her in the firebombing.

Fear that they might find some reason to arrest her. Fear that whomever had done this, that sinister voice on the phone, might actually find her as he had promised.

She couldn't tell the cops of the threats he had made. Right now they wouldn't believe her if she told them the sky was blue. She thought of people she could call for help or comfort. Her mother was an emotional infant and would need more comfort than Lainie if she heard what was going on. Lainie's little sister was little more than a teenager, freshman at UCLA. Lainie'd spent all of her waking hours concentrating on school and simply hadn't had the time nor, frankly, the inclination to make many friends. She had never before felt as alone and friendless as she did now.

She parked in the spot stenciled with her apartment number and ran up the stairs. All she wanted to do right now was curl up in bed and shut down mentally until everything blew over. She unlocked her door, slipped in and locked all three locks, the knob and two deadbolts, before falling against it and letting out her first small sob.

Lainie hated to cry, but if ever there was an excuse to let herself, she couldn't think of a better one. But tears didn't come. The anger in her was still too close to the surface for the grief and fear to get a solid hold on her tear ducts. Pushing away from the door, she decided that honeyed tea sounded good about now. Maybe spiked with some vodka, she had about a tenth of a bottle she'd filched from a party months ago.

It wasn't until she was halfway to the kitchen that she felt the other presence in the apartment. She hadn't turned on any lights yet and only the parking lot lights filtering in through the vertical blinds of her front window penetrated the gloom. Terror gripped her heart and she froze. She nearly screamed, but instinct stopped her. She waited until she could speak without her voice breaking into a million tears.

"You found my address in the company records." Her voice trembled.

"Umhum," he said. It was the voice of the second man on the phone that night, the killer.

"That's why you were there."

"Umhum," he said again.

Over by the TV. Or maybe the bedroom door. She couldn't tell which. Could she make it to the front door, unlock three locks and run out before he got to her? Impossible.

He killed them for no better reason than so he could get to me.

"How did you get in my apartment?"

"Baby," his voice oozed with sensual violence, "as you're about to find out, I got me all kinds of skills. I always win."

Definitely the bedroom door, only now she heard the susurrus of clothing as he moved. She forced herself not to bolt for the kitchen, much as she wanted to. Blind panic wouldn't save her now. Instead she tried to concentrate on the sound, track him wherever he moved to.

But she couldn't. She simply wasn't used to using her senses in that way. The blind children she had worked with during her dissertation research were very good at it, but they'd had every reason to practice and hone that skill. What she wouldn't give to have one of them with her now.

"You're going to kill me, aren't you?" She heard the despair in her own voice.

"Umhum." He was somewhere by the TV now, she was sure. "Have to, to win." He was trying to get between her and the front door. She began to slide-step slowly toward the kitchen, separated from the living room by nothing but a chest-high bar counter.

"Well that will certainly clear my name," she said, trying to match his jaunty tone. "Cops think I killed Kim and Mitch at the office."

"Really," he said, sounding truly intrigued. "Glad to be of service."

She reached the kitchen. There was a knife rack by the stove. She reached for it. Every knife handle was missing. He'd been busy in her absence. She tried not to let the whimper of fear that vibrated in her throat escape her lips.

"Have you tried the phone," he asked, "or did you go for the knife rack first? I'll bet it was the knives, wasn't it?"

So he'd disabled her phone, too. This shook her but didn't surprise her, it was logical. Her cell phone would be of no use either – he'd be on her before she could finish dialing. She had only one more trick up her sleeve. She hoped to God he hadn't found that, or her last chance was to leap from her window and hope she landed on a bush in the narrow strip of lawn between the sidewalk and the parking lot pavement.

He was on the move again. Apparently guessing she wasn't going for the door, he seemed to be going around the other side of the bar counter, toward the breakfast nook. She knelt and crab-walked to one of her lower cabinets. Opening it, she tried to rummage without making any noise.

Where was the damned thing?

She bumped a pot with her elbow. It fell out with a loud, hollow rattle onto the tiles.

Abandoning all stealth she began pulling anything and everything out of the cabinet. She heard his heals on the floor as he rushed into the kitchen to investigate. She could feel him behind her. The beam of a flashlight backlit her and washed the interior of the cabinet in concentric circles of light. What she sought was there, tucked around the edge of the cabinet opening to the right. She snatched it and rolled away.

There was a hoarse cough and a Dutch-oven kettle on the floor where she had been a split second before rang loudly with the impact of a bullet and flipped back up into the cabinet. She'd heard silencers before on TV, and this sound was just like that.

Lainie gave the valve of the propane torch she'd retrieved from the cabinet a twist and was pulling the trigger of the lighting flint in front even as the beam of light centered on and blinded her. Another bullet splintered the cabinet beside her head as the torch leapt to life with a good-sized ball of yellow flame.

She had bought the torch to make *Crème Brule*, her favorite desert.

Blood red flame briefly illuminated the room, in which she caught a glimpse of a huge hulk of a large, burly man dressed all in black before he lifted his arm to his eyes and backed away from the burst of heat. The gun coughed again, but no sign or sound of where the bullet went. A can of oven cleaner had also been in the cabinet and now lay within reach. Lainie snatched it up and crossed the sprays of propane and sodium hydroxide, increasing the reach of the homemade flamethrower as well as filling the room with lung-scorching fumes.

He fell back, gagging and coughing. Lainie, who was holding her breath, threw the torch at him, hoping to catch him on fire, and did a summersault into the breakfast nook. The torch went out as it struck him. Rising to her feet, she sprinted for the door. She only got one of the deadbolts unlocked before he was on her.

He slammed into her, pressing her against the door, covering her with his bulk and knocking the wind out of her lungs. The fumes rising off of him burned her eyes and her nose and she was grateful that for the moment she couldn't inhale.

"Okay, Bitch," he hissed in her ear. "You've made your escape attempt. Now you can die with a clear conscience."

Lainie felt a cold, hard cylinder pressed to the right side of the base of her skull. He kept pressing, hard, forcing her to tilt her head to the left. Still he pressed, until her head would cock no further and the sharp edge was cutting into her scalp. Her hands were free, but could only scrabble uselessly against the door. Lainie winced and gasped for breath.

"I love it when they fight," he hissed. "Because it pisses me off, and when I'm pissed off, I make it last longer.\"

Lainie was gathering her breath, preserving the tiny gasps his weight would allow her for one, good blast of alarm that would, hopefully, awaken somebody. She was just about to cut loose with the scream when he punched her kidney on the left side and forced it all out again in a silent *whoosh*.

"Nah-uh," he scolded her, his breath hot against the back of her neck. "No fair screaming. Not yet, anyway."

"Why?" she managed to wheeze.

"Because," he said. "You heard me kill him, and you called the cops, which was...inconvenient. I had to track you before they tracked me. I always win."

His explanation only left more questions.

She struggled again and he pressed harder against her, grinding his erection into the crease of her butt, breathing onto her cheek and leaving wet condensation.

A firm and insistent knock caused the door to vibrate and Lainie felt her attacker start in alarm. She tried but was unable to push back away from the door even just enough to fill her lungs and scream. The killer froze, pressing her, waiting.

There was another authoritative lock on the door.

"Ask who it is," he whispered. "Say anything else and I pull the trigger."

"Wh-who is it," she wheezed.

"SFPD," the detective's voice came from the other side. "It's Gilis, Ms. Parker. I need to ask you some more questions about tonight."

Suddenly the pressure was gone, and Lainie was panting to regain her breath, trying to regain enough quickly enough to scream. By the time her breath had replenished itself the killer was gone and Lainie stumbled backward, almost falling to the carpet.

She cast about her but he'd vanished. The blinds over the front window clashed and swung against each other, the window open, letting in the night air. She opened the door and, ignoring Gillis's impatient expression, she ran to the window to see how the intruder intended to get down two stories. He was climbing down a series of decorative mortar blocks that protruded from the wall, seemingly placed perfectly for just such an escape.

Damn, he was nimble.

"Here," she said, motioning to Gillis with urgency.

He stood in the lit doorway peering into the gloom of her apartment as if waiting for his eyes to adjust.

"Come here, now," she demanded. "He's getting away."

But by the time Gillis staggered to the window, the intruder had reached the bushes below and was gone.

CHAPTER 8

"Well, they certainly look like bullet holes," Detective Gillis said, slipping the tip of his pinky into the one in the cabinet door. He bent further to look at the back of the cabinet. "Unfortunately, the bullet went right through the wall. That's an outside wall. Convenient, that."

"Why do you keep saying that," Lainie shouted at him.

He fingered the dent in the pot made by the first bullet while looking all around him as if in search of something. "This one ricocheted. No telling where it went. So no proof that either one was, indeed, a bullet."

"What else would they be," Lainie shouted again.

He turned and looked past her and nodded to the officers at the door, who turned and left. Still, was there a shadow of self-doubt in his eyes? Was he finally beginning to believe her?

He said, "These would appear to be the same caliber as the gun that killed your boss and coworker tonight."

"Well they would be, wouldn't they?" Lainie said, "since it was the same guy."

"Well it's certainly likely to be the same gun, anyway." Gillis watched her.

She glared back.

"If this is an attempt to get attention, Ms. Parker..."

"It isn't."

"If it is, I hope you're not getting your fill just yet, because there's an awful lot more to come once we tie you to some physical evidence at the crime scene."

"And what are you going to do about what happened here, tonight?"

"Well, no evidence except a couple of bullet holes and a scratch on your scalp you claim he made with a gun, but could be anything. Blinds knocked down, could've been anyone. Climbing down the wall? Maybe it's possible, but I wouldn't want to try it. So I'll add this incident report to the growing case file and let you know."

"And what about police protection?"

"Oh, you're being watched," he said, nearly smiling. "Have no fear about that."

He headed for the door.

"By the way," he said, turning back. "Got a lawyer yet?"

"In the last hour? At four-thirty in the morning? No."

He tsked. "Still, I gotta ask. My original reason for coming here. Would you be willing to submit to a gunpowder residue test? Shows whether you've fired a gun. Got a technician waiting outside. Won't take a minute."

"Of course," she said.

"I'll send her right up."

"Thanks for nothing," she said.

"You're very welcome," he said, and left.

CHAPTER 9

The technician swabbed sour-smelling chemicals liberally on Lainie's hands, examined them under some sort of special light and photographed them. Throughout the entire process the blond CSI specialist said nothing, and when she was done she left without giving Lainie any indication whether she had passed or failed the test.

As if there was any doubt.

Lainie was trying to straighten the blinds when she saw the technician leave the building below. Gillis waited for her in the parking lot. Lainie saw them exchange words. Gillis shook his head and scratched it, then nodded to the technician, got in his own car and drove away, the technician soon behind.

It took Lainie thirty minutes to pack and leave the apartment. As she drove to the Holiday Inn on 8th near Market she watched her mirrors almost more than she did the windshield. There was a heavy morning fog clinging to the street corners and lampposts graying out the early light, but it didn't seem as if anyone was following her. Least of all any cop supposedly assigned to keep tabs on her, her one hope for some sort of protection.

She checked-in using the Mastercard she'd gotten just for enrolling in school eight years ago, and found her room. It was clean and neutrally austere, as such rooms are. She stripped, took a shower as hot as she could manage it, then climbed between the crisp sheets and tried to sleep.

A hulking beast chased her out of her dreams and into a waking cold sweat almost every fifteen minutes. The clock advanced slowly in the strobe of her eyelids. It was not a restful sleep at all, and after four hours, at around 9 AM, she finally sat up and stared at the rectangle of light outlining the curtains of the only window.

This couldn't go on. She was so tired she felt like taffy in a pulling machine, all stretched out and aching in the shoulders and neck. What was her plan, to wait here until either the cops arrested and charged her or the murderer found her?

The attacker had nearly pressed the anger out of her last night, and with it her will to fight. But the thought of conceding defeat rekindled her rage again. Lainie wasn't one who could just sit and wait for things to sort themselves out. She was impatient, and she hated being bullied.

She went to the table where she had set her laptop when coming in and that also held the phone. She'd paid extra for WiFi access when checking in, so as she booted the computer she got immediate access to the Internet.

She pulled up the document in which she had made note of Micheal Gaston's stolen identity and stared at the American Express number for a moment. Then she picked up the phone and dialed the front desk.

"Yes, what is your fax number here?" she asked. She jotted this down on a pad of hotel notepaper.

Then she dialed the number of the real Michael Gaston in Del Mar again. Before he answered she reminded herself that she had spoken to him before and that he had Caller ID.

"Hello?" A woman's voice this time.

"Hello, ma'am," Lainie said, putting on a harsher, more businesslike voice a notch or two lower in register than her natural one. "This is Samantha Porter from American Express. May I please speak to Michael Gaston?"

Porter had been Kim's last name. Poor, brown-nosing, harmless Kim.

"Why, yes, of course."

Mr. Gaston was apparently nearby. "Hello?"

"Mr. Gaston, I'm Samantha Porter, Fraud Investigator with American Express. It's my job to travel around the country investigating incidents of identity theft and other fraud."

"Oh my."

"Yes, Mr. Gaston, I'm afraid I'm here at the Holiday Inn in San Francisco investigating a case and it seems that our perpetrator has several other cards on him than just those we were initially investigating. One of them has your name on it. I need to get some personal information from you."

"What kind of information?"

"Well, let's start with your full name and address, date of birth, Social Security Number, and mother's maiden name."

"Why do you need my Social and mother's maiden?"

"Because that information is required for us to issue a credit card. If he used a bogus Social Security Number, then all we will have to do is cancel the card. But if he used your actual one, then we can send you a letter that will help you clear your credit with the reporting agencies."

"But I don't even *have* an American Express card."

This stopped Lainie for a second, then she pressed on, "Yes, we know. But it appears that he had the account opened in your name just the same."

He was silent, hesitating.

"Mr. Gaston," Lainie pressed, "more senior citizens are victimized by these criminals than any other sector of society. I'm trying to help you here, and in return you could help put one of these bad guys in jail."

"Oh my," he said finally, sounding distressed. "Of course, I suppose."

She typed the information into an open document on the laptop as he recited it to her, then she read it back. "Thank you, Mr. Gaston. We will get back to you if we need anything else."

"Well, was it the right number?"

"We don't know yet. We'll get back to you."

She hung up.

She hadn't brought her printer with her, so she transferred the information that she'd typed to a notepad provided by the hotel. Using the Internet yellow pages again, she found the American Express toll free number.

She picked up the phone and dialed again. She answered the automated prompts, was placed on hold for two and a half minutes, then got an operator.

"I'm Michael Gaston," Lainie said. She put a soft croak into her voice to age it. She already had a low voice, what one of her phone sex regulars had called smoky. Some men had softer voices. She hoped it was enough. She figured the trick was not to overdo it. "I've come to suspect my son may have put some charges on my card that I didn't authorize. Can you fax me copies of my statements for the last year?"

This was likely more than she needed, but better more than not enough.

"Certainly," the operator said. "Can I get the card number? I'll also need the last four numbers of the cardholder's social security number."

*   *   *

Lainie let herself back into the hotel room, sheaf of official-looking fax pages folded once in her hand. She'd had them faxed to the hotel, by room number and not by name, which would have been hard to explain to the AmEx operator. There were nearly fifty pages, which gained her an acrid look by the desk clerk. Still, it was frightening how easy it was to get them. She'd been right, the social security number had been the key element to gain her credibility. Identity theft was just that easy.

Now, Lainie sat down to her computer again and for the rest of the day she hunched over the internet tracking down the addresses of the places the card had been used, beginning with the most recent, the motel in Commerce City, Colorado, and working back. There was precious little activity, mostly up and down the Eastern seaboard, up until about three months ago. In the time since he'd certainly gotten around – Paris, London, New York, Baltimore, Chicago, St. Lois, Colorado...moving progressively westward.

Probably some sort of sales route or something.

Lainie leaned way back over the backrest of the desk chair and stretched, moaning. Her next step was to trace the imposter-Michael's steps and poke around until she uncovered something to indicate who he really was and who may have wanted him dead. At some point she was going to have to involve the authorities, but given their current state of almost studied obtuseness, she was going to have to find some evidence that her version of events was true before they'd lift a finger to help her.

First stop, Commerce City, Colorado.

She reached for the phone and dialed.

If she could slip away without the murderer tracking her...

"American Transit Airlines. How may I help you?"

...or the cops trying to stop her...

"I'd like to get a ticket to..." Lainie trailed off.

"Yes, Ma'am?"

The top page of the credit card statement sat propped up next to her computer. Each page had a header with the card owner's name, address and account number on it.

"Ma'am, where was that flight to?"

It was the address that had caught Lainie's attention. It wasn't Del Mar, California.

"Ma'am?"

It wasn't even Commerce City, Colorado.

"Ma'am."

It was...

"Maryland," Lainie said. "I want to fly to Baltimore, Maryland."

CHAPTER 10

I don't even have an American Express card, the real Mr. Gaston had said.

Most identify theft was motivated by greed, the chance to purchase big ticket items while passing responsibility for the bill to some innocent victim. But what if your motive was not greed, but disguise? Imagine you only wanted to operate under a *nom de plume*, for example to call phone sex services anonymously. The old trick of using the name and Social Security Number of an old deceased person to open a credit card account was one to which the authorities had already long since been hip.

Instead, what better way than to use the name and Social Security Number of an existing person? Rather than simply let credit card bills be delivered to the unfortunate victim of your identity theft or permit marks against their credit to appear, thus alerting them to the fact that their identity was being borrowed, how much better to give a real address elsewhere, accept the bills yourself, and keep them paid? If careful to prevent any alerts or alarms from being seen by the real person, you could conceivably use the assumed identity almost indefinitely this way.

It was a hunch, but one that Lainie felt strong in following.

Lainie called the school to report an invented family emergency that would keep her away from classes for at least a couple of weeks, checked out of the hotel, and parked her Blazer in long-term parking at the airport in Oakland.

Still no sign of any police surveillance.

The phone sex gig had paid extremely well, so she had some money to play with. She just hoped her investigation wouldn't take too long. However long it took, her life was on the line, whether stagnated by jail for arson and murders she hadn't committed or cut short by a homicidal maniac desperate to remove the only witness to his vile crimes. Detective Gillis was focused on her and not even following the right leads. She simply had no choice.

It was a long flight with a one-hour layover in St. Louis. By the time the plane landed at BWI Airport in Baltimore, Maryland it was late Wednesday morning and Lainie had gone four consecutive nights without a quality 8 hours of sleep. She felt like a zombie and was certain she looked like one. Taking a cab to one of many chain hotels around the airport, she was barely conscious as she followed first the elevator and then a rather long hallway to her room. She collapsed on the bed and was snoring even before the door whispered closed on its hydraulics.

*   *   *

She awoke disoriented. For a long minute she cast about her in a panic wondering where the hell she was and how she'd gotten there. As the events of the past several days came back to her she slowed her breathing and focused on the digital clock by the bed.

10:00 PM. She'd slept for almost eleven hours.

Lainie called a cab and jumped into the shower. Refreshed, if not entirely rested, she dressed in jeans and a maroon cowl-neck sweater and met the cab outside. She gave the driver the address printed at the top of the credit account statement. He drove her through business districts toward downtown and deposited her outside a moderately ritzy upscale apartment high-rise.

There was a fine rain falling, more a mist than a shower that looked like fog under the ranks of street lamps. A phosphorescent sky hung high and haughty over the humid and somewhat shiver-inducing night, chilly even to a native San Franciscan like Lainie.

There was a glass outer door in front of the building, a dimly lit security vestibule and then an inner, locked door. She could see a security guard inside the lobby reclining in his chair behind a high desk. There was a bank of call buttons to her left inside the vestibule. She located the one she sought, the apartment number on the account statement. The name wasn't Gaston.

It was Brandt.

She pushed the button, preparing herself for a story should there be an answer. There was none. She looked at the guard. He was preoccupied with something below the level of the desk and didn't see her. A laden ring of keys hung from his belt on the right side. She slipped back outside and walked up the block a short distance to think.

What she was planning might work, but she'd have to move fast and be deft with her hand-work. She'd played flag-football for several years at the YWCA when she was in elementary school and she remembered the coach telling them not to grab for the flag. "Grab for the flag and you're liable to miss it," she'd said. "But grab for their pants where the flag is and you'll get the flag every single time."

Lainie pulled the cowl neck of her sweater over to the side to reveal her shoulder, then she rubbed her neck hard with the heels of her hands until it stung, certain it must be quite red. Finally she mussed up her raven hair. There were no reflecting surfaces nearby to look at herself but she thought this might do the trick.

She ran in place as fast as she could, kicking her knees up high for about a minute, enough to make her thighs burn, then she ran to the vestibule of the building, stumbled in and collapsed against the inner door gasping for breath. She banged on the door with limp hands as if she was weak from running.

The security guard was there in an instant. "What's going on," he shouted through the door.

"Man...tried to mug...chasing...let me in," Lainie called.

"Wait right there," he said, "I'll call the cops."

"No," she said, throwing a panicked sob into her voice. "He's coming...let me in first."

"I can't," he said.

"Then at least go and see if he's coming before you leave me here," she said. "Please...going to kill me..."

The guard, a red-headed man with buzz-cut and hard features, nonetheless looked momentarily indecisive. Finally he stepped out into the vestibule and past Lainie toward the outer door. Lainie snatched at the side seam of his pants and caught the keys firmly in her grasp. Slipping through the inner door just before it closed, she yanked the keys free of his belt and threw her body against the door, shutting it firmly.

The guard turned to look at her through the glass of the door in surprise, and then a stern anger blanketed his face. "Okay," he said, "just what the hell are you going to do now?"

Lainie was about to turn and make a run for the elevators when she noticed why he was just standing there, instead of running to a pay phone to call the police. The keys she held in her left hand were still linked to a small round case clipped to his belt by a long, thin, retractable cable that had been trapped in the jamb of the security door. She at one end, he at the other, the door between them.

He chuckled without humor as she examined the key ring she held for a way to detach it from the cable. It was looped in place by a very strong-looking crimp-clamp. There was no detaching the ring, and with about fifteen or twenty keys on the ring there was no time to try to find the one she needed.

"Well conceived plan," he said to her through the door, "poorly executed."

She gave him a sneer.

"Not all contingencies were accounted for," he said,

"and no avenues of escape scouted."

Ex-military, no question, by his vernacular. He was telling her she was trapped.

"Might as well surrender." He mocked her by throwing up his hands in a shrug.

Grabbing the key-ring in both hands, she planted her left foot up on the door jamb and pulled as hard as she could. Taken off balance, he stumbled forward, slamming his face into the glass of the door. Blinking, he reached up to feel his nose, check for blood, then he roared in rage, twisted the cable in both hands and yanked back. Lainie let the keys go, the cable slipped through the crack and when the key-ring came up against the door jamb with the full force of 200 lbs. of ex-marine rage, the crimp-clamp slipped with a metallic screech, the cable slipped freely out of the door jamb, and the key ring, keys all linked, fell to the floor with a jingle.

Lainie and the security guard stood opposite each other for a beat, gazes locked. Then Lainie snatched up the keys and the guard roared at her again, rattling the door much as she had a moment ago but considerably more power. They turned away from each other simultaneously, he presumably to go find a pay telephone to call the police, she to find the elevators.

The elevators were around the corner, and she held her breath in trepidation as the lift doors closed on her and whisked her up to the eighth floor. During the ride she searched the keys on the guard's key ring for any sign of which one she needed. Conveniently, one of them was labeled with a small sticker, "Master."

Apartment 8-B was one of four on the eighth floor, two to the left and two to the right. The hall was clean with windows at each end, each fronted by an elegant mahogany table set with a flower arrangement.

Lainie unlocked the door with the master key, slipped in and closed it behind her, pressing her back against it. The room was dark, but she could see the starry night sky through the widely open curtains of a huge bay window across the room and the huddled silhouettes of furniture between here and there. There was the vague smell of furniture polish and other cleansers.

Carefully wending her way through the obstacles she reached the curtains and searched first one side and then the other for a draw-cord but found none. She'd hoped to close them before turning on any lights, but there didn't seem to be a way to do it. Working her way back to the front door she felt the wall for the light switch. There was a bank of three rocker switches. She tried the first one and nothing happened. The second one turned on a spotlight directly over her head, which she turned off again immediately. The second turned on a light in a passage to her left leading deeper into the apartment.

The living room remained dim, lit only indirectly by the hall light. The couch, love seat, and chair were leather of a dark, rich chocolate brown. The tables were textured gunmetal frames with glass tops. There was an intricately detailed rug turned askew of the room stylishly. In front of the window there was a table with two chairs, a half-finished chess game in progress. A wet bar stood near a grey-marble faced fireplace, and a squared archway leading into what appeared in the gloom to be a formal dining room.

She nearly cried out as the phone rang. She held her breath as it rang on for what seemed like forever but was really only four rings before falling silent again. She guessed he – Gaston/Brandt – must have voicemail.

On the coffee table was a book on championship chess games throughout history and on top of it was a hand-held electronic chess game. Nearby clustered a collection of remote controls. Lainie went to these, examined them, picked one and pressed an indicated button. She smiled as the curtains hummed closed, swinging pendulously. She pressed and held another labeled button and watched the lamps in the room slowly fade into illumination, stopping before they were at full brightness.

Lainie took a quick tour of the apartment, turning on lights only long enough to survey each room. The place was decorator-elegant, with high-end furniture and artwork. Through the arch was the dining room and kitchen, the furnishings plush, the appliances restaurant-style.

She was crossing the living room once more to the hall on the other side of the apartment when the intercom by the door beeped. The guard was back in the entry vestibule again pushing the call button.

But how did he know what apartment she was in?

CHAPTER 11

She calmed herself by an act of will – he didn't know, he had to be hitting all of the call buttons in the vestibule trying to get someone to let him in. Once they recognized that he was their security guard someone was likely to buzz him in. Lainie needed no further reminders that her time was short before the police arrived. She guessed maybe ten minutes. At that time they'd probably start a room by room search of the building, and there was no telling how much time she'd have then.

"Let them come," she said to the empty room. But she only half meant it. True, she was deliberately leaving a trail plain enough for a blind man to follow. If the cops wouldn't investigate her story, then by God she'd lead them by the nose. But she hadn't found any decisive clues yet and a premature arrival of the cavalry would only land her in deeper trouble.

If she was going to be caught, she was damn well going to make it worthwhile. She needed to find whatever she was going to find here to put the cops on the trail of the real killer. She hurried into the hallway. There was a guest bedroom on the left and a guest bathroom on the right, both clean and stocked with soap and linen, but otherwise barren. There was also a weight room with universal gym, a rack of dumbbells, and a huge mirror on a wall above a tumbling mat.

There were wooden martial arts practice weaponry hanging on the wall. She noted this and moved on.

The final room was the master bedroom, and for the first time she encountered signs that a person lived here amid the showroom-perfect interior designer's wet dream. The room was neat, clean and organized, but it didn't match the rest of the house. On one whole wall hung a vast collection of framed paintings, each a treatment on a different chess piece. The book on the nightstand was entitled *"Chess: Opening Books, Gambits and Endgames"*.

There were all sorts of toiletries on the counter of the master bathroom. The cologne was expensive, but he apparently used disposable razors. In the cabinet there were no prescriptions, but there was a bottle of Rogaine. On a small table opposite the toilet was another hand-held electronic chess game, of different make and styling than the one in the living room, on top of a magazine, *Chessmasters*.

She went to the closet in the bedroom which, when she opened it, was a walk-in style so large it was nearly a room unto itself. He had taken pains to organize his things, indeed, not only hanging his clothes in order from office formal to casual, but he had clearly placed all of his summer fabrics on the right and his winters on the left. His shoes were neatly stacked on risers on the floor and his ties hung from specially designed hangers.

So far she'd found nothing in the apartment that would tell her anything about him except that he seemed preoccupied with chess. What bothered her most was that she hadn't found a desk with bills or correspondence on it. If he had a computer, even if just a laptop, like her, where did he sit to use it when home? Aside from the martial arts equipment in the gym and the chess stuff, well, everywhere, she'd seen no signs of hobbies or diversions.

She was missing something critical, she knew, and she was running out of time. She wasn't a detective, but she was observant. Stubborn, she toured the apartment again, looking for something, anything out of place or odd. She was looking in the gym again and had almost turned to leave when she stopped. Certainly the architect of the building hadn't built this room in this one apartment to be a gym. Like most apartments, all such rooms would be initially designed for use as bedrooms.

But this room had no closet.

Could it be that simple?

She walked along the walls, looking for some sign that Brandt had either torn out or closed up a closet. She focused most of her attention on the dumbbell rack, pulling on each dumbbell as if she expected it to trigger some sort of secret passage. Feeling stupid, she stepped on the tumbling mat and backed up against the mirror to scan the room again.

The mirror.

She turned and examined it. The mirror was in nine sections making one large rectangle and joined so closely together she couldn't see between them. Under the outer edges she found no sign of hinges. She went to the left side and tugged, once, then again harder. Nothing.

She went to the right side and tugged hard. There was the click of a latch and the entire right-hand section of the mirror swung outward.

CHAPTER 12

The room was a walk-in, like the other closets, but there were no hanging racks for clothes. Lined with one continuous waist-high work-shelf on all three walls and with shelves above that, the room revealed to her a computer, a printer, a scanner, and a bunch of other esoteric electronics equipment at whose function she could only vaguely guess.

A glass enclosed gun case loomed on one wall, in it a daunting array of weaponry. Most were handguns but there was also a shotgun; a long, scope-mounted rifle that said *AK47* on the side; and an ugly, boxy looking weapon she'd never seen before in any movie embossed with the name *P90 cal .5 7x23*, whatever that meant. Boxes of ammunition were stacked like sentries at the bottom of the cabinet. She didn't touch any of the weaponry – she didn't know a thing about guns, much less what bullet would go with what weapon.

In a jumble near the computer were the bills she knew had to be there. She thumbed through them quickly and finally discovered the faux-Michael's real full name: Sean Brandt.

Sticky-notes and other things were pinned to a corkboard in a clutter. Little of it made much sense to her but one. Hanging from a pushpin on a chain dangled an ID badge. It bore the photo of a man who might have been thirty. He had a pleasant if round face, sandy hair and dead gray eyes. The name on the ID badge was Sean Brandt, and his job title, Consultant/Analyst. Behind the name and barcode was a watermark - big, blocky letters over an official-looking seal.

N.S.A. The National Security Agency.

She felt a chill. She couldn't remember what the agency did, exactly, and maybe no one really knew for sure, but she remembered hearing the acronym used in movies in hushed tones of reverence and fear. What came to mind was a movie in which Will Smith ran from black helicopters and exploding buildings as high-tech satellite surveillance equipment systematically brought his life crashing down around him.

She backed away from the badge as if it was a snake. Her surroundings had taken a sudden sinister aspect upon opening this door, as if a portal into hell, and she began to suspect she was in over her head. She turned as if to leave, run and never look back, but one thing stopped her.

Mitch, often insensitive and driven primarily by greed, had nevertheless been a decent and evenhanded man. Kim, though weak-minded and prone to gossip, had had the personality of Christmas all year round. Not only was Lainie afraid of going to jail for murders she didn't commit, she hated the idea that the man who had killed them and had almost killed her, as unsavory a human lizard if ever there was, would go on with his life as if they and Lainie had never existed.

So she forced herself to turn to the secret room once more. Under the lower shelf was a safe. It hung open as if someone had already been here, picking locks and searching the place. The only thing remaining inside was a black vinyl folder with ranks of pockets all along the inside. In these pockets were rows of cards and documents. As she looked closely she recognized driver's licenses from several states, all with Brandt's picture but with different names. A matching social security card, birth certificate, credit cards and other identification accompanied each one. Further along were others in foreign languages, French, Russian, Chinese or Japanese or both, and one that she suspected was Arabic, or

Farsi.

She wasn't sure what a Consultant/Analyst did at the NSA, but she suspected that if it involved guns and false international identities, then *analyst* was another word for *spy*.

I killed my first man at the age of twelve, Michael's/Brandt's voice rang in her head as if she was hearing it through the phone again. *I love the smell of burnt gunpowder.*

Lainie dropped the false identities and continued to explore.

Hanging-folder racks burdened with file folders were so full of dry, technical jargon that she barely gathered what they said, but while no doubt related to national security none of it seemed particularly telling in regards to why Brandt had been in Colorado and who may have followed him there and killed him. Frankly she was holding at bay the overwhelming thought that since he was a spy it could be just about anyone.

But what was a spy doing using a forged identity to call a phone sex service?

She came to a stack of what appeared to be personal correspondence, weighted by a heavy book with a cushioned binding of what felt like soft leatherette. She lifted it to flip through the letters, mostly things related to travel or intended purchases of furniture and such, a pricing guide for rare or highly artistic chess sets, etc. She opened the book and glanced at it.

Dated entries written by hand, scrawled the pages and a multitude of folded and dog-eared documents stuck out between the pages. Very quickly she recognized it as a personal journal. She tucked it up under her arm.

She turned on the computer, but after booting the machine requested a password, so she shut it off again. She had neither the skills nor the time to hack into it.

She glanced around. She had no idea whether any of the bills or the journal would help her track down the killer, much less prove her own innocence, but she knew that the rest of the stuff in this room was beyond her comprehension and so would be of no use at all.

Making one last circle in the center of the room, she turned to the door and looked directly into the bluest pair of eyes she'd ever seen. They were looking out of a tanned, rugged face with sandy hair, a lock of which hung into the eyelashes, jumping when he blinked like an insect caught in a web. The rest of his athletically muscular form was dressed in black slacks, a grey shirt and a brown bomber jacket with dun colored fur at the turned-up collar.

She'd never seen him before in her life, but he was blocking her only escape.

CHAPTER 13

Panic almost took her, but this wasn't Michael's/Brandt's, Kim's, and Mitch's murderer, that man had been huge with a square head and hulking shoulders. This man wasn't menacing her, in fact his mouth was quirked in a wry sort of crooked sneer as if amused to find her here.

"NSA?" he asked her.

"Um, yes," Lainie said, glancing at Brandt's ID badge where it still hung from the pushpin on the corkboard. "Who are you?"

"CIA," he said. "Find anything?" He pointed to the bundle under her arm.

Her mouth went dry. One read about spies, saw them in movies, but here standing before her was a real life, flesh and blood secret agent, and he'd caught her rifling through the secret room of another dead secret agent. What was he going to do about it? Kill her? Torture her? Something worse?

"Not sure," she said, clearing her throat and trying to keep her voice level. "We'll see." He was going to have to take the journal and bills from her, she wasn't going to give them to him.

"Why don't you just let me have that?"

"I can't. I need this." She tucked the journal more snugly under her arm. She knew she'd lose a struggle with him, but he didn't move to take the bundle from her.

She was about to explain that what she found here might help her clear her name and find a murderer when he took a step toward her. Reflexively she flinched back a step, but he was only offering a gloved hand for her to shake.

"Cord Steele," he said.

"Samantha Porter," she said, shaking the hand. She'd used the stage name reflexively. "I was expecting the cops."

"When you opened this room," he explained, "the all-clear signal was sent to the entry alarm system."

She nodded. "And set off a whole other alarm, bringing you here." It was a guess, but he didn't contradict her. "But the doorman called the cops directly."

"We pulled rank, got them pulled off the call." He shrugged as if it was no big deal. "I was expecting you. NSA said they'd be sending someone over to look around. I expected you sooner."

He wasn't making any sense to her.

"Now what?" she asked.

"I've been waiting to talk to you," he said, "see if I can reason with you. Don't you think we're taking inter-agency rivalry a little too far? Instead of covering the same ground, in effect duplicating each other's efforts, what do you say we, the NSA" - gesturing to her - "and the CIA" – gesturing to himself – "work together on this?"

She understood.

When he had said NSA the first time, he wasn't asking if Brandt had been an NSA operative, but if she worked for them. In saying yes, she'd inadvertently misled him, and now wondered if she should go on with the ruse or fess up. Would it change his attitude toward her? Would he just kill her out of hand if she admitted she wasn't his counterpart at a rival agency? How much trouble could one get in impersonating a spy?

"S-since when?" she said, trying to sound professional.

"How about now?" Steele said. "Don't you think it's time we stopped getting in each other's way and started benefiting from each other's expertise?'"

"You first," she said.

"Let's get out of here, *first*," he said. "Go somewhere where we can talk."

Motioning for him to step back she slipped out and closed the mirror-door behind her. They left the apartment and he made no comment as she locked the door with one key jangling on a ring with several others. The lobby was only just visible around the corner when the elevator doors opened, and Lainie saw it was full of people shouting, most in their pajamas and robes, demanding what the hell was going on.

"This way," Steele said, pulling her by the arm.

She caught a quick glimpse of the security guard trying to get control of the situation and looking harried. She pulled back on Steele just enough to drop the poor doorman's keys next to the plant on a table by the elevators.

Steele led her through some back corridors past a fitness room, sauna and Jacuzzi to the laundry room. He opened a door marked "Superintendant Only" and that led into a small room with lines of furnaces and water heaters and an old incinerator long since dormant. Steele picked up a small shovel leaning against the monstrous oven and used it to hit a small lever hidden in the shadows against the wall. A four-foot trap door opened in the wall about a foot above the floor.

With a flourish Steele motioned for Lainie to go first. Watching her head, Lainie stepped through and found herself in a musty foul-smelling room with sloping walls on three sides and no ceiling, the night sky visible above her. After closing the trap door behind them Steele motioned her toward a ladder leading up. It was a short climb and at the top she found herself looking out into an alley. She stepped over the rim and onto a loading dock. It wasn't a room she'd climbed out of but an old, long disused coal-hopper from the days when the building had been heated by steam.

Steele climbed out behind her, then he grabbed her hands. She almost pulled away, but he had a handkerchief and was wiping the soot off of her hands with it. She looked up at him and he was giving her a crooked smile. Those eyes, even here in a dim alleyway, shown quite blue.

"My grandfather once told me," he said, "that any man who leaves the house without a handkerchief is no civilized man."

"Old fashioned," she said.

"Ex Green Beret," he said.

His ministrations on her hands were getting too slow, a little too intimate. She pulled at them until he let them go, but it was he who broke their gaze first. He turned and led the way down a ramp and to the end of the alley. Steele led her to a silver Lexus IS 250C convertible parked on the street a block away and opened the passenger door for her.

Lainie hesitated. There could be no doubt she was out of her element, in view of which getting into his car with a strange man whose identity she couldn't verify seemed beyond reckless. She had no doubt he could present any number of false ID's every bit as convincing as those she'd seen upstairs in Brandt's secret room.

"Well?" he said, his smile patient and inviting.

On the other hand she needed information, and he was a resource she couldn't afford to squander. Had she really come this far to balk just when she got her first break in the case? If he'd wanted to kill her he could have done so upstairs, or in the basement when they were alone.

"What?" he teased, "You don't trust me?"

Behind those blue eyes she got no clues at all, he was completely inscrutable.

She sighed and slid into the car, forcing herself not to jump as he slammed the door on her.

He drove very fast and aggressively and it didn't take long for Lainie to give up trying to play it cool. She clung to the shoulder strap of her seatbelt like a lifeline. He only glanced over once with that crooked smile of his, then kept his eyes on the road.

He pulled up outside an elegantly landscaped restaurant whose name she hadn't been able to catch as they fishtailed into the drive. A valet opened Steele's door and Steele circled the car to open Lainie's, offering her a hand to step out.

"I'm not dressed for..." she protested.

"Shh," he said, tucking her wrist in the crook of his arm and leading her inside. "It's all attitude. Act like you belong, and you do."

She comforted herself by noting that he was dressed quite casually as well.

The place was every bit as swanky as the exterior promised. There were four bars on a raised perimeter opposite the foyer where the coat-check and *maitre 'd* awaited them, then a pair of arching staircases that parted to left and right as they descended and met again on the floor of the dining room half a story below. Elegant bolts of fabric draped the walls, the carpet a mocha-tan, the tables covered in cream-colored linen and the chandeliers were amber and dim. On the far side of the sunken dining room was a dance floor backed by a low stage upon which performed a band playing soft jazz and a singer torching it up big time.

In the western states, restaurants closed around 9 or 10 PM, but she knew people on the East Coast dined late, sometimes quite late, so it was not surprising to find this place open at...what was it, 11:30, midnight?

A host showed them to a dark booth at the edge of the dining room furthest from the stage. Steele ordered coffee for both of them.

"Crème Brule," Lainie blurted before the waitress could walk away.

Steele pulled the cord on the velvet curtains to give them some privacy from the rest of the patrons, all the while studying her with that crooked smirk.

"Sweet tooth, huh?" he observed.

Here she felt more in her element. Here, they were just a man and a woman, he trying to impress her and she measuring out admiration in stingy doses, the ages-old game of seduction. Lainie had played this game countless times before.

She said, "Don't think your suicidal-homicidal driving skills and a hoity-toity restaurant are going to make me forget that I said 'you first.'"

"Let's wait till the coffee and Brule comes," he said. "Meanwhile, tell me about you."

"What do you want to know?" she said, still cautious.

"I don't know. Tell me something...surprising." His bluer-than-blue eyes made her fidget.

She wanted to shock him, regain some ground. "Okay. I worked as a phone sex girl to put myself through college." Putting it in the past tense like that didn't make it any less true.

His broad grin was so warm and genuine she knew it had taken him as much by surprise as it did her.

"Really? That's definitely surprising."

"What about you?"

"I was never a phone sex girl."

"You know what I mean."

"Mowed lawns summers."

"I meant tell me something surprising about you," she scolded him, "and you know it."

"I like country music."

"Really?" she laughed.

"Really."

They locked eyes for a beat.

"You are having Brandt's apartment watched," she said.

"Naturally," he shrugged.

"That's how you knew I was there."

"Bugged, too."

"How did you get in without tripping the alarm?"

He didn't answer, but his smile took a mischievous turn.

The waitress came with the coffee and the Brule.

"Enough stalling," Lainie said when she'd gone.

Steele parted the curtains with a finger, then let them close again. He turned to her, all signs of the game gone from his eyes, strictly business now.

"Okay, you know that Sean Brandt went dark two or three months ago, dropped off the grid, no communication, and that he missed a rendezvous at which he was supposed to turn the formula over to us. I know NSA is pissed at us for waiting until last Saturday to tell you, but that's water under the bridge. The bottom line is we are no closer to finding him than we were two months ago. So what I want to know from you is anything that you've been able to find out in your investigation that might help us. We're both looking for the same guy, so why not give each other a hand?"

Lainie hadn't touched her dessert, she was concentrating on not showing any of the shock she felt. She *was* in over her head. She had to force herself to appear casual. She needed to be careful what she said, not to reveal how ignorant she truly was. But the three months that Steele referred to corresponded to the sudden increase in activity on the forged Gaston credit card account Brandt had used to call her phone sex agency with. Whatever Brandt had been up to, he was using that card to finance it.

But the nagging question in her head became even more strident: what business did a spy, one on the run from his own government, have calling a phone sex outfit, of all ridiculous things?

"Brandt was an analyst for the NSA...for us." If she repeated facts she knew, perhaps it would get Steele to talk.

"Yes, and he was one of the CIA's best assassins," he nodded. "I know moonlighting is frowned on by you guys, us too, but let's set aside the recitation of regulations for just a moment. Can't you see we have a stake in his disappearance, too, maybe even a bigger stake than you?"

Assassin? Lainie filled her mouth with toasted custard to hide her horror. "Why would he work for both government agencies?" she asked after she'd swallowed.

Steele shrugged. "I won't lie. Gets us nowhere at this point. The NSA has the single largest, most complete, and most accurate digital repository of intelligence in the world. Any of us – State Department, FBI, CIA – have to come to the

NSA hat-in-hand if we want any meager sliver of that for our operations. It gets...cumbersome...so it served us to have our own operative inside your organization to...let's just say expedite our intelligence data needs."

"The CIA put a spy inside the NSA?" Lainie asked. Even to her, unschooled as she was in these things, that sounded messed up.

"We aren't the only ones," he said. "But now I need your help."

She wasn't sure what she could offer him that would sound credible. "Brandt has disappeared," she said. When Steele gave her a puzzled look she hurried to add, "He was killed in a motel in Colorado very early last Sunday morning."

"What?" Steele's eyes were wide as he leaned forward to whisper. "How do you know?"

"He was on the telephone with me when it happened."

"Shit. And the formula?"

"He didn't mention it."

"Well what were you talking about?"

"Just things," she shrugged. "Personal...nonsense."

Steele sat back. "Were you...involved with him?"

"We had...a unique relationship."

"I'm sorry, Samantha. And the NSA put you on his case, knowing how well you knew him?"

"W-who else?"

Steele nodded, as if that made perfect sense to him.

"Only I didn't really know him that well," Lainie amended. While bluffing, she didn't want to overdo it. "We'd only just started to get to know each other."

"Met him once," Steele said. "Seemed like a boring guy. Kind of dead. Zombie. You know, like most of them get."

"He seemed lonely to me."

"Did he tell you why he missed our rendezvous?"

"No," she said. "He didn't mention it, and at the time I didn't even know about it."

Steele shook his head ruefully. "We don't tell the NSA

about his rendezvous with us until Saturday, and you guys don't tell us about his death until now. Fair enough. Did you check out the motel?"

"Sent a guy," Lainie said. "Place was completely cleaned. Not even an eyelash, so I was told."

"Damn," Steele shook his head. "So someone killed Brandt, got the formula from him, and now we have no way of finding out who has it."

"That isn't exactly true," Lainie said.

Steele's arresting eyes went wide again. "He traced you, the shooter, because you were on the telephone and you overheard the killing."

Lainie nodded, deciding the details of the shootings and firebombing at Capri would only confuse the issue right now. "He showed up at my apartment early Monday morning and tried to kill me. I...changed his mind." Lainie knew what she was implying, but she couldn't very well tell him a rumpled, grumpy old police detective had shown up and scared the attacker away.

Steele didn't react to this at all, as if he expected nothing less from a NSA Investigator. This automatic acceptance of her ability to defend herself, fiction though it was, notched up her respect for him. The sexism she encountered on nearly a daily basis in the world of academe was either dead or dying in the government services these days, or so it seemed.

"Did he say anything that gave a clue to who he worked for? Who might have the formula now?"

Lainie shook her head. "He was big, I mean really big, with a street-slang accent. Couldn't have been more American. Other than that, nothing."

"Doesn't mean anything," Steele said, mostly to himself. "Could be any government or terrorist organization. This guy could be a mercenary, for that matter. Do you think you could pick him out if you saw him again?"

"I imagine so," she said. She *knew* so.

"Well, keep an eye out for him. Meanwhile I guess

we're back to square one."

"Which means?"

"Which means keeping our eyes on the usual suspects and our ears open on the usual channels for any chatter about the formula and who may have it."

"There may be another way," she said.

She told him of Brandt's cover, Michael Gaston, and the credit card statements she'd gotten copies of. She showed him the bills and the journal she'd picked up at Brandt's apartment.

Steele seemed impressed.

"You're right, retracing Brandt's steps might give us a clue to who he's met with and where he met them. Can I see those?"

He reached for them.

She moved them from the table, out of sight to her lap. These items were a thread that could lead to her proof of innocence. She dared not let them out of her sight.

Their eyes locked for a moment and though his remained smiling she sensed, if only for a moment, just how deadly an enemy Steele could be, if enemy he became. But then the sense was gone and the warmth behind his smile seemed to become genuine where moments before it had been tightly wound whipcord.

"Of course it's late," he said. "I can see you're tired, and I need to check-in with the office. Let's finish our coffee, then regroup tomorrow to look at what you have."

She hoped her smile remained as neutral as his as she used a spoon to crack the last remaining crust of the Brule.

She knew he hadn't given up that easily.

CHAPTER 14

Lainie had Steele drop her off at Brandt's apartment building to hide the fact that she didn't have a car of her own. The lobby was empty again with no sign of the night's earlier chaos. The doorman sat once again behind his desk. Staying out of his line of sight, it took Lainie fifteen minutes to hail a taxi. The cab let her out by the pay phone she'd asked him to find for her and drove off a distance to wait. The phone kiosk stood outside a convenience store that was just shutting down its lights and closing up as she dialed the San Francisco Police department and asked for Detective Gillis.

"Where the hell are you, young lady," he demanded when picking up the call.

She could have used her cell phone, but couldn't risk that they wouldn't trace the call. This way simple caller ID would show them the area code, at least, of the city she was in.

"Miss me? I thought you were having me watched."

"It took me twenty minutes to put a guy in place. You were gone by the time he got there. We traced you to the Holiday Inn but you'd already checked out."

"Inspector Clouseau has nothing on you."

"Don't fuck with me, Ms. Parker. Where are you?"

"I'm doing the investigation you should have done."

"God damn it. We have reason to believe you've left

the state. If you've left the state, missy, you're in a lot of trouble."

"How much trouble. Hmm? As much trouble as, say, oh, being accused of murder?"

She could hear his teeth grinding even over the phone. She could picture him in his rumpled suit and perpetual five o'clock shadow pulverizing his nicotine gum in anger.

"I'm just calling," she went on, "to tell you that the guy who was shot, Michael Gaston, wasn't Michael Gaston after all but a spy for the NSA and an assassin for the CIA."

"Oh Jesus Christ." His voice bristled with irritation.

"Fine, you still think I'm delusional? Well I'm going to bring this case down around your fucking ears, Flatfoot."

She slammed the handset down so hard the ringer dinged once in protest. As she feared, she was going to have to get some hard evidence to get the authorities to believe her.

FBI Agent Peck, when she called him next, was only slightly less cooperative.

"My suggestion, Ms. Parker, is that you leave Baltimore immediately and go home," he said in his characteristically tired voice. At least he'd bothered to look at the number she was calling from. Still, knowing he knew what city she was in made her glance over her shoulder.

He was still scolding her, "Even if any one thing you're saying is true, however unlikely, you're in over your head and are liable to get yourself killed."

She hung up on him, too, though less violently. He knew she was calling from Baltimore. He could trace her to the very hotel through her credit card. But by telling her to go home he seemed to be hinting that he wasn't going to move on that information. At least not yet.

It appeared she was still on her own.

*   *   *

Back in her room, Lainie undressed and climbed into the bed, leaving the lights off. Her mind was reeling with the revelations of the evening. She was in awe of her own audacity, barely able to believe that she'd had the gall to impersonate a spy, and more than a little frightened of what might come of it. Steele's frequent references to a stolen formula were ominous.

She reflected on Cord Steele, Secret Agent. That he was dreamy had not escaped her notice, but she had more pressing matters to contend with. Could she keep up her brazen masquerade right under his nose? Or was she doomed to slip up and set off his highly trained and honed instincts?

Unable to sleep, she turned on the lamp and reached to the nightstand where she'd left the things she'd taken from Brandt's apartment. The bills were in his name, mostly electric and cable television charges. Among them was a cell phone bill that itemized calls. She put this on top of the stack and returned the mail to the nightstand.

The journal she put in her lap and opened.

The entries started with a series of names and dates. She flipped through the pages and found that spanning ten years about five or six names were scattered over each year. After that he had begun to add details under each name. At first only ages, then increasing details, weird ones.

Sphigniu Kilnchmskev, 10/12/1997, 78 years old, eating a spumoni.

Jean Beaumaire, 12/15/1997, 32 years old, urinating in an alley.

Janice Kleimore, 1/27/1998, 39 years old, mother and Catholic, window shopping.

As the dates progressed, so did the details, clearly details about the person belonging to the name, though the last note on each was usually some odd activity. Then she came to the first one that explained all of the others.

Miles Pomskew, 6/9/2001, violin virtuoso, hopeful of winning a seat in the London Philharmonic, loves carnations, drinks soy milk, looks like a young Tom Hanks, shot him while feeding ducks by a lake.

Each entry after this one gave ever-increasing details, the last detail always a note on what the person had been doing when Brandt had killed him.

Lainie stopped reading. The pages of the journal

rattled in her trembling hands. She swallowed several times before saliva would return to her mouth. She reached for the phone by the bed and dialed the number on the card Steele had given her as they left the restaurant earlier that night. After a single ring he picked up.

"Hello?"

"Weren't you asleep?" she asked.

"Yes. What is it?" He didn't sound it.

"I was looking through the journal."

"And?"

She read him some of the entries, finishing with the last one she'd read. "It's clearly a catalog of his assassinations." Her years in academic psychology had kicked in. "The increasing details are a tell, the killings were beginning to take a toll on Brandt's conscience."

Steele cursed. "Writing them down was a serious breech of his security clearance."

"But I'm betting an increasing need to confess had led him to do it," she explained. "If he couldn't tell someone, not even a priest, then writing it down was the next best thing. Perhaps there had even been a latent hope that someone would discover the journal and expose him."

Steele cursed again.

She went back to flipping through the pages. "The entries stop almost exactly three months ago. No reasons given for why each person had to be killed, only that he'd done so."

"He wouldn't have been given a reason for each target. That information is on a need to know basis."

"They didn't deem it necessary that he know why each person had to be killed?"

"No."

"All they cared about was that he kill them. Without any explanation as to why, that could only add to a growing sense of guilt."

"They're supposed to weed out people prone to that kind of sentimentality."

Maybe Brandt had called Capri Entertainment out of

genuine loneliness and angst. Lainie wasn't sure it seemed likely a trained assassin would be so careless, but she thought it possible. Maybe he was tempting himself to confess to a perfect stranger.

"He joked about suicide," she said. "On the phone. Before he was shot."

"Maybe he really was contemplating suicide," Steele said. "He had disappeared for nearly three months by then, and that's how most of them, assassins, go out."

This seemed more probable to Lainie the more she thought about it.

"God, if he only had," Steele said.

"That's a terrible thing to say," Lainie scolded him.

"It would have saved a lot of trouble looking for the damned formula."

She didn't answer, dared not risk revealing her ignorance on the matter.

"Go to sleep," he said. "Don't take it to bed with you. You'll go crazy."

She said good night and hung up.

Lainie didn't have such a defense mechanism, an ability to turn off her brain to sleep at night. She supposed someone in Steele's line of work developed it, though. She set the journal aside and sat staring at nothing, unable to sleep. A horrified sort of pity for all of those victims consumed her, as well as disturbing, persistent sadness for a haunted killer who had, himself, been killed in his turn, who should have deserved no mourning.

CHAPTER 15

Lainie tried the website for Capri Entertainment in the morning and as expected she got a server fault error. Capri Entertainment was out of business. Her life had certainly taken a turn since Michael's/Sean's murder - the firebombing of the office, her visit from the murderer. Here she was in Baltimore, a fugitive from justice and impersonating a spy.

A week ago her biggest worry had been how to tactfully fend off the unwanted advances of her teenaged male students.

She spread out the phone bill from Brandt's apartment. Printed at the top was the number for the cellular telephone on the account. She picked up the hotel phone and dialed.

"Who may I say is calling?" A woman's voice, firm, crisp, officious.

"Who is this?" Lainie asked.

"This is his friend, Julia," the voice said.

His friend?

"Whose friend?" Lainie asked.

"Who's calling, please?"

Something was wrong. This didn't sound like someone's friend. Julia sounded too carefully neutral, too impersonal, like a secretary. Someone who didn't dare state a name because Brandt had so many aliases. Someone meant to intercept calls.

Why?

Lainie hung up.

She was so stupid. Of course those looking for Brandt would intercept his calls in an attempt to get clues to where he'd disappeared. Julia, definitely not her real name, was some minor functionary whose job had been to answer the calls.

Answer and do what?

"Of course!"

Lainie rushed to the closet, threw her suitcase on the bed and scrambled to stuff her clothes and other things in as fast as she could, taking no time to fold or organize anything. She rushed to the bathroom and tried to scoop up deodorant, shampoo, brush, makeup, etc., dropping some and having to come back for a second load. Jamming the case closed, she struggled with the latches.

She paused, not wanting to leave anything behind. How much time did she have before they got here?

Looking around again, she almost convinced herself she had everything before she noted the most glaring blunder of all – her laptop, on the table next to the phone. She rushed to shut it down and stuff it into its customized carrying case, expecting at any moment to hear the door rattle and raised voices outside demanding she open up.

She was fully packed now and no such knock came.

As much as she wanted, needed the authorities to follow her footsteps, she couldn't afford to be arrested just yet. She had no idea who it was that she feared might be coming for her, it could be anyone from the CIA to the NSA to those from whom Brandt had stolen the formula of which Steele spoke.

Leaving her card key behind – she had no intention of returning here - she ducked out the door and started up the hallway toward the elevators, suitcase in her left hand, laptop in her right. She passed a young, swarthy man who watched her in alarm but didn't move to stop her. As the chime sounded announcing the arrival of one of the elevator cars she skidded to a stop and watched two men in suits and sunglasses step out and look both ways.

She turned and walked back up the hallway, trying to remain casual, passing the young, confused man again while trying to hide her haphazardly packed luggage in front of her.

"Miss?" one of the men in sunglasses called. "Ma'am," The second was even closer. They were hurrying up on her.

Lainie sprinted for the other end of the hall, toward the stairwell. She heard their footsteps beating a hunting rhythm against the carpet behind her as she slammed through the stairwell door and threw herself down the stairs.

She thought she heard too many echoes for only her two feet alone. Pausing she listened to at least two other pairs of feet rushing up the stairs from below toward her. Turning she watched the two from the hall above enter the stairwell and stop, looking down at her. One of them murmured something into his sleeve.

Turning once again she saw another pair of men round the landing below her and stop at the bottom of the stairs, looking up at her. She threw her suitcase at them, clutched her computer case to her chest, and vaulted the partition wall to the next flight down, but her luggage only stopped one of the men as he tried to intercept it. The other bore down the stairs after her.

She only reached one more landing before he caught her, grabbing a fistful of her pony tail and dragging her back, yanking a yell of pain from her, driving her to the hard floor. She lost her grip on her laptop and didn't see where it landed.

She stopped struggling and grit her teeth helplessly as he rolled her over onto her stomach, put a knee between her shoulder blades and forced her wrists into a pair of handcuffs.

CHAPTER 16

Lainie was frightened and damned determined not to show it. She sat in the interrogation room with her cuffed hands in her lap, sipping occasionally from a straw stuck in the mouth of a Coke can. The can sat on a nondescript oval table. A man in a suit sat opposite her reading a paperback novel with the cover torn off, glancing up at her occasionally to make sure she hadn't escaped yet. The room itself was bare, institutional green walls and tiles enough shades darker to cause a nauseating contrast. Centered high on the door was a wire-mesh reinforced window. A small surveillance camera mounted high in the corner facing her kept watch.

After being dragged from the service tunnel of the hotel and stuffed into an unmarked forest-green van, her captors sat her opposite this same guard. The two of them sat on hard benches ranked along each side. A reinforced wall completely sealed off the cargo area of the van from the cab area except for a small, wire-mesh reinforced sliding window through which eyes obscured by sunglasses watched her periodically. Her luggage was not with her and she hoped they hadn't left it behind.

The drive was maybe a half hour long, after which the back doors were snapped open and she was dragged out again, up a loading dock and hauled through a series of offices until she'd been deposited in this room. Sitting here for what felt like another hour, she'd long since missed her rendezvous with Steele this morning.

Now when the door finally snapped opened she humiliated herself by crying out and nearly jumping out of her chair. Two cold, stone-faced men came in and relieved her guard. One sat in the chair just vacated. The other, carrying in another chair, perched opposite her. He ignored her while he arranged his notes on the table in front of him.

Finally, he looked at her.

"Elaine Janine Parker," his voice was dry and toneless, "born twenty-six years ago in Oakland, California to Aldred Pritchard Parker and Jane Freda Trudeau Parker, preceded two years by Donald Aldred, deceased, and succeeded eight years by Kim Cynthia Parker."

Lainie wanted to throw something at his smug face, but didn't dare even if she could put enough pepper on the throw with handcuffs fowling her. The man proceeded to peel back the admittedly few layers of her life, laying out all the details in such a way that made them seem pitiful and unimportant, small and insignificant. He even knew her bank balance and how many refills she had left on her current birth control prescription.

"Stop," she said desperately, her fists clenched on the table, the cuffs cutting into her wrists.

He looked up for the first time as if surprised to see her sitting in front of him, as if he'd simply been reading for his own entertainment. He slowly closed the folder in front of him and sat back.

"So how do you know Sean Brandt?" he asked.

"You can dissect my life all you want," she said. "I'm not saying a word until I know who I'm talking to."

He waited.

"Fine," she said, sitting back. "You might as well go back to reading out loud."

He studied her, his companion matching his gaze over

his shoulder like a reflection. Finally, he reached to his breast pocket, pulled out a billfold and flashed an ID: NSA. His shadow did the same.

She snorted, sitting forward and sipping from the straw to keep her throat from seizing up. "Figured it was you guys monitoring his calls. You knew Brandt was moonlighting for the CIA, that he went missing three months ago after getting some formula they were after but before delivering it to them. What you don't know is that Brandt is dead. At least it came as a surprise to the CIA."

They didn't react at all.

Lainie didn't hold back anything. She told them everything from the first call to Capri Entertainment by Michael/Brandt to her encounter with Steele the night before. She had nothing to hide and every reason to try to get some government agency, no matter who they were, to believe her.

Still, they called a halt to the interrogation rather abruptly. She'd expected it to go on for hours, with much repetition, shouting, threats, etc. Like on TV. Instead after only an hour in which they simply asked questions to clarify parts of her story, they left.

She thought her guard would return, that she had another long wait ahead of her. Instead after only a few minutes another man in a charcoal suit came in smiling at her and waving a handcuff key as if it were her gold star for doing well on a test.

"Agent Sumner, Ms. Parker," he said warmly as he unlocked the cuffs. He had smile-wrinkles around his eyes and smelled of mellow cologne. "Sorry for all the problems. Your story checks out, of course, thanks to a call we got from the FBI last night, apparently after you'd called them."

Lainie rubbed her wrists. So Peck had at least made an attempt to check out her story. "Then you told them everything I said was true?" she asked in relief.

"Of course not," he said with the stern frown of a caring uncle. "We feigned no knowledge of any of it."

"But they think I killed..."

"Tut, tut, tut," he said, patting her hands and kneeling in front of her. "I'm sorry we can't get involved, and you've been a naughty girl, getting mixed up in international affairs way beyond your understanding."

She pulled away. "Don't patronize me. So what, you just cut me loose? Let me be arrested for murders I didn't commit?"

He stood and shook his head sympathetically. "Our business is none of yours, and yours is none of ours. I'm sorry."

"What kind of people are you?"

He took a sheet of paper out of his breast pocket folded once lengthwise, unfolded it and placed it on the table and snapped a pen down on top of the document.

"What?" she demanded.

"Before you go, we need you to sign this."

"What is it?" she asked, not reaching for the pen.

"It's a form 312," he said. "Classified Information Nondisclosure Agreement. Standard Form. We ask all citizens who have inadvertently crossed paths with national secrets to sign it."

Her name was already carefully printed by hand at the top.   She tried to read the one-page document: "Intending to be legally bound, I hereby accept the obligations contained in this Agreement in consideration of my being granted access to classified information. As used in this Agreement, classified information is marked or unmarked classified information, including oral communications, that is classified under the standards of Executive Order 12356, or any other Executive Order..." Blah-blah-blah...after that it got *really* dense and dry.

"You want me to promise not to tell anyone what I know. To in effect sign this agreement *after* the fact?"

"Would you?"

"Is that, y'know, strictly speaking, legal?"

He said nothing.

She nodded. "I'll sign it. If you clear my name with the cops in San Francisco."

He *tsked* at her again. "You have the wrong end of the horse, dear. You'll sign it or rot in Leavenworth." He continued to smile indulgently.

She stared at him. With his jaunty demeanor and condescending attitude he was the perfect heavy, one who gave her nothing against which to fight or struggle. Spitting an unladylike expletive at him, she reached for the pen.

After she signed, his mock-friendly manner vanished and he was all business. "Wait here," he said so firmly she froze. He left, locking the door behind him.

In moments her stoic guard returned. Without a word he took her by the arm and yanked her to her feet. She cried out with the pain. Then he led her out the door and into a corridor.

"Where are you taking me now?" she demanded.

He didn't answer, but pulled her down toward a darkened end of the hall.

CHAPTER 17

Her guard took her out another tunnel to an underground parking garage and put her in the back of a car with no handles for door or window operation on the inside. A grate separated her from the front seat. He drove. Her luggage was already here with her, and she did a quick inventory. Everything seemed to be there, including her laptop.

He took her to the airport. He carried her suitcase in one hand and kept the other clamped to her arm as he walked her to the ticket desk of United. She held her laptop case to her chest and went where he guided her, still too shaken to resist or try to get away. She was caught, and fighting now would be futile and might even get her shot.

He bought them both tickets to San Francisco and checked her bag for the flight. He let her hold on to her laptop as carry-on. Clearly he was to escort her home, and she didn't doubt that once they got there he'd turn her over to the police, one certain way the NSA could be sure she'd be too busy to meddle in their affairs again, or at least for a while.

After registering his gun with airport security Lainie's guard took her to the VIP lounge to await their flight, the first time she'd seen the inside of such a place. They were the only two there. He sat ramrod straight in his chair, his hand clamping her wrist firmly to the arm between their seats, staring off into space, lost in his own, stern thoughts. She slumped, trying to appear meek and submissive while she searched her mind and the room around them. She was pretty sure she was looking for a means to break free of him, useless as such an exercise seemed.

Plush lounge chairs reclined in little groupings facing each other around low tables, magazines and bookracks stood laden with reading material. A piano waited in one corner without a player, and a bar, which had remained unmanned until now, occupied an opposite corner. She barely took notice as a man backed out of the back room behind the bar, arms laden with a tray of clean glasses, she continued to scan the room.

On one far side was a hallway that led back to the restrooms. She'd given up the bathroom gambit as the oldest one in the book. He wouldn't hesitate to accompany her and watch her, and it was doubtful there'd be an exterior window that would open and allow egress anyway.

The bartender approached them with a tray. "Would you like something?" he asked, his familiar low, wet voice seizing her heart in a block of ice.

"No," her guard said firmly.

Lainie snapped her head around and screamed.

The knife in the large, muscular killer's fist – Brandt's killer, Mitch's killer, Kim's killer, and Lainie's waking nightmare – arced down and sliced through her guard's throat. Her guard gurgled, one hand going to his gushing throat while the other hand grabbed for the gun at his hip. Lainie pulled free and would have run but in reaction to his sliced throat the guard had slumped over, his legs crossing hers, tripping her to the carpet. The killer's hand reached to stop the guard's gun hand, holding it down so the dying man couldn't pull his weapon from it's holster. Lainie lunged for the weapon as well.

The three of them struggled. The guard's grip weakened and gave first as he died. The gun handle was slippery with blood and getting slipperier. Having gotten there a split second before Lainie, the bartender had a better grip on the butt than she did and he wrenched it out of the holster and her grasp.

Lainie looked up into the face of the man who'd attacked her in her apartment two nights ago, murderer and firebomber. The NSA agent rolled out of his chair and on top of her with a groan. Screaming, she tried to crabwalk backwards, but the body was too heavy. Blood covered her while only splattering the killer's left arm. He cast the knife aside and leveled the gun at her over the guard's cooling body. The murderer wore a white smock over his clothes and baggy, clear plastic gloves, the kind fast food employees sometimes wear.

"Amazing," he said. "So much security to keep weapons out of an airport, and yet bartenders still need to cut their lemons and limes."

Faced once again with this man, Lanie couldn't bring herself to beg him for her life, not him. Instead, voice edged with a mixture of terror and anger, she demanded, "How did you find me?"

"It wasn't hard," was all he said. She saw his finger begin to contract on the trigger. The barrel of the gun grew huge and black in her vision, any second to be lit by a bright flash and the roar of expanding gasses.

"I always w..."

Then his grip relaxed, the gun drooped.

She focused on his face. Was he toying with her again?

No, his face had gone lax. A small ball of what looked like fluorescent yellow lint appeared at his throat. "What the f...?" he murmured, his face melting downward as if paralyzed. He let the gun drop from his grasp, closed his eyes and fell toward her.

Somehow she rolled out from under the dead man quickly enough to be out of the way of the killer as he slumped over the guard's corpse where it lay, the gun trapped between them. Lainie get to feet, horrified. She turned to look around her, trying to clear her shock-numbed mind and decide what to do. Standing in the main entrance was a girl with jet black hair hanging down past her shoulders and wearing an olive green jacket. She lifted something to shoulder height, arms length, aimed at Lainie. There was a soft sound, like a child spitting a sunflower seed, and Lainie felt something sting her neck, just to the left of her larynx.

She reached up as the room stretched and turned around her and felt something soft with a hard-core sticking out of her throat. Her vision narrowed steadily to a single circle encompassing the girl's pretty if rugged face. Lainie felt herself falling.

CHAPTER 18

Lainie was jostled awake.

A vibrating surface rocked her unevenly. The floor of a vehicle as it careened through traffic. She smelled stale gasoline and some other bitter odors she didn't recognize. She opened her eyes.

The back of a van, cluttered with pillows and cushions, the engine roaring, strange music in the background. Music in a mysterious, middle-Eastern flavor. Two people in front, driver and passenger, driver big, passenger small, slight of build, feminine. They talked in low tones.

The girl in the passenger seat looked at her wrist, a watch, and turned to look back at Lainie. Murmuring to the driver, touching his arm, she came back, steadying herself on opposing walls. It was the girl from the airport, the one in the green jacket.

A scream rising in Lainie's throat, tears in her eyes, hot, not wanting to let the scream loose. She knew her eyes must have betrayed her struggle with rising hysteria, because the girl rushed to her and backhanded her across the mouth, hard.

Lainie felt rage drown out the panic and she glared at the girl. "Who the fuck do you think you are?"

"Ah," the girl said in disgust. She followed the

exclamation with a string of words in a language Lainie didn't understand, then said in heavily accented English, "You Americans cannot express yourselves without filth," She wiped the hand with which she'd hit Lainie on her leg as if it had been soiled.

"Where is my father," the girl demanded.

"What," Lainie said.

The girl slapped her again.

Lainie had had enough of being pushed around.

She launched herself at the girl with such sudden ferocity that she bore the smaller girl up and over onto her back. Lainie could quickly tell the girl was the better fighter, ropey and strong, using some sort of martial arts that would easily overcome an unskilled opponent, and Lainie hadn't been in a fight since junior high.

On the other hand, the close quarters and the countless cushions scattered in the van hindered the girl and she was clearly completely unprepared for the sheer suddenness and wild ferociousness of Lainie's enraged attack. Lainie slammed the girl's head into the bare metal floor of the van and watched her blink as if stunned. Lainie began to pummel the girl's face, ignoring the yells of the driver.

When he pulled the van over and set the parking break Lainie launched herself at him as he rose from his seat, bearing him back before he could gain his balance, throwing him against the center console. She scratched at his face, venting her rage at Kim and Mitch's murderer, her frustration at authorities, her horror at what was done to the guard from the NSA back in the lounge at the airport.

The girl grabbed Lainie from behind. Lainie felt a sharp edge at her throat but she didn't stop, somehow couldn't. She felt blood trickle down her skin and still primal hysteria would not let her stop. The girl ordered her to stop or she will die and Lainie still didn't stop.

Lainie felt a grip at her armpit. Her right arm went numb. Immediately after came a pinch to her hip-joint and her right leg went numb. She went down to one knee, then was born back in a headlock, the blade no longer threatening to spill her life.

She continued to struggle.

"Why don't you stop," the girl demanded.

Lainie roared and fought on, fear and ire mixing to create a sort of violent fight-or-flight hysteria.

The man was on her, now, his dusky face striped with bloody scratches and twisted in pain. Lainie got an arm free and began hammering his body with it. He tried to press her down with his weight. Reaching around behind him, Lainie found and grabbed something that seemed to be wedged into the waistband of his pants. Immediately his face showed alarm and he struggled back away from her.

Lainie found herself in possession of a handgun.

Without thinking she fired into the ceiling. The deafening sound reverberated off the metal walls.

In the moment left by the shock of the other two, she sprung off the girl and backed up against the side wall where she could keep them both in sight, holding the gun in both hands. It was heavy and felt hot.

"Who the fuck are you?" she asked again.

They looked at her cagily. Fear, but also clear calculation. They weren't stopped, only paused, seeking an opening to regain the upper hand. They were both clearly of Middle-Eastern stock, brown skin and dark hair, and bore a resemblance to each other, though whether due to heritage or actual blood relation Lainie couldn't tell.

These were dangerous people.

"You are a good fighter," the girl said.

Lainie could have laughed, if not for the grimness of the situation. If it hadn't been for a sudden rush of adrenaline she would not have surprised them as she had.

"Why are you trying to kill me?" Lainie demanded.

"I could have killed you," the girl said. "While you slept off the tranquilizer, or with the knife just now. I didn't."

Lainie blinked. "Then what's going on?"

The driver said something to the girl in the same

language the girl had used earlier, but she cut him off with a gesture. "We want to know where our father is. We know Sean Brandt took him, we know he is hiding him." Defiant still.

"Took who," Lainie demanded. "Hiding who?"

The girl gave her an as-if-you-didn't-know glare and said, "Dr. Faisal Al-Sehremni."

"I've never heard of him. What makes you think I know where he is?"

"You people took him. Kidnapped him."

"Me?" Lainie demanded, confused.

"That —" a word in her own language "- American, Sean Brandt. We saw you go into his flat and come out with another man."

Brandt's apartment. Steele.

"The restaurant, the hotel, then the NSA office parking garage. And then you left there with the other man, the one killed at the airport. Then we were sure, you are one of them. Spies. Assassins. Do not deny it."

The driver – her brother? – said something to the girl in their own language, which sounded like Arabic to Lainie. Now Lainie recognized him, the young man in the hallway of the hotel who'd watched NSA agents chase her and take her. The girl answered him, then turned back to Lainie.

"I do not know who it was that tried to kill the two of you at the airport, I do not care, you Americans have earned many enemies. But I could not let him kill you. You must tell us where you have taken our father."

"What happened to him?" Lainie asked. "The man with the knife?"

"He sleeps as you slept," the girl answered.

Not dead, too bad. But perhaps discovered by Airport Security before he woke up. Lainie hoped so.

As if reading Lainie's thoughts the girl added, "I would have killed him had I been able to bring any other weapon through the security checkpoint."

"How did you get me out?" Lainie asked. In spite of her more urgent need to ask other questions, she couldn't think clearly.

"Easy," the girl said. "Ibrahim, here, carried you out over his shoulder and we laughed loudly the whole time as if it was a game. People let us pass without question."

The driver - Ibrahim – lunged for the gun. Lainie raised it and he hesitated, then smiled. "She will not shoot," he said with derision. Then he simply snatched it out of her grasp.

But Lainie had developed another plan while talking to them. The van had matching doors on each side that slid back on tracks. Reaching behind her Lainie pulled the handle to the sliding door at the port side of the van. As it rolled open precipitously it caused her to spin. Suddenly she was stumbling out into the blinding light of day as they yelled at her to stop. They may have tried to catch her, she couldn't tell.

A horn blared as Lainie spun out of control and the huge grill of a giant truck bore down on her. Clearly Ibrahim had parked the van on the shoulder of a highway, onto which Lainie now fell, sprawled out into the middle of the slow lane. Tires squealed and stuttered on the blacktop. Lainie curled up into a ball. The sunlight was blotted out by noise and stink.

CHAPTER 19

She smelled oil, gas and burnt rubber. Traffic shushed by, but a giant engine idled directly over her head. She opened her eyes. She lay under a semi tractor. She gasped back a sob of terror. She turned her head away from the heat and could see the lower portion of the van on the shoulder of the road past a huge tire, as the door slid shut. The van's engine roared, its tires squealed, and it peeled away at speed.

"Hey," someone yelled, a male voice, gruff, filled with alarm.

She heard heels hit the pavement. She craned her neck to the other side where a pair of worn cowboy boots were visible near the other front tire. Then a grizzled face appeared as the trucker bent down to blink at her.

"How are you?" he asked as if surprised she was alive at all.

"F-fine," she said. "How are y-you?"

*   *   *

"Jesus, is that blood?"

The truck driver had helped her out from under his truck but was now looking at her in horror, covered as she was from chest to knees in sticky, drying blood. She almost told him it wasn't her blood. Through her trembling she somehow realized this would raise more questions than she was prepared to stand here in the middle of the highway answering at the moment. Already the cars backed up behind them were honking and veering around them, drivers shouting expletives and waving fingers.

Instead Lainie said, "It isn't real."

The driver looked as if he wanted to ask questions, then clearly decided not to get involved. It wasn't hard to talk him out of calling the police, scratching a stubbly chin he seemed reluctant to involve himself in anything that would delay his schedule. She did accept his offer of a ride, however.

They had been taking her somewhere out of town, her two kidnappers, and Lainie had no idea where she was. The trucker had been leaving town as well and wasn't about to turn around and take her back. He said the nearest place he could drop her was a truck stop that he said was about fifteen miles outside Baltimore.

He drove with a fast-food paper cup clutched in his right hand into which he frequently spat tobacco juice. He showed a concentrated lack of interest in how she'd come to be thrown out into traffic, covered in muck as she was. As if to fill the silence, he talked about his truck, describing the horsepower and torque with pride and finally launching into a brief primer on how to drive a vehicle with 18 gears, a complex process involving switches on the shift-head itself called *splitters* which multiplied the gears themselves. Lainie rode in the passenger seat listening and nodding politely. His voice became hypnotic and she found herself listening intently, suspecting she was in shock but unable to shake out of it.

The driver seemed relieved to drop her at the truck stop and be on his way. Before she climbed down from the truck she asked him if he had a spare shirt she could borrow. Looking at her askance, he sighed and reached back behind the seats through a little trap door into the sleeper compartment and rummaged. He pulled out a red flannel shirt, rumpled and looking worn, seemed reluctant, then thrust it at her, mumbling something about punishment for good deeds.

In the ladies restroom she tried to remove most of the dust and grime from her hands, face and hair, but she knew she still looked a fright. She had scrapes and bruises all over, both visible and hidden by her clothing. The shirt her rescuer gave her covered the bloodstains nearly to her knees, at least enough to escape casual notice.

She had no one else to call, so using her cell phone, returned to her by the NSA along with the rest of her belongings, she called Steele.

Her bags were on their way back to San Francisco without her. She had nothing to wear. Her laptop was presumably still in the lounge at the airport, or in a police evidence room. She ordered some coffee without a cent in her pocket and took a booth to wait for Steele.

She'd seen more blood in one day than in her entire life, drugged, beaten, and nearly turned into road kill. Badly shaken, Lainie was convinced she should go back to the airport and make use of the ticket the NSA had bought for her.

Nearly.

Steele appeared in thirty minutes, a silver streak fishtailing into the lot and into a parking slot without slowing down. In the face of what had just happened to her there was still an irrepressible part of her that willfully noted his walk. He had a nice, firm butt and long, straight legs. He waved at her through the window and came inside, joined her at her table.

"I take it you've been busy," he said. "Are you all right? What are you wearing?"

"Who's Dr. Faisal Al-Sehremni?" she asked him, ignoring his question. Perhaps her fake spy persona should already know who the doctor was, but she wasn't in the mood to play spy just now. Just now, she was tired and pissed off and sick of secrets.

"He's the scientist who developed the formula," Steele said readily, not at all surprised that she had asked. "Why?"

"I just had a run in with his kids?"

"Really?" he said, frowning. "Simi and Ibrahim? I

didn't know they were in town. Don't guess I should be surprised. I suppose they want the formula back."

"They wanted their father."

"What?" he said.

"They seemed to think Brandt had kidnapped him."

Steele's brow stayed furrowed. "That doesn't make any sense. I don't suppose they said what made them think he'd been kidnapped?"

"I didn't get the chance to ask."

"I don't imagine so," he said wryly.

She wasn't sure what he meant, but again there was that instant acceptance of her ability to handle herself in dangerous situations. Even the initial concern he'd shown over her obvious condition was more professional than sympathetic. He thought she was as highly trained as he. Training or none, after what she'd been through she felt she had earned that respect. That he granted it so readily made her like him against reason.

"Still," he went on, "they should have found the body by now."

"Whose body?"

"The doc's. Brandt was supposed to get the formula out of him, then liquidate him."

Lainie felt a chill, hearing it put so clinically.

"This is all fucked up," he puzzled. "Hold on a moment."

Steele got up and stepped out into the parking lot. She watched him place a call on a cell phone. She glanced at the TV behind the breakfast bar. The sound was low. It appeared to be some trashy talk show. She turned back to watch Steele hang up before coming back in, taking his seat, shaking his head.

"Paris station reports that the body of the Doc has not been found by authorities. If it was at his office a janitor would have found it, if no one else. If at home, his kids wouldn't be here looking for him. Someone's trying to pull a fast one.

"Do you think it was them, Simi and Ibrahim, who

killed Brandt?" he asked her.

She shook her head. "I don't know, but I don't think so. It seemed as if they grabbed me because they couldn't find Brandt *or* their father. They think the government is holding their father somewhere."

"Why would someone on the other side hide the doc's body? It seems even more questions would be raised by a disappearance than a simple murder."

"Maybe Brandt didn't kill him," Lainie said.

Steele's piercing eyes focused on her intently.

"I think from his journal," she went on, "that Brandt was laboring under a huge burden of guilt for all of the killings he'd done. Maybe he was tired of the life of an assassin. Maybe instead of killing him Brandt took the doctor with him, and the formula."

"Why?" Steele asked.

Lainie shrugged.

"Okay, where?"

Lainie had already guessed, and she watched Steele, waiting for him to make the connection himself. Finally, his head snapped up, his eyes meeting hers, and she saw the same idea come to life in his eyes.

"The motel..." Steele began.

"In Commerce City, Colorado," Lainie finished for him.

CHAPTER 20

A waitress came while Steele was on his phone again, calling information to get the number of the motel and speaking to the clerk, so Lainie ordered him a coffee. When Steele snapped off the phone Lainie looked at him expectantly.

"You're right," he said. "An elderly middle-eastern gentleman checked in with Brandt. The clerk remembers because they stayed a week and almost never went out. He thought they were father and son because the younger man seemed very protective of the older man. He got the impression they were hiding from something. Or someone."

"Why didn't the clerk tell that to the investigator who was sent?" Lainie asked.

"The clerk said because the agent didn't ask," Steele shrugged wryly. "He didn't strike me as very bright."

"So Al-Sehremni was Brandt's prisoner?" Lainie asked.

"Doesn't sound like it," Steele mused. "More like Brandt fakes up some papers for the doc, brings him across and takes him someplace no one is likely to look for him. Instead of killing him like he was told to. Why?"

"Political asylum, maybe?"

"There are channels for that, and Brandt knows them. Knew them. When Brandt found Dr. Al-Sehremni, he was In Paris, of all places, working at a legitimate lab outside the city.

He was a guest of the French government working and exchanging ideas on immune systems and stuff like that. Political asylum would have been easy to arrange from there. Anyway, that wasn't the assignment. No, Brandt was up to something else. He had his own rogue agenda."

"Dr. Al-Sehremni was working on the formula in Paris," Lainie said, incredulous.

"Exactly. Last word we had from Brandt, he had a plan for infiltrating the lab, getting the formula and an exit strategy for getting out of the country. He was supposed to meet me in New York to deliver the formula two weeks ago, but he didn't show."

"Why New York?"

"Because you folks at the NSA still didn't know he was working for us, too, at that time." He gave her a rueful look. "Anyway, Paris Station couldn't find him, so to find out if the NSA knew anything we had to come clean with them. A few days later you showed up at his apartment. I expected someone sooner."

"So now," Lainie said, "it looks like he didn't kill Al-Sehremni, but took him to Colorado, where someone tracked them down and killed them."

"Killed Brandt," Steele said, "we only know that much, if that much."

"You don't believe me, either," Lainie said, unable to keep the anger from her voice.

"Easy," Steele said, "easy. I didn't say I didn't believe you. Why, don't your superiors believe you?"

Lainie stayed silent, realizing she was on the verge of blowing her...well, she supposed spies called it a cover.

Steele said, 'I believe that you heard something, but your own man said the motel room was clean. You know as well as I do we can't assume anything. Maybe it was part of his attempts to duck everyone, fake his own death."

Lainie forced herself to admit that in light of everything she'd learned so far, what Steele said seemed most likely. "Who was Al-Sehremni working for?" she asked.

KEVIN PAUL TRACY

"The same prominent Arab investors paying his grants have also been tentatively linked to support of prominent terrorist organizations, deep ones, the ones you don't necessarily hear about on the news every night."

Lainie's blood, already running cold, froze solid. What had she gotten herself into? She was hoping to find something to clear her name, but not only did everything she found out only sound more and even more incredible, it only served to set her back further and further from what she came here for, to clear her name of arson and homicide. Certainly nothing she'd found out so far were things she could take to Detective Gillis back home in San Francisco with any hope of convincing him.

She wasn't sure she wanted to know the answer to her next question. "What, exactly, does the formula do?"

He gave her a puzzled glance that told her this was something she should already know. Thinking quickly, she said, "I have the file on my desk but things have been moving pretty fast and I haven't had a chance to catch up."

He seemed to buy that, nodding. "Okay, well we've been calling it a formula, but it's more than that. It's a formula combined with an engineering schematic combined with an ordinance blueprint. It's supposed to be a revolutionary new delivery system for chemical warfare. It sounds like something out of Star Trek, but I assure you it is one hundred percent real. He's developed a means of bonding almost any chemical or biological agent to highly focused energy beams."

Lainie felt her eyelid twitch. "A l...laser?" Lainie asked.

"Particle beam," he answered seriously. "Completely invisible, highly focused with range and accuracy enough to be deployed on any satellite and used to target specific individuals or whole neighborhoods. By sweeping you could devastate a city in minutes. It can also be vehicle- or tripod-mounted. Botulism, anthrax, serin, you name it. He had particular success with HG3000."

"HG3000?"

"What we call Horror Gas. New, nasty. It attacks the

96

mucous membranes the way salt attacks a snail, only more violently. The eyes swell and pop like rotten grapes, the tongue swells, blisters and cracks open in seconds, blood spurts out of the ears, the body reacts like...I don't know, like a sack full of rats fighting or something."

Steele must have heard Lainie's gorge rise with an audible *urp* because he stopped and looked over at her.

She swallowed. "So the killer who's after me killed Al-Sehremni when he killed Brandt." Her voice was shaking. "Or they faked their deaths on the phone with me and slipped away."

"No," he shook his head. "I've been trying to tell you the last thing the clerk at the motel told me. He said Brandt never checked out, but a day or so later, the older gentleman who'd checked in with him did."

"What?"

"The doc's still alive."

"So Brandt faked his own death and left the scientist behind?" she asked.

"Well, possibly" Steele said, "but not likely. Why would he take the doc all the way from Paris to Colorado just to ditch him in the end?"

"Then whoever came after them," Lainie said, "killed Brandt but not the doctor."

"At first I was thinking," Steele said, "that it was the people financing the doc who tracked them down."

"If so," Lainie said, "then after killing Brandt and they would have taken Al-Sehremni with them, not left him behind to wander into the motel office later looking for Brandt."

"Maybe it was someone who didn't know that Brandt and the doctor were together," Steele said. "Or knew but didn't care, or had other reasons for leaving the doc alive."

"Like what?" Lainie asked.

Steele leaned forward intently. "Say Brandt was stupid enough to buy whatever sob story Al-Sehremni told him and helped the doc fool customs to get over here, but the doc's plan all along was to develop the formula here and use it. So the doc made his contact here, and the contact came and killed Brandt."

"But again," Lainie said, "if that was the case, why would the doc wait two days to check out, risk being linked to Brandt and hauled in?"

"I don't know," Steele said.

Lainie thought out loud, "The man sent to inspect the room didn't mention Al-Sehremni, which means the doctor wasn't there. Maybe he wasn't there when Brandt was killed, either. Maybe the doctor was as baffled as everyone else about what happened to Brandt."

"Seems a stretch to me," Steele squinted at her. "I like the doc for some sort of involvement in Brandt's murder, and now the killer's after you because you overheard the hit."

"But why would they send him after me?" she demanded. "Why not just all disappear?"

"Loose end? Who knows?"

She shook her head. "That guy, this assassin or whatever he is, seems awfully determined just to tie up a loose end, and he seems pissed. Almost as if it's personal between us."

Steele's cellular telephone danced briefly on the table where he'd left it and he looked at the display screen. She heard it vibrate again. He said, "I have to take this," and stepped outside once more.

She sat staring at nothing. Other things didn't make sense to her, either, things she couldn't mention to Steele. As always the core question of why Brandt would call a telephone sex line with so much else going on around him. She was sure most men wouldn't make such a call with other men in the room, which means that the doctor hadn't been with him at the time. Where had he been?

Was it all a ruse? Had Brandt merely called Capri Entertainment to stage his own death, as Mitch and others suspected, maybe to shake off any pursuit as Steele thought? If so, then why use an assumed name? In fact, weren't there better ways to fake one's own death, ways that simply made more sense? And putting the final nail in the coffin of that theory was the killer still stalking her.

Everything was happening too fast. She felt as if she couldn't catch her breath.

"Lainie Parker."

Lainie turned to look at the television from which, impossibly, it seemed her name had just come. She saw her face displayed prominently on the screen. She strained to listen to the low-volume audio. It was a special breaking news report.

"Police are seeking Lainie Parker in connection with the brutal murder of a government functionary in the VIP lounge of BWI Airport today."

CHAPTER 21

Lainie watched horrified as the image on the television behind the breakfast bar shifted to a cartoonish silhouette cut-out of a man with a large question mark in the center of its head.

"Police are also looking for a witness to the crime who apparently tried to intervene in the murder and was knocked unconscious for his trouble. After questioning by the police he disappeared. Police describe him as African American, large build, approximately six-foot-two, with a crew cut and close-cropped goatee."

Lainie's stalker.

"Want another one?" Lainie turned to see Steele walking toward her again. "Another coffee?" he elaborated.

Lainie ducked her head, panic struggling to take her screaming out of the diner. *I didn't kill him. The man they say was a witness did. That's the guy. The one that killed Brandt and Kim and Mitch...and tried to kill me.*

"You look pale," he said. "But I don't know you well enough to know if that's a good thing or a bad thing."

She looked at the TV again and there was a frozen image of the Capri Entertainment offices, burnt and blasted, no longer smoldering. The voiceover was saying, "...is also urgently sought for questioning in connection with the firebombing of these offices in San Francisco, California, which performed phone sex services..."

"What's up?" he asked, glancing at the television as well.

"Can we go," she blurted, snapping his attention back to her. Trying to smile, she said, "Do you have some place I can get cleaned up?"

*   *   *

Steele took curves with dizzying speed, slipped over hills and bumped through dips as if on a cushion of air, and took straight-aways as if they were a challenge to see who'd quit first. This time Lainie didn't mind. Chill or not, she welcomed the play of the wind through her hair, across her face. The air passed over her nostrils with enough force that she barely had to inhale at all.

The knot of fear in her gut had found no respite since Brandt's call to Capri, and now it threatened to unbind her resolve entirely. Instead of clearing her name she was in worse trouble now. Speeding along in the Lexus felt like escape.

It was over too soon and she felt the car slowing as it climbed a hill. She opened her eyes and saw that the car was now spiraling up a slope with an ivy-covered brick wall on the left side and a view over Baltimore to the right. The road terminated at a garage, which was already opening. Steele pulled in next to a motorcycle with the BMW logo on the gas tank and set the parking break.

He hopped out over the car door and ran around to let Lainie out. She felt intoxicated from the speed. As the garage door closed itself, he led her through an interior door. She found herself in a mudroom with coats hanging on hooks, a water heater and furnace and a dark hall leading further back. Rising up toward the light was a cast-iron spiral staircase and he motioned for her to go on ahead of him.

The next floor was a workshop with benches and tools and the smell of wood and fragrant oils. Steele encouraged her on to the next floor where she found a kitchen and dining room and, through another door, a sitting room. On this level he told her to wait as he went on up the last flight. The kitchen was small but functional, the counters cluttered with appliances including a small indoor electric grill and, of all things, a cappuccino machine. She turned a knob and a spout of steam was so loud she hurried to shut it off again.

The dining room presented a round wood-plank table and captain's chairs. On the table waited a bowl of fresh fruit and the remains of the morning paper. Realizing she hadn't eaten yet Lainie took an apple and bit into it absently as she walked through to the sitting room.

Here one entire curved wall was made up of glass panels overlooking Baltimore, the morning fog having burned off and the afternoon smog just beginning to settle in. The furniture was plush and cushiony, cream-colored coarse fabric and lots and lots of pillows. An entertainment center dominated one wall with a huge flat-screen TV and audio system.

Munching on the apple, she hit the power switch on the audio system. The CD player picked up where it'd left off and she recognized the voice of Willie Nelson singing *Crazy*. Lainie shook her head and turned back to the stairway as Steele reappeared carrying a white first aid kit with a red cross on it and a clean shirt draped over his arm.

"Sit down," he said. "Let's play doctor."

She sat on the edge of one of the chairs, putting her half-eaten apple on an end table.

He knelt in front of her and opened the case, preparing a cotton ball with hydrogen peroxide. He reached for her left hand and applied the cotton ball to the scraped heel. She sucked in a breath with an audible hiss on first contact, then forced herself to remain silent. He was gentle, but determined as he used his fingernails to work gravel free of the wound. His hands were strong, economical in their movements, confident.

As he proceeded with her right hand she looked at the part in his hair. It was rakishly crooked, but the hair was thick, strong. His shoulders weren't particularly broad, but neither were his hips.

The feel of his firm but soft hands caring for her wounds countered by the brief sting of each scrape as it was treated was becoming erotic. He sat up on the coffee table, his knees intermittent with hers, and looked into her face. He was studying her contusions with a critical, piercing blue gaze.

He pressed a spot on her forehead and she winced.

"Bruise," he said. "Can't do much about that."

He applied peroxide to a scrape on her right cheek.

"What is this place, anyway?" she asked.

"It's where I live. I call it The Lighthouse, but only because that's how it seems from the inside. From the outside it just looks like some windows built into the rock of the bluff. The architect designed the house to blend with the natural environment completely except for the windows. He designed it for this lady artist. When she refused to leave her husband for him, the architect had no use for the place. I got it for almost a song."

Lainie was only half listening.

For whatever reason, Brandt didn't kill Al-Sehremni, but brought him back and hid him in a motel in Commerce City, Colorado. The murderer who'd killed Brandt while he was on the phone with Lainie, if murder there really was, left the scientist alive. Why? Because they were working together, or was it merely because the doctor wasn't in the room to be killed?

The killer also went to a lot of trouble to track Lainie down, covering his own tracks with such extreme measures as firebombing the offices of Capri Entertainment. He tried twice to kill her. Why? That she was a loose end just didn't seem enough of a reason.

Suppose the murderer had tracked her to Baltimore in much the same way she had tracked Brandt, through credit card receipts. At her apartment her knives had been moved and her phone disconnected, and if he'd had time to do that it was reasonable to assume he'd had time to dig for her personal info. It hadn't occurred to Lainie to hide such information before so it wouldn't have been hard to find.

In order to track her from her hotel to the NSA and to the airport he had to have been close when the NSA came to get her. He must have tracked her credit card to the hotel, been waiting for her to come out, Just like the young Arab man, Ibrahim. Must have seen the agents chase her or carry her through the lobby and out the back, or perhaps he was waiting in a car outside. The NSA may have just saved her life by taking her when they did, because the murderer would most certainly have gotten to her soon if they hadn't. Would the scientist's son have intervened?

Lainie was aghast at her own luck, and at the string of shadows she'd unknowingly had trailing her during the last two days. She'd had no clue she was being followed, by the motel killer, or Simi and her brother. Who else'd been following her without her being any the wiser? It all brought into stark relief just how inexperienced she was at this cloak and dagger shit. Dangerously inexperienced.

"Samantha?" Steele was calling her by her stage name.

"What?"

"Where were you," he said. His face was so close to hers, his breath like the warmth of a spring breeze on her skin. "You were a million miles away?"

She didn't answer.

He looked at her lips, then back to her eyes. She knew he was about to kiss her just as surely as she knew she would do nothing to stop him. But just as his dry, warm lips brushed hers, she unexpectedly flashed on an unwanted image of the NSA guard, his throat a gaping black gash, blood fountaining from it in a brackish torrent. She grunted, pushed Steele away from her and ran into the kitchen to heave over the sink. Truck stop coffee and apple chunks came up, then nothing but the taste of bile.

"Not quite the reaction I was going for," he said from the doorway. "Are you all right?"

Embarrassed, Lainie trembled as she rinsed her mouth

and the sink out. She was angry with herself. She couldn't let her guard down like this. It was seductive, tucking herself under Steele's protective arm, letting him make the world go away like this. But he was as great a danger to her as the murderer was, should he discover she wasn't who he thought she was. She hated the part of her that wanted a rescuer, a knight in shining armor.

Pointing to the shirt he'd brought down, still draped on his arm, she asked, "Is that for me?"

He stood at the foot of the stairs until she finally met his gaze impatiently. Shrugging, he nodded, "It is. That one smells like a bus driver."

She snatched the shirt from him, doffed the one she was wearing and the bloody sweater underneath, not caring that he saw her bra, then put on the one Steele give her. It was a light blue button-down of some sort of crisp linen fabric and she had to roll up the sleeve to free her hands.

"Do you have any idea where we can find Simi and Ibrahim?" she asked.

"Some," he said. "I know what you're thinking. I was thinking the same thing. Sooner or later their dad is going to find out they're looking for him and try to contact them, to either have them join him or to tell them to go home. Clearly they aren't in on whatever he's up to or they'd know where he was and what had been done to Brandt."

"Right," Lainie said.

Steele wanted Al-Sehremni in order to get the formula, Lainie thought. But for her, the only link to proof of who'd firebombed Capri and killed the NSA guard at the airport was the scientist. The question was, could she get that proof before Steele spirited the doctor away?

Or worse, finished the job Brandt had been paid to do.

"But when he contacts them," she said, "Simi and Ibrahim won't lead us to him. Not willingly."

"Or not on purpose," he said. "Samantha, what was wrong, just then?"

She stopped and glared out the window. "I saw a man die today. I...just need some time to process that."

"I understand," he said. "Who was it?"

Omitting the interrogation scene at the NSA she told him about the attack at the airport, ending with Simi's interruption.

"What I don't get," Lainie concluded, "why still try to kill me? If he is with terrorists why wouldn't he be trying to lay low after killing Brandt? Why risk being caught and jeopardize whatever operation they have going by coming after me? I mean, I'm not that big a loose end after all."

He shook his head.

"I'm asking," she snapped.

"I don't know," he said, holding up his hands in defense. He came forward to take her in his arms and she pushed him away.

"This is a mistake." The last thing she wanted was Steele feeling like he had to protect her. She had as much to fear from him as anyone else she'd met so far. "Can we just forget this happened?"

"You're welcome to," he said, drawing back coldly, his eyes going to slits.

"To find out why the killer is still after me I need to find Dr. Al-Sehremni, and the only way to do that is to get to the doctor's kids before he does. You coming?"

She marched back down the stairs, not looking to see if he followed.

CHAPTER 22

"They're students," Steele said. "Simi and Ibrahim. Attending New York University on student visas. Are you sure you don't need to pack?"

Lainie clung to her seatbelt as he drove Interstate 95 north bound for New York with the same blacktop-skimming, speed-shifting verve he had shown off before.

"No," she said. "But what makes you think they went back to New York already?"

"They have to keep regular attendance in classes to avoid drawing the attention of authorities. They watch these Student Visas pretty closely these days. Grabbing you the way they did, they're desperate. They're running out of time, and this is the direction they were taking you when you escaped."

"They were taking me to New York?"

He nodded his head, the oncoming terrain reflected dizzyingly in his mirrored sunglasses. "Chances are they were going to interrogate you on the way, dump you somewhere once you told them what they wanted to know."

"Kill me?" Why should they be any different?

He didn't answer at first as he fit the Lexus diagonally between two semi trucks and pasted her to her seat again with even more added speed. Finally he shrugged, "Hard to say. On the surface they're just two kids worried about their dad, not terrorists. Not murderers."

"But...?"

"Well, there are some questionable distant family ties to some known terror cell leaders and even some higher-ups. But it's on their mother's side, not their father's, and their mother died soon after she gave birth to Ibrahim."

"How do you know?"

"I did the background work on Al-Sehremni for the dossier we gave Brandt."

"If you had all the background, why didn't they send you?"

Steele looked at her and smiled. "I'm not an assassin, Samantha. Oh, I'll kill someone if I have to. Have done, as a matter of fact. But it's not my specialty."

"What is your specialty?"

Though he frowned as he studied the traffic ahead of him, probably planning his next stunt of automobile acrobatics, his voice was playful. "Being one sneaky son of a bitch, that's what."

"What does that mean?"

He crossed two lanes to the right, down-shifted around the back of a moving van towing a Volkswagen Beetle, then crossed back one more lane and picked up speed again. She wished he drove a tank instead of a convertible.

"You'll see." He winked at her.

*   *   *

The US Highway Safety Commission estimated New York was nearly a three hour drive from Baltimore, Lainie read in the atlas she'd found in the Lexus' center console. By experience she knew these were conservative estimates, she probably could have made the drive in just over two hours herself, speeding a little.

Steele made the drive in ninety minutes, flat.

It took inner-city traffic to slow him down, but he didn't become impatient. He relaxed, almost reclined, with one hand on the wheel and the other over the back of her seat, humming with the crooked hint of a smile that Lainie had come to associate with him.

Simi and Ibrahim lived together, Steele told her during the drive, with a cousin named Sayed in an apartment off 8th near Washington Square in Greenwich Village. They had been out of town for the summer break, but clearly they were back, looking for their father.

"Unless you have a better one," he said, "the plan is to bug their apartment and maybe their van, then set up shop somewhere nearby and wait. I'd like to get a bug in a coat collar or a book bag or something, but reception is unreliable and they're too easily discovered."

"No," she said, feeling gloomy.

"No what?"

"No, I can't think of a better plan."

"What's wrong, then?"

"Sounds time consuming. I was hoping to have some concrete evidence...sooner."

"You've been watching too many James Bond films," he said. "If that's what you expected, you got into the wrong business. Most of our job is boring. If you're not gathering data you're analyzing it, and vice versa. You should know that by now."

Analyst, Brandt's NSA security badge had said. So it *was* synonymous with spy, after all.

Steele parked at the curb and pointed at a thirty-story high-rise apartment building across the street and a block away. Half-way up this side someone had painted a bright mural, a stylized depiction of images from the writings of John Irving – the plane crashed into the roof of the house from *The World According to Garp*; Susie the Bear from *The Hotel New Hampshire*; several baskets of apples from *The Cider House Rules*, etc. Otherwise, the building was yellow brick and bleached-white concrete. Outward facing shops formed the foundation, a book store, a coffee house, an art gallery, and then windows ranked regularly up the sides and front.

"C'mon," he said eagerly, like a child at Christmas.

They stepped out of the car and he opened the trunk. Inside were several cases, hard and soft. He took out a black vinyl one the size of a shaving kit and closed the trunk again. They crossed against traffic and walked casually to the building. He led her once around the block and through the alley as if on a casual stroll around the building. Out front again Steele opened the door to the coffee joint for Lainie and followed her in. The place was half-full of patrons. They ordered coffee and took a table.

He unclipped a small garage remote from the side of the vinyl case and handed it to her.

He pointed out the window. "I'm sure you saw what I saw. That's the main entrance" - pointing the other direction – "and that's the alley that leads to the parking garage. If you see their van, or see them coming on foot, push that button."

Lainie thought he needed a warrant to bug someone's place. Clearly not.

He slipped out of his chair.

"What if they're already in the apartment?"

He gave her his rakish grin again and ducked out of the store. She watched him disappear toward the building entrance. He was having fun. How could that be? A dark cloud had enveloped Lainie's life ever since Michael/Brandt had entered it and that thunderhead gave no sign of letting up.

But Steele seemed to only truly come alive when risking his neck, which clearly played a part in why he drove the way he did. He was a danger-junkie, she thought, but whatever, his enthusiasm was beginning to be infectious. Lainie found herself hoping Simi and Ibrahim did show up.

Almost.

When she saw Simi outside the coffee shop window, Lainie immediately regretted the wish.

CHAPTER 23

It was inevitable that one of them would appear, Lainie supposed. Steele had been gone a scant ten minutes, the shop had begun to fill up with students when the diminutive dark-haired beauty appeared outside the window wearing jeans and the same olive-green jacket over a NYU sweatshirt. She walked and talked with another man of decided middle-eastern features that was not Ibrahim. Her companion wore black slacks, a black shirt and carried a single textbook in his left hand, his face a stone carving of guarded grimness behind a beard no less wild than Br'er Rabbit's briar patch. He listened attentively while Simi spoke animatedly.

Lainie was about to push the button on the device Steele had given her when the pair paused while Simi made some salient point, then turned and came into the coffee shop. Lainie sat still, not daring to make a move to the exit for fear of drawing attention. She watched them order, pay, then turn and search for a place to sit.

Simi scanned past Lainie, did a double-take and looked directly into her eyes. The fact that Simi's face blanched with fear mirroring Lainies own, only slightly mollified Lainie's beating heart. She saw the girl hesitate, clearly debating whether to turn and run or stay. Lainie saw her set her jaw and march directly toward Lainie's table.

"What are you going to do to me," Simi said, "in public like this?"

Funny, Lainie thought, I was just going to ask you the same thing. She was gratified to see Simi's right eye swollen, almost closed, a respectable shiner she must've earned as a result of their tussle earlier.

Lainie didn't push the button, which she held under the table. That would bring Steele down, interrupting things, and as long as she kept Simi here he was presumably still safe from discovery. Meanwhile, if she played it right, she had a chance to get some of her own questions answered.

"Sit down," Laine said firmly, using the tone she used with the children she'd taught as a teacher's aide whenever they got unruly.

Simi did as she was told.

The stranger said something to Simi in an Arabic dialect and she answered without taking her eyes off Lainie. His eyes widened and he looked at Lainie with more interest than fear.

"Would you mind giving us some privacy?" Lainie said to him.

Lanie watched indignation, anger and resentment slide across his face, then he hid them under a veneer of compliance, murmured something to Simi and moving over to the coffee bar to sit down.

"That is Sayed," Simi said. "He is my cousin."

Lainie didn't say that she already knew the name. Instead, uncertain where to start, she asked, "Where'd you get the nifty tranquilizer gun?"

Simi seemed to consider lying, then glared at Lainie as if refusing to be as secretive as the spies she hated. "Sayed gave it to me." She gestured back without looking over at him.

Lainie glanced at Sayed. He watched them under stormy brows.

"It is made from a pen and pencil set," Simi went on. "The handle of a hairbrush is a CO_2 cartridge."

"Where did he get it?" And why?

"He wouldn't say where he got it, but it got past airport security today without a glance." Simi glared at Lainie as if defying her to make an arrest. Then, keeping her voice low, she said, "You can deport me if you want, but I will find out what you have done with father. You will not get away with killing him, and if you have him prisoner I will make the press make you release him. Where is Jean-Pierre? Or should I say Sean Brandt? Where has he taken my father?"

The press? Jean-Pierre "What makes you think someone took your father?" Lainie asked.

"Because he was being watched by someone. By men. Then father and Jean-Pierre, AKA Sean Brandt, disappeared at the same time."

"How do you know Sean Brandt?"

Simi gave her the same look she had before in the van, the look that said she did not believe Lainie did not already know. "I knew him as Jean-Pierre. In Paris he posed as a friend of my father's, then he kidnapped him for your government."

Lainie sighed. "Start from the beginning. How did you meet Brandt?"

Simi folded her arms as if resigning herself to playing things Lainie's way.

"Fine. Father was living in Paris. He buried himself in his work after Mother died. They sent him to Paris to work with other scientists there. He wouldn't tell us what he worked on or who, exactly, was paying for his Fellowship, but it consumed him. Ibrahim and I went to Paris to be with him for Ramadan instead of home to the UAE. He had a new friend, a man he came to know from the pub he frequented on his way from the labs each day."

"Brandt," Lainie said.

"Jean-Pierre. They were very close, talking philosophy and playing chess until the small hours every night. Through father we came to like and to trust Jean-Pierre as well. He seemed truly fond of father, even waiting on him in his own home because father has a bent back...spine...and doesn't move very well."

This had been part of Brandt's assignment, to befriend the scientist in order to get access to the formula.

"Chess?" Lainie asked. Chessboards of various design littered Brandt's apartment, as well as books, magazines, catalogs...

"Yes. They played chess constantly, every time they sat down together. They read the chess problems in the newspaper every morning and tried to solve them. They were obsessed with the game. Jean-Pierre was the first friend I ever knew father to have."

Lainie saw the girl's love for her father in her eyes. She felt pangs of sympathy herself, not having spoken to her own father for nearly three months before he died. Though he'd divorced her mother, for which Lainie couldn't blame him, and lost custody, Lainie and her father tried to stay close in the years before he died of a heart attack, but life intruded for both of them.

Then in an intuitive flash Lainie said, "You loved Brandt...Jean-Pierre."

Simi's face colored, though with anger or embarrassment was difficult to tell. That face was beautiful, but also hard.

"He spoke love to me," she said. "He was so kind to father, so respectful of our home and our customs, and I soon came to have feelings for him as well. As a brother, an uncle."

Lainie doubted the last part, Simi said it with much too empathy.

"Then what?" Lainie pressed.

Simi hadn't touched her coffee. "When we returned to Paris for summer break there were several messages on Father's answering machine. The lab was looking for him. That morning father had never reported to work. We called the police. An investigation found no sign of either of them. You know this."

"What made you think Brandt took your father against his will?"

"Because father would never have gone voluntarily,"

Simi said. "Not without letting Ibrahim and I know where he was going and how to contact him."

Unless he thought you were safer not knowing, Lainie thought.

"When father disappeared," Simi continued, "I went to Jean-Pierre for help. When he didn't answer for two days I talked the landlord into letting me into his place – I was afraid he, like father, had met with foul play. The pace showed no sign of him, no sign that he'd been there, ever."

Any number of questions vied for attention in Lainie's mind, she didn't know which to ask next. In the end she asked, "So what made you think I'd know where your father is?"

"We saw you come out of his, Sean's, Baltimore apartment with that CIA agent."

"How did you know the apartment was Sean's," Lainie asked. "For that matter, how did you learn Sean's real name?"

"Jean-Pierre gave me the address," Simi said, now frowning at nothing past Lainie's left shoulder, as if confused by this part of her own story. "The apartment in Baltimore. One night after the Ramadan dinner and my father had gone to bed – he did so earlier these days than before – we sat by the fireplace and Jean-Pierre told me about the apartment he kept in Baltimore, Maryland, United States. He gave me the address and said that if I ever needed to send him a message to mail it there."

That Brandt had broken his own cover, giving Simi his home address, further confused the issue to Lainie. Why would a spy and assassin do that?

"The Paris authorities had no luck finding Father or Jean-Pierre," Simi said. "In fact they had no record of Jean-pierre, no ID, no passport, and he always paid the rent on his Paris flat in cash. There was nothing else for us to do, and we had to return to school or risk losing the university's sponership of our student Visas. When we got back to the states, I sent a message to Jean-Pierre's Baltimore address, asking him where he'd gone and if he knew where my father was."

When Brandt gave Simi his real address he must not have yet been planning to disappear with the scientist, Simi's father, or he probably wouldn't have done it. God knows why he gave it to her, but Lainie kept thinking back to the journal entries and her suspicion that the murders Brandt had committed in the name of his Government were wearing him down. Maybe he harbored some vague hope of retiring and eventually pursuing a normal life, perhaps with Simi as his wife.

"Instead of an answer to the message I sent," Simi went on, "two men showed up here in New York, saying they worked for ICE and asking the three of us – me, Ibrahim, and Sayed – a lot of questions. Too many of the questions had to do with father for there not to be a connection."

"You went to the Baltimore apartment," Laini said. To Simi's raised eyebrows, she said, "You don't strike me as someone to be scared off by a visit from an ICE agent. After he left, you went to Brandt's apartment in Baltimore."

"Only then did we find out Jean-Pierre's real last name was Brandt," Simi said, "from the name on the call button to the apartment. I looked over the mailman's shoulder when he came placing mail in the boxes to find out Sean's first name, too. I am not stupid. I knew my father was working on something of great importance, if by nothing more than his evasions whenever we asked him questions about it."

"After he disappeared," Lainie said, "and your message to Jean-Pierre brought government agents to your doorstep, albeit immigration agents, then you discovered that Sean had an entirely different name...well, it was not a great leap to imagine that your father's work might have been something in which governments would take an interest."

"Especially your government," Simi said, "who consider it their calling to take what they want at will. At any rate, we resolved, Ibrahim and I, to watch Sean Brandt's place for any sign of he or father, and we did so for many days. We saw no sign of them, but last night we saw one of the men who'd come to us claiming to be ICE agents. He came out of the back of the building, got in his car, and drove away. You were with him."

"You followed us to the restaurant," Lainie said.

"When you parted ways," Simi said, "we split up, too. Ibrahim followed you to your hotel and even walked behind you, watching as you let yourself into your room. I hailed a cab to follow the ICE man. Only he wasn't ICE after all. He drove for one hour straight, directly to CIA headquarters in Langley, Virginia. That scared us. A little. But we thought we had leverage. You."

"But how did you show up at the airport," Lainie asked. "When I left the hotel I was in the back of a van myself."

"When I returned to meet Ibrahim at your hotel," Simi said, "it was 2:30 in the morning. We decided to wait until the morning for you to come out, but after sunrise when we saw the van with the government license plate go to the back of the hotel we grew suspicious. Ibrahim ran up to your room to see if you'd gone and saw the men chase you and catch you. So he ran back and we followed the van. When it left the hotel it led us to the NSA complex at Fort Meade."

"You couldn't have known I was in that van," Lainie said.

"It was a hunch that paid off. After some hours we saw you come out of the gates in a car. Yes, riding in the back like someone important. We followed you to the airport. You know the rest."

"Why did you tranquilize me," she said, "kidnap me."

Simi shrugged. "At first we thought you might be a cherished one of the CIA spy we saw you with, whom we could use as leverage to get him to reveal where father was. When we discovered you were a spy yourself, and one quite highly placed, worthy of riding in the back of a limousine as you were and accompanied by a body guard, we realized that you could not only tell us where father was, but that you could issue orders to have him released."

"Then how do you explain the men who were after me?"

"We assumed it was part of your cover," Simi said. "Get arrested to allay suspicions that you are under cover."

This made Lainie want to laugh, but she recognized it for the hysteria it was and bit the laughter back. The thought of the way she'd blundered from one point to the next in this affair, completely unaware of the danger that followed her, of the merry caravan she'd unwittingly led this morning from the hotel to the NSA complex to the airport, made her want to vomit.

"It was lucky you intervened when you did," Lainie said.

"Clearly you have made many enemies," Simi said. "But I couldn't let the man with the knife kill you before we got the information we needed."

Lainie glanced over, but Sayed was gone. Quickly she cast around and saw his back as he ducked out of the coffee shop. How much had he overheard? Under the table, Lainie pushed the little button Steele had given her. As an afterthought, she pressed it several more times, then held it down.

"He got tired of waiting," Simi said, following Lainie's gaze, "and I'm tired of talking. So if you are going to arrest me and deport me, do it now."

Lainie didn't have the authority to do that, of course, and wouldn't even if she could. She didn't want to do anything to keep Dr. Al-Sehremni from contacting his children, so that Steele could intercept the call. Still, she thought it best to distract Simi a little more while Steele contended with evading discovery by Sayed.

"What does Sayed know?" Lainie asked.

"All of it," Simi answered. "But he does not help us. He is a distant cousin. He is no blood relation to us or my father. He wishes to help, he gave me the tranquilizer gun, but Ibrahim and I will not let him do more, to risk his visa as we do."

Desperately trying to think of other questions, Lainie said, "You claim you never knew what your father was working on."

"Yes," Simi said defiantly. "He wouldn't tell us. But don't believe me, because I wouldn't tell you even if I did know."

Oddly, Lainie did believe her. Simi had no clue what her father was into, and the scientist was not likely to involve his daughter. But, perhaps his son was another matter.

"Where's Ibrahim?" Lainie asked.

"Behind you," Simi sneered.

Lainie very nearly turned in terror, before realizing there was no way the girl's brother could have come into the store and gotten behind her unseen. However, it did make her realize that she'd been concentrating on Simi this whole time. Ibrahim could have slipped past outside and entered the building without her noticing.

She pushed the button again, several times.

"So are you going to arrest me," Simi asked. "If not, then I am done here. I have to find my father."

Lainie hesitated. Simi took her silence as an opportunity to stand and march out of the café, leaving her coffee behind.

Simi was no spy, no terrorist, Lainie realized. She was just a girl looking for her missing father, culturally suspicious of Americans and to some degree understandably so. Lainie asked herself what lengths she would go to in order to find her own father. He died of a heart attack, but under other circumstances wouldn't she have given her own life if it could have saved his? Lainie liked Simi, grudgingly, in spite of the tranquilizer and the kidnapping. She pitied Simi and felt compelled to give her some hope that her father was alive. A real spy would not, but Lainie was not a real spy.

Lainie stood, stuffed the button-device into the front pocket of her jeans, and hurried after Simi. Out on the street, a chilly dusk draping the city, Lainie lost the girl in the sparse crowd, then saw her turning into the alleyway that Steele had said led to the parking garage. Rushing, Lainie only just caught up to Simi as she was turning into the garage entrance.

She touched Simi's shoulder and the girl spun around, backing away a step defensively.

"You should know," Lainie said to Simi, "I...we have no idea where your father is, either."

Simi snorted in derision and looked away.

Lainie shrugged. "Believe me or not, your choice. But it's true. We're looking for your father just as urgently as you are."

Now Simi studied her with some doubt, as if wondering whether it could be true. Her lower lip trembled, but that was the only sign of emotion.

"Lies."

This hissed condemnation came from behind Simi. Lainie looked past her into the gloom of the garage. Sayed stood there, looking at the two of them with an expression of utter disdain. Simi turned her back to Lainie to face him.

"Sayed?" she said. "What...?"

"Lies," he said again. Striding indolently toward them he lifted his light jacket so that they could see the gun tucked into his pants, then covered it again.

Past Sayed, loitering near the elevator, Lainie saw another man looking around as if ready for trouble. She turned, and coming into the garage behind her were two others. All three appeared to also be of Middle Eastern descent, like Sayed.

Lainie backed up until she was heel-to-heel with Simi.

"Sayed," Simi hissed angrily, "this is none of your concern. Go back to the apartment."

Sayed used a word from his own language to address her that made Simi gasp. "Alter your tone, woman," he continued. "Living among these Americans, you forget your place."

Lainie had the device Steele gave her in hand once more, pumping the button frantically at her side. She glanced over her shoulder as Sayed pushed Simi out of the way firmly. Lainie tried to duck quickly away but he gripped her arm hard and pulled her back up against him, prodding her spine rudely with a knuckle. He snatched the button-device from her.

"What is this?" he whispered urgently, chin on her shoulder, mouth near her ear.

She locked her teeth and continued to look forward.

She heard the plastic casing hit the floor, heard it crunch under his heel.

CHAPTER 24

Sayed's breath on Lainie's neck was hot, redolent of heady exotic spices she didn't recognize.

Simi marched around them and confronted Sayed.

"I asked you what you think you are doing. This is not your concern."

Sayed released Lainie and stepped past her. He struck Simi, backhanded, so hard she nearly fell, but the two other men that had followed Lainie and Simi into the garage were suddenly flanking Simi, holding her arms as much to restrain as support her. Lainie could see that Simi's face was flushed with shock and rage. Sayed said something in Arabic and Simi stared at him as if seeing him for the first time.

Lainie pivoted on her heel and fled. Confronted by the man in front of the elevator, crouched as if to intercept her, Lainie ducked left between two cars, keeping low and hidden. She ran in a crouch, not daring to peer up. She turned left again and was running between the facing grills of parked vehicles back toward the alley exit.

Seeing Sayed abruptly loom ahead of her made her stop in alarm. Thinking quickly, she turned left between two cars again, but it wasn't quickly enough. The man from the elevator was closer than she thought and she felt him clamp the back of her neck and bring her up short. Lainie tried to resist, but the man's stone-grip prevented much movement. When she tried he squeezed harder, making her ears roar and the edges of her vision fold in on themselves. He pushed her forward, back out into the open area again where Simi was held by the two and Sayed joined them.

At Sayed's command the men led Simi and Lainie along the ranks of parked cars, deeper into the parking garage. Lainie knew she should stop struggling, hope to lull their captors into a false sense of her helplessness, but the urge to get away was primal.

Though Simi walked ahead of Lainie, she sagged between the men holding her. It seemed irrational given what Simi had done to her, but Lainie hoped Simi's cousin hadn't hurt her too badly. She'd developed a grudging respect for the tough young girl.

However, Simi proved more adept at misdirection than Lainie. As they approached a van — the van Simi and Ibrahim had taken her in earlier this morning, Lainie realized — they paused to tie Lainie's hands with a length of clothesline drawn from Sayed's pocket. Lainie fought them now in spite of the white-hot pain delivered to her vertebrae. While this occupied Sayed, Simi seemed to stumble, and then sprung back up and began to *whirl*. She became a dervish of motion, flying fists and feet impacting their captors with solid, painful-sounding hits that sent them scattering.

The men closed on their diminutive target relentlessly, taking hits and delivering some of their own. Lainie wanted to help the tiny lone figure but, her wrists now tied, the man holding her neck forced her to kneel. She strained her eyes around for some sort of weapon that she might lunge for if she could break free, but there was nothing in sight.

Eventually Simi ran out of steam. Two of the thugs finally held her, squirming, while Sayed retrieved jumper-cables from the van. At first Lainie thought they were going to whip the girl, but instead her cousin used the cables to tie her hands and her knees together, hog tying her with some difficulty as she struggled. The captors hoisted Simi up and tossed her into the van. Lainie climbed in when directed to and waddled awkwardly on her knees to Simi's side.

Two of the men reclined in the back, sitting among the pillows and cushions on either side of the two women, while the other two men stepped up into the cab, Sayed in the passenger seat. The van roared to life, pulled out of the parking slot and took a speedy course, where Lainie had no way of knowing.

"What do you think they want," Lainie whispered.

Simi turned her head, matted with her wild black hair, and bared her teeth at Lainie. "I do not know," she said. Then she screamed an expletive toward the front of the van in their language, bringing a brief glare from Sayed.

"Shh," Lainie urged her. "Think. What could they want?"

Lainie knew the two men in back were listening, but it didn't matter.

"If they had only taken you," Simi said, "I would have thought Sayed was trying to help us find father. But what he said..."

"What did he say?"

"He called me...never mind. It is our word for traitor."

"He thinks you have betrayed your country somehow?"

"Not a traitor to country," Simi grated. "Traitor to Allah. To God."

Laine sat back and left Simi to her fury.

She knew she'd squandered her chance to get away back at the garage, circling back as she had. She had no idea what Sayed and his friends wanted, but she didn't need to guess that it wasn't good. Perhaps she and Simi were enemies, but as captives they had become sisters – the enemy of my enemy, etc. Lainie might be of no use to the girl wherever the men were taking them, but to leave Simi alone in the hands of these men, even if Lainie could get away, would be worse than cowardly.

The two men watching them had hard, grim faces.

They looked too old to be college students. Their dead eyes reminded her of someone. She flashed on the necrotic look in the eyes of the photo on Brandt's ID badge and realized this was the look of deadly men on deadly business. Men who had seen too much.

Lainie thought she knew who they might be - the men after Sean Brandt and the scientist.

For most Americans the word *terrorist* had taken on the same dark connotation as *demon* or *devil*, epic in their monstrosity and evil. Now, faced with flesh-and-blood men who wore the word like a shroud, Lainie realized the reality was even more terrifying. Men ready to kill anyone to vent their rage, and eager to die doing so.

Simi ground out between her teeth another string of words unrecognizable to Lainie, and Sayed turned again to answer Simi in the same venomous tone. They went back and forth like this for some time and as much as Lainie wanted to ask what they were saying, she didn't interrupt.

The drive was long, and it was night when the men flung the van doors open and hauled the ladies out. Simi, carried by two men, cried out with the strain this put on her bound wrists and knees. The same man who'd held Lainie's neck gripped it again and twisted her bound arms behind her back. She saw that the men carried their guns openly here, no longer tucked under shirts and jackets.

Some sort of compound enclosed them. They walked in the valley between small hills of gravel and sand interspersed among the huge orange hulks of strange machinery and the shadows of giant, crouching, insect-like construction vehicles. Lainie smelled the salt of the ocean, but it was tainted, rotten somehow.

Sayed and his companions took the ladies to a large, hangar-like metal building, a hulking shadow in the moonlight, and led them through the narrow gap between a pair of two-storey-tall sliding doors into the dark interior. Sayed lit a camp lantern and a ring of light gradually encircled them.

He issued an order and the men carrying Simi dropped

her. The girl cried out in pain but her cousin ignored her. He marched up to Lainie and without ceremony slugged his fist into her midsection.

Lainie wanted to gasp but no air would fill her lungs. The man holding her let go and she went down, struggling to inhale and finding it impossible. She knew she was foolishly opening and closing her mouth like a grounded trout but she couldn't stop. Her vision clouded with dark shrouds, threatening to dowse her consciousness.

Lainie heard herself whimper as Sayed twisted his fingers in her pony tail, straining her neck back. He bent down on one knee and placed his nose against hers and looked directly into her eyes. "Let us not mistake each other, American spy," he said through clenched teeth. "You have perhaps wondered in the course of your life when your death would come. I assure you, the wait is over. You die, here, this night."

Her ability to breathe was coming back, but reluctantly. She hated the mewling sound she made as she took the tiny gasps her lungs would allow.

Sayed went on, "You have also perhaps wondered *how* your death would come. I will be merciful. I will permit you to choose the method of your own death. Isn't that kind of me? Am I not generous, to hold your life in my hands and yet to permit you to decide how it shall end?"

"Fuh...fuh...y...y...," Lainie managed.

He released her hair and stood, stepping away. Lainie curled into a ball, a position she found made it easier to nurse her lungs back to full capacity.

"If you tell me what I want to know," he said, voice now echoing into the shadows, "I will tranquilize you before I place a single bullet into your brain."

Lainie felt the cold steel that could only be the barrel of a gun as Sayed illustrated what he intended to do. She'd felt this once before, in her apartment what seemed ages ago.

"If you do not tell me," Sayed told her, "I will cut you at least a thousand times before I let you die."

Now Lainie felt the icy heat of a razor-sharp edge placed against the back of her neck and her stomach rolled.

Her breath was returning, but she held her tongue. A killer had threatened Lainie before, and she was learning something about men who made such threats. They fed on fear. It made them feel powerful. She would not give him the satisfaction of voicing the gut-clenching terror she felt.

Simi shouted words Lainie didn't understand, then her groan followed a solid-sounding thud.

Lanie straightened enough to look to where Simi curled on the floor. "Leave her alone, you goat-fucking towel-head. It's me you want."

Sayed, standing over Simi, turned once more to Lainie with a look of surprise and fury. "What is she to you?" he asked. "Because I will tell you what she is to me. She is a westernized gutter slut. She and her father and her weakling brother are traitors to Allah. We told Faisal Al-Sehremni that if he tried to run from us we would kill his family."

He turned to Simi. "Either he did not take us seriously, or he does not care what happens to you. Which is it, dear cousin?"

"He didn't run," Simi countered, trying unsuccessfully to leverage herself into a sitting position with her elbows. "You know this. The Americans took him."

Sayed turned to Lainie once more. "When Simi and Ibrahim left New York and went to Baltimore, we awaited them, hoping they would return with their father. But instead, they return home with stories of the bitch spy who escaped them before they could find out where their father was hiding."

"Hiding?" Simi demanded. "He does not hide. He is held prisoner by Sean Brandt, who kidnapped him, and the Americans. I told you this."

"Shut up, Simi," Sayed snapped. "You are so stupid. The American didn't take your father against his will. Your father left with Sean Brandt willingly. Our Eyes-and-Ears saw them at the airport. Sean Brandt waved at our men as if he thought it was a joke as they boarded the plane."

"Lies," she hissed. "He would have contacted us, let us know."

"He tried," Sayed said. "But I intercepted the telegram."

"You," Simi said, glaring up at Sayed. "You are with those who would steal my father's work?"

"We paid for your father's work," Sayed told her. "Paid him well."

"No," Simi grated. "No."

"So Dr. Al-Sehremni knew who was paying his grants after all," Lainie said.

"Not at first, of course," Sayed answered. "Or he would not have taken the work. But later there was less reason to keep it from him."

"Because you were here, with Simi and Ibrahim."

Simi shouted something at him in their language and Sayed casually kicked her in the face, rolling her over to her other side where she curled up again in agony.

The other three men stood back, half hidden by the shadows.

"When you appeared at the coffee shop," he said, "and Simi told me who you were, I was amazed to be granted the chance to question you myself. You know my question to you, don't you? The question that stands between you and your audience with Allah."

"I don't know where Al-Sehremni is," Lainie said.

Sayed smiled. "Good. I am glad you have chosen the hard way. Babysitting these -" an Arabic-sounding curse "– I haven't been called upon to bathe my knife in infidel blood in the name of the almighty in much too long."

CHAPTER 25

Sayed made a gesture and two of the men came out of the shadows to take Lainie's arms and hoist her to her feet. They backed her up against an iron mesh grate behind which were ranks of empty shelves extending away into abysmal blackness. They lifted her arms above her head. She struggled but they were too strong.

Shoving the gun he held in his left hand into his belt, Sayed used a big Bowie knife in his right to cut several lengths of nylon cargo net that hung nearby, from which fell a clutter of metal rebar making a terrible clamor. Using this nylon as rope, he tied her hands to the mesh over her head, his body against hers, his pungent breath on her face.

She would have spit on him had she any saliva left.

The men stepped back and Lainie strained against the bonds. The nylon knots pulled tighter and she stopped when her fingers began to throb, starved of blood flow.

Lainie swallowed back a scream. How could she tell him something she didn't know?

Sayed pointed to two of the men and sent them away with instructions she didn't understand but from the gestures she assumed they were to set up watch outside. Sayed then ordered the third to keep an eye on Simi.

Sayed approached Lainie in an exaggerated stroll, as if

he had all the time in the world. He studied her face. Not her eyes, but her skin, as if picking his place. Then he raised the knife and held it next to her right temple, the edge like a thin hair lying across her skin. Only then did he meet her gaze.

"Where is he?" he asked.

Lainie was breathing in huffs, like a steam engine. Tears came to her eyes, but she set her jaw and tightened her lips, trying to bore into his head with her eyes.

He smiled. He drew the blade in a slow arc across her forehead from temple to temple. At first she felt nothing, then a line of searing fire sliced across her scalp. Her abject scream of pain sounded distant to her own ears, as if she were hearing herself from the bottom of a deep chasm.

Warm blood oozed, parting at her eyebrows and running down the sides of her face and her nose. She shook her head to keep it out of her eyes and saw droplets of it scatter from her peripheral vision like crimson raindrops.

Sayed had stepped back to watch her as if studying a painting he had started before adding more strokes of the brush. She looked at him, hatred and fear, rage and terror warring for possession of her mind.

Then his face went slack and his hand dropped.

She'd seen that expression before.

At the airport, on the face of a murderer.

As Sayed slumped to the floor Lainie saw the glint of the make-shift tranquilizer gun in Simi's hands, between her knees where they were bound. The girl's nose looked crooked, the lower part of her face painted in blood, but she smiled like a feral animal.

Simi's guard was watching Lainie's torture with a salacious grin on his face, his back to his charge. Now he turned and aimed his gun at Simi. Lainie flinched at the expected blast, but it didn't come.

A shadow moved within other shadows at the edge of their little circle of light. The guard stiffened, dropped the gun and put his hands to his throat, making sounds like a clogged sewer drain. Out of the darkness came Cord Steele, reeling something in hand-over-hand as he came.

In the light Lainie saw a thin, silvery line glint between Steele's hands and the frozen guard's neck, some sort of snare.

Seeing Steele, Lainie nearly cried out in relief.

"Don't move," Steele said to the ensnared killer, and Lainie had never heard his voice so cold before, so deadly. He was behind the man, his back to Lainie. "I don't have to do anything. Pull the wrong way and you'll sever your own neck. Now kneel down, slowly."

As the man did what he was told, Steel bent with him. He wrapped the snare-wire around the heels of the man's shoes behind his back and used a small pair of wire-clippers to cut his spool free.

A figure moved out of the shadows from behind Lainie, one of the men sent to stand sentry. He moved quickly as he brushed past in front of Lainie, clearly expecting her to raise the alarm. He had his gun drawn and was lifting it to aim it at Steele's back. A mere word of warning wouldn't stop a bullet from killing Steele. Lainie thrust her foot out desperately with all of her strength and slammed the side of the gunman's knee. A mute crack sounded from the joint and he cried out. He fired, but the bullet ricocheted off the concrete floor, kicking up a cement divot about two feet from where Steele stood. Then the shooter crumpled.

Steele lept on him instantly. Kicking the gun from the fallen man's hand, Steele placed his foot at the back of the man's neck and pressed him into the floor.

"Don't move if you want to live," he said dangerously.

Steele glanced at Lainie and his smile was genuine as he said, "Thanks. Nice footwork."

"Thanks yourself," she winced back. "I could really use some help here. My hands are about to fall off."

"Sorry," he said, "hang on."

Steele used more wire to bind this man's hands. Hurrying over to Sayed's prone form, Steele picked up the dropped Bowie knife and took the gun. He had the three guns, Sayed's and those of the two others, shoved into his belt as he came to cut Lainie loose with the Bowie knife.

"There's another guy," Lainie whispered to him as he worked. "Outside, I think."

"I know," he said as her hands came free. "I'll be right back."

He slipped into the shadows again.

Lainie rubbed her wrists, then she put her fingers to her face. She felt it gingerly. There was a lot of blood, but the wound didn't feel deep, and in fact as she explored it with more confidence it didn't feel any deeper than a scratch a cat would make. Scalp wounds bleed worse than others. She had no doubt that Sayed intended to cut deeper later, that he only started small to prolong the torture.

Her stomach still cramped from the earlier blow from Sayed's fist, she staggered over to Simi. The girl lay holding the tranquilizer gun loosely. Just as Simi had described it, two pen-casings screwed end-to-end formed the barrel of the weapon, and the small, oblong bulb of a CO_2 cartridge attached below functioned as handle and fuel for firing tiny darts.

"Where'd you have this stashed," Lainie asked, "your socks?"

Simi didn't answer, but lay passively as Lainie worked the knots of the twinned cables loose.

"Is it true?" The girl's voice came out rough, as if under constraint. "Did father leave with Sean Brandt willingly?"

"I don't know," Lainie said as the cable came free. Then, to Simi's smoldering glare, she hurried to add, "It's one of many working theories, yes."

Simi stumbled twice but finally stood, if unsteadily, apparently by sheer force of will. "Then where are they, Sean Brandt and my father?"

"Sean Brandt is dead."

Simi's head snapped up and her face bore unveiled shock. Her eyes filled rapidly and she turned away, lifting her hands to her face. Lainie placed a hand on the smaller woman's shoulder.

Simi shrugged the hand off and spun back around again, her wet eyes defiant. "Don't touch me," she spat. "My father. Is he dead as well?"

"No," Lainie said. "At least, I don't think so. I think he is here, in the country, somewhere."

"God damn it," Steele cursed from behind her.

Lainie turned. Steele stood just inside the circle of light. Behind him he dragged another man, trussed ankles to wrists like a Cornish hen with his own belt. Steele's face was a storm.

"Where in hell is the other guy?" he hissed.

Lainie noticed for the first time that where Sayed had lain was now empty floor.

Sayed was gone.

CHAPTER 26

"Get out of the light," Steele whispered urgently, backing away himself.

Before Lainie or Simi could move, the darkness outside the ring of light was blasted by the sound of a large engine starting up. Lainie barely heard Steele's warning to get out of the way over the roar of the engine as he dropped his prisoner and took his own advice. Lainie grabbed Simi and the two of them dove to the side as a huge hulk leapt out of the depths of the hanger.

A monstrous semi-tractor-trailer thundered by where they had stood, Sayed behind the wheel. The huge truck mowed down the three other helpless men trussed in the middle of the floor and slammed through the doors at the entrance, blasting them outward, twisted and shattered. The sound made Lainie cover her ears.

Steele led the charge as Lainie and Simi followed out the entrance of the hangar. The van that Lainie and Simi had been brought in still sat with its doors negligently open and the semi clipped it, sending it tumbling into another abandoned piece of giant machinery. The van exploded in a ball of yellow heat.

The semi pulled a flatbed trailer behind and a heavy canvas tarp shrouded whatever was strapped to it. The vehicle picked up speed as it headed toward a gap between rusted equipment and stacks of warped and moldy lumber.

"To the Bat Mobile," Steele called as he ran, motioning Lainie to follow.

The truck rounded the obstacles and was quickly out of sight, but Lainie could still hear it working up through its gears as she followed Steele at a sprint through other stacks of detritus to where he'd parked his Lexus. When they jumped in, Simi appeared and leapt into the narrow space behind the two front seats.

Steele glanced at the girl as he turned the key, then at Lainie, who shrugged back at him. Steele fishtailed over the hard-packed dirt and wove among the hills and stacks and piles of refuse.

"How did you find us?" Lainie called over the rev of the engine.

"First thing I did was put a tracer on that van, before I went upstairs to the apartment." He said this only loud enough for Lainie to hear but low enough to exclude Simi. "When you started hammering on that button I gave you I came back, but you were gone, so I checked my scanner and sure enough, the van was on the move. So I tracked it."

They caught a glimpse of the back of the flatbed trailer before it disappeared behind more rubbish, but they were going the opposite direction. Steele slid to a halt, reversed, made a U-turn, and rejoined pursuit.

"What happened upstairs?" Lainie asked, hoping to distract herself from his driving.

"Peachy," he said. "Ibrahim was there, but I was able to bug the place anyway."

"Was he asleep or something?"

"No, he was applying alcohol to those scratches you gave him on his face. Nasty. Good work there."

"Thanks," she said, queasy and not the least proud. "So you planted bugs even with him there?"

He spared her that crooked grin. "Told you: sneaky son of a bitch."

His enthusiasm was infectious, Lainie couldn't help but smile and shake her head.

The trailer came in view again as it slowed to bob over some speed bumps just inside a gate in the perimeter fence. It was pulling out onto a dark, deserted road when Steele hit the speed bump at full speed.

"By the way," he said. "You should know that the alarm I gave you, the button, is designed to alert me without giving me away. The receiver connects to a wire hidden on my inner thigh that gives me a slight electrical zap when the button is pressed."

"So when I was pressing the button over and over..."

"And holding it down..."

"...it was zapping you...down there?"

He nodded.

In spite of the chase Lainie smiled again. "Sorry."

When she turned her head forward again the cut on her scalp stung her and she felt dizzy. She stopped smiling then, shuddered and swallowed back a sour taste in her mouth as she traced the cut again with her fingers.

"I'm sorry," Steele said. "I would have acted sooner, but I wasn't in position yet."

She didn't answer and used her sleeve to start scrubbing the sticky blood from her face, carefully voiding the cut itself. She paused to ask him if it was his favorite shirt.

"Not any more," he said dryly, looking askance at the smear of blood she'd already soiled the sleeve with. Then, "Shit."

"What?"

Steele pointed ahead, "He's getting on the highway."

He gunned the car and it raced along the shoulder of the onramp to the left of the truck. Steele drew one of the guns from his waist and as the car pulled ahead he cut the truck off and fired up into the cab. Looking back, Lainie saw Sayed through the oversized windshield fighting desperately with the steering wheel as he swerved away from the bullets. The truck went off onto the embankment, yawing wildly, and Lainie was sure it would pitch over. It didn't, but rumbled down the patchy grass slope and back onto the surface road.

The Lexus was leaning steeply as well, but Steele's grin was a rictis of determination as he brought the car back to the road behind the trailer once more. It was a two-way road but Sayed drove down the center to prevent Steel from passing him again.

"That was close," Steele said. He had shoved the weapon into his belt.

Lainie glanced back at Simi. The girl crouched behind them like a panther, brooding, with dark bruises developing around her eyes, one of which was already grey from the punch Lainie herself had delivered earlier that morning.

"Where are we, anyway?" Lainie asked.

"New Jersey," Steele said, checking the mirror for other cars.

"Where is he going?"

"He wants to lose us. He'll get desperate here any minute, start trying something stupid."

"How long were you listening?" she asked him. "At the warehouse, or whatever that was."

"Just long enough to see him tie you up and..." He gestured to her forehead.

She resumed cleaning her face with the sleeve as she filled him in on what Sayed had said, still talking so that only he could hear her over the wind.

"So Dr. Al-Sehremni didn't know who was paying for his research," Lainie concluded. "Or not at first. Then later, they blackmailed him through his kids. Sayed wasn't here in New York to go to school. It was his job to hold an axe over Simi and Ibrahim's necks to keep Dr. Al-Sehremni in line."

"Doesn't change anything," Steele said, keeping one car-length between the Lexus and the trailer ahead. Every time he tried to pull along one side or the other Sayed would swerve to block him. "Brandt didn't do his job. Instead, he left a mess behind for us to try to clean up. We still need to find the doc before the other side does."

"And do what," Lainie asked, "*liquidate* him?"

Steele glanced at her with raised eyebrows. "What the hell's wrong with you?"

"Nothing," she said, looking back at Simi.

Simi looked down and met Lainie's eyes briefly, then looked away. She, too, had used a sleeve to remove most of the blood from her face. She had also clearly righted her nose herself while Lainie and Steele had been talking, because though badly swollen it was no longer crooked.

That must've hurt, but the girl remained stoic.

Simi was small, still young by American standards, and yet her face already bore the stony resignation that hardship and disappointment usually only etched on older countenances. Lainie saw for the first time what it was that had drawn Simi and Brandt together. Simi was beautiful, but there was an underlying sadness, a latent burden of experience, so like that hinted by Brandt's journal. They perhaps understood each other much deeper than some people normally ever do.

Turning back, Lainie nodded forward. "Do you think he's calling for back-up?"

"Sayed?" Steele shrugged. "Hard to tell. You NSA folks know better than anyone that these guys have pretty much stopped using cell phones because they've learned we can track them. They still use them in emergencies. Whether this qualifies as an emergency, or whether he even has one at all..."

The truck slowed.

"What now?" Steele groused.

Veering left so sharply it went up on two wheels, the semi pulled the trailer around a corner onto a cross-street and under the highway overpass. Steele tried to take the opportunity to pass on the left again but the underpass was too narrow and they nearly got squashed against the side.

The new road struck out away from the freeway into what looked like farm country, fences to either side, cows lowing, some even startled away from the road as the two vehicles roared past.

"Why don't you shoot out the tires?" Lainie asked.

Steele looked at her with wide eyes. "Have you ever tried shooting at one moving vehicle from another moving vehicle? It isn't as easy as they show in the movies, even for an expert marksman. Which I'm not. Are you?"

At first the question sounded facetious, until she looked at him and saw in his eyes that he was genuinely asking. She shook her head and shut up.

Suddenly Steele swerved off the road. Flame erupted on his side and he flinched while struggling to maintain control of the car on the soft shoulder, muscling it back onto the road again.

"What was that?" Lainie shouted.

"Granade," he answered through clenched teeth, "white phosphorous."

He swerved again. This time the eruption rocked the car and sprayed it with shrapnel.

"Motherfucker," Steele cursed venomously.

The truck had pulled further ahead. As it sped onto a picturesque old wooden covered bridge, Steele stood on his accelerator, hitting the bump at the edge of the bridge so hard the Lexus lifted off the road.

This time Lainie saw the small black sphere in the Lexus' headlights, tumbling behind the trailer, before an explosion blanketed the wooden bridge in white flame and black smoke. As the plume of inky smoke billowed up and away Lainie saw that the entire surface of the wooden bridge was aflame.

"Stop," Lainie screamed, ducking her head. She felt heat so intense she knew her hair must be singed, then the heat was gone. She looked up, but aside from some soot on the hood and windshield they were unscathed. Looking back she saw they were rapidly leaving the wall of fire behind.

"Shit," she said breathlessly. "Do we really need to kill ourselves just to get this one last guy?"

Steele spared her an iron look.

"Didn't you wonder why he drove away in that thing

instead of the van, which would have been faster?" he asked.

Lainie gave him a blank look, ashamed to admit that she hadn't wondered that at all.

"Three guesses what's on that trailer," Steele said.

CHAPTER 27

"Where does this road go?" Lainie asked.

Steele pressed a panel on the dashboard. A GPS screen mounted on an extendable arm sprung out. "Can't tell," he shook his head as he drove with one hand and tapped the scroll key with the other. They watched the map slide by on the screen. "It's a maze of interconnecting rural roads out here, some of them not even mapped."

Steele slowed a little further behind the trailer to give himself time to react if Sayed threw any more grenades. Whether Sayed had used all he had or he was trying to lure them into thinking so, no more grenades tumbled toward them.

Simi leaned forward to peer over their shoulders, her face a mask of anger and humiliation. "He tried to warn us," she said through clenched teeth, shaking her head.

"What?" Lainie asked. "Who?"

"My father," Simi said. "He sent a telegram, but Sayed said he intercepted it. Papa tried to warn us about Sayed."

"Yes," Lainie said.

Steele gave Lainie a stony look.

"Sean Brandt did not kidnap Father," Simi said. "He was trying to help him get away from them."

"I don't know," Lainie said, "but it seems more and

more possible."

Steele tried to shush her with a soft hiss between his lips, but she ignored him.

"And now Sean Brandt is dead," the girl said miserably.

Lainie knew Simi was only voicing the thoughts that had been going round and round in her head, saying them aloud in an attempt to come to grips with the information.

Steele looked at Simi in the rear-view mirror with wide eyes. He turned to Lainie. "What did you tell her?" he said openly.

"Everything," Lainie told him defiantly. "Or almost."

Steele ran a hand through his hair and shook his head.

"What will you do to my father if you find him?" Simi asked Steele.

The CIA man looked to Lainie for help, but she just looked back expectantly. "Yes, Cord. What will you do to Al-Sehremni if we find him?"

Steele turned his eyes to the road once more. "We will try to finish what Brandt started. We'll protect your father from those who want to use him."

"Is this true?" Simi asked Lainie.

"No," Lainie said.

"Whose side are you on?" Steele snapped at her.

"Oh he's not lying," Lainie went on. "At least I don't think so. But he isn't telling the whole truth, either. It isn't all up to Cord, and it certainly isn't up to me. I think they'll try to use your father to flush out these guys. They'll also want him to give *them* the formula and the schematics that he's trying to keep away from these other guys. Whatever they do, your father's life and comfort will be of only secondary concern to them."

"Why are you telling me all of this?" Simi asked her.

"I'd like to know that myself," Steele said under his breath, as if to himself.

"Because you deserve to know the truth," Lainie held Simi's gaze with hers, "if you are going to help us find your father."

"After what you have told me why would I help you find him?" Simi asked.

"Because your father trusted Brandt. He knows he has a better chance with us than with them. He went with Brandt because whatever quality of life he could expect as an expatriate in our country, he knew it would be vastly superior to what Sayed and his superiors would do to him if he didn't hand over his research to them. It's clear now he didn't want to do that. You should trust your father's judgment."

Steele was glancing at Lainie, shaking his head, jaw slack.

Simi lowered her head, deep in thought, her hands working against each other in indecision. Finally she looked up. "You ask too much," she said.

"What else are you going to do?" Lainie asked. "You can't go home. Not now. Can you? After what you've learned? The minute you show your face Sayed and his buddies'll come down on you like an avalanche, and this time you might not get away."

Simi's hands continued to grind each other and she looked away. In spite of dry eyes her lip trembled. Finally, she said, "Under one condition."

"What?"

"After you get what you want you leave us alone. Give us the money to hide ourselves, it is the least you can do, then leave us alone."

Lainie turned a pleading look on Steele.

"Done," he said loudly, nodding in his mirror to Simi.

The girl sat back again, the wind whipping her hair wildly around her lined and conflicted features.

"Can you do that?" Lainie asked Steele quietly. "Make a deal like that?"

"Course not," he whispered jauntily, "but she doesn't know that."

"Cord," she said in protest.

"What?"

"You can't..."

Two motorcycles, black and sleek, went past them going in the opposite direction, one on each side, and the wasp-whine of their engines drowned out Lainie's voice. Steele stiffened and looked in his rear-view mirror, adjusting it to get a better view.

"Simi, get down," he shouted.

"What?" Lainie asked.

"They're turning around. I think this is Sayed's back-up."

"What do we do?" Lainie's chest hammered with panic.

Steele shrugged. "Wait and see what they are going to do. Here." He drew one of the three guns from his waist and placed it, balanced, on her leg.

Lainie looked at the weapon as if it were a scorpion, just landed in her lap, and her heart quailed.

"What about me?" Simi called.

"Can you shoot?" Steele called back.

"Point the end toward your enemy and pull the trigger, right?" Simi answered.

Steele handed a second gun back to her, then drew the third for himself. There was still one in his belt.

Lainie picked up the gun in her lap and held it awkwardly in two hands. She had fired another gun, a similar one or maybe the same one, in Simi and Ibrahim's van that morning on instinct, out of desperation. Now, with time to think about it, she found the thing bulky and heavy, off balance and clunky. She didn't want to shoot anyone.

The trailer rumbled on ahead of them.

"Get ready," Steele said. "Here they come."

The Motorcycles pulled up behind them. In the moonlight, behind the face screens of their helmets, it was impossible to see the riders' faces, but they lay low, nearly prone across the aerodynamic bodies of their cycles. Lainie recalled hearing this design of motorcycle referred to as a crotch-rocket.

Simi fired, but no one went down. One of the riders lobbed something small and black toward them. It tumbled forward off of the back of the seat and landed at Lainie's feet.

"Grenade," Steele bellowed, fumbling at his door handle as if he intended to make a dive for it.

Lainie bent and picked it up and threw the thing back over her head without looking, like a hot potato. It went off with a skull-crushing bang high over the heads of the cyclists. One went down with a screech and crash of metal and plastic, and the other swerved so badly it appeared as if he might join his partner, but he recovered, zipping under the rain of fire. Tendrils of white-hot magnesium chased the Lexus and Steele only just outran them.

"You've got balls," Steele chortled, "I'll give you that."

Lainie didn't respond. Calm settled over her and she wondered if this was what shock felt like. She took a breath and squared the gun in her grasp, turned and fired past Simi. The girl cried out and covered her ears, but then fired her own gun as well. The lone motorcycle gained on them rapidly, unhit.

"Told you," Steele said. "Shooting out tires isn't so easy, is it?"

Lainie returned his grin with a hard glare. What did he find so damn amusing? She fired again, careful to aim wide of Simi.

"Can't you go faster?" Simi asked.

"Weight to power," Steele yelled back.

"What?"

"Weight to power ratio. No car's a match for a motorcycle, no matter how suped-up the car is."

Another grenade sailed over their heads, seeming to hover as it matched their forward momentum. Simi reached up with a bare hand and batted the thing back, then ducked. The motorcycle swerved and backed away and though the grenade went off above him again he was well behind the explosion and able to circumvent the smoke and flame. Then he was gaining on them again.

Simi cried out, holding her left arm. A slit in her jacket emitted a thin line of smoke.

"What is it?" Lainie yelled.

Steele glanced back. "Shrapnel. Get that coat off before it catches."

Simi struggled out of her green jacket. Blood oozed out of shallow gashes and punctures in her arm, but she ignored it and slapped at her jacket, which was smoldering, belching more and more smoke in the wind, smoke coming from the cut in the fabric. When, stoked as it was by the wind of their speed, the smoking ember burst into flame Simi threw the jacket out of the car.

The cyclist ran over it and rode on.

"The tranquilizer gun was in there," she said ruefully, wincing as she studied the speckled wound on her arm.

"Here comes the other one, again," Steeled called, looking in the mirror.

"He's still alive?" Lainie asked incredulously.

"Guess so."

Then there were two cyclists once more.

"Where did these guys come from?" Lainie asked, firing again.

"Some place ahead," Steele said. "Sayed knows where he's going after all. Some fall-back staging position, I'm guessing. Since he's leading us right to it, it stands to reason he called ahead to make sure we didn't live to tell anyone."

"Staging for what?"

"For what's on that truck."

"The laser beam."

"Particle beam," he corrected her.

Simi was taking her turn to shoot, kneeling and facing backward.

Steele suddenly swerved. The rear of the Lexus hit the front wheel of one of the cyclists who'd been pulling up along side them. Lainie watched the machine flail end-over end like a pinwheel, the rider flying loose and wrapping himself around a roadside reflector pole like a rag doll.

146

"That one's not getting up again," Lainie said.

The remaining cyclist threw another grenade. This one bounced off the trunk and into the street behind them, but when it exploded it rocked the convertible forward. Flame and white-hot phosphorous licked up the back and sides of the car. Simi had curled into a ball, hands over her head and Lainie ducked, too.

"Enough," Steele said, balancing his gun on his thigh so he could take a pair of gloves from a pocket inside his jacket and don them. What hell, Lainie thought.

He drew his snare out of a pocket and fashioned a loop with one hand, eyes on the road as he slowed and swerved to force the cyclist to pull up to his side. The rider wore a black jumpsuit and black helmet, and he kept away from the Lexus as he drew up, presumably in order to maneuver in case Steele tried to sideswipe him as well. Simi fired at him...but nothing happened and she mumbled to herself in her own language as she dropped the magazine into her palm and looked at it forlornly.

Lainie didn't want to risk her lack of skill with a gun by firing between Simi's and Steele's heads, so she waited for a cleaner shot.

Seeing Simi was out of ammo, the cyclist nodded as if laughing behind his face-shield. He drew another grenade out of his pocket and popped the pin out with his thumb. Holding it like an egg he tried to veer closer so that he could just lob it easily into the convertible. After several tries, as if working up his nerve, he brought the bike up to the side of Steele's Lexus and reached out.

The CIA agent tapped the brakes, dropping back, and threw the loop of the snare over the rider's head. He then slammed the brakes, almost standing on them.

The Lexus skidded, fishtailed, corrected, came to a rest. Lainie and the others watched the cycle continue up the road. When it came to a curve ahead it kept going straight, careened into the fence and tangled in among the barbed wire. The grenade dropped from the gloved hand and seconds later

KEVIN PAUL TRACY

erupted in a starburst of yellow flame and tar-thick smoke, followed quickly by the blast of the motorcycle's gas tank.

Meanwhile, the rider's helmeted head, severed by Steele's snare, slowed its spinning in the center of the road about two yards in front of the Lexus, wobbled, then simply rolled lopsidedly off the blacktop and into the ditch.

CHAPTER 28

It took Lainie several minutes to be sure she wouldn't vomit if she tried to speak. Her voice still trembled when she asked, "Why are we going so slowly?"

Steele had turned off the headlights and was trolling along the road with only moonlight to navigate by, barely breaking twenty miles per hour. He seemed relaxed, even contented as he watched the road ahead. Killing a man in such a gruesome way had no more effect on him than cracking the shell of an egg and spilling its guts into hot grease.

"We lost the truck while we dealt with the motorcycles," he said. "Sayed doesn't know who came out on top. If the riders don't report in, he and his cronies won't know what the outcome was. They'll still be alert, but with any luck, we can sneak up on them."

"What if he turned off onto another road?"

Steele didn't answer.

She watched his profile. She'd always known she was in danger with him, masquerading as she was, but the reality of it sometimes receded in her urgency to prove that Michael/Brandt was murdered, that she did not kill Mitch and Kim and firebomb the offices of Capri Entertainment, and she did not slice the throat of the NSA operative at the airport. Now the danger that Steele presented struck her again. If he found out who she really was, he'd be pretty well pissed. And, she had to admit, rightly so. Would he use his snare to decapitate her as unemotionally as he had that rider?

Given the peril he presented for her, the primal, physical attraction she felt to him perplexed Lanie. His dark hair was roguishly ruffled, a lock of it brushing the eyelash of his right eye. His smooth face held that perpetual smirk, a strong chin and sparkling eyes so blue Lainie felt flustered whenever he turned them on her.

He glanced at her, eyes glinting in the twilight, and she looked away quickly, feeling the heat of the blush on her cheeks, grateful for the dark and hoping it hid the color of her face from him.

"There," Simi said, her extended finger appearing between them like a barrier. "Do you see?"

Steele nodded.

Lainie peered ahead. There was a side road to the left, not unlike any of a hundred they'd passed without remark. But giant tire-marks gouged the dirt here where they curved sharply. The ghost of a dust cloud still lingered from the passing of the veering truck. Off the road about a half a mile in that direction were a cluster of amber floodlights and the vague shadows of buildings.

Steele took the turn slowly, the grit of the road crackling under the tires of the Lexus. He pulled off the road and parked with the car canted on the incline of a shallow embankment, then hopped out. Lainie got out and Simi leapt from the back.

"How many bullets do you have left?" Steele asked as he unlocked the trunk of the car.

"I'm empty," Simi said.

"Me too," Lainie said, not about to reveal that in actuality she didn't know how to open the gun to check.

"Good," he said, snatching the gun away from Simi. He took Lainie's away more gently. He tossed them in the trunk and closed it, then he drew the last remaining gun from his waistband, jacked the action with a sinister clack, and handed it to Lainie.

"I'll call for back-up," he said to Lainie, showing her his cell phone. He put the keys to the Lexus in her free hand. "Anyone comes that doesn't have siren and lights blazing, you take off, and keep running." He chucked his head toward Simi. "And keep an eye on that one."

Simi's face clouded with resentment.

"Where are you going?" Lainie demanded.

Steele pointed toward the cluster of amber lights. "Scouting. Sneaky son of a bitch, remember?"

"Be careful," Lainie heard herself say as he ducked into the night.

Simi said, "This is how you ask for my help? By holding me prisoner?"

Lainie looked at the gun, then stuck it behind her in the waistband of her jeans, adjusting it awkwardly to find the least uncomfortable spot to hold it. "No," she said.

Simi studied her for a moment. "Why trust me, after what I did to you?"

Lainie shrugged. "I don't trust you. Not yet. Because you haven't learned to trust me, yet. But I hope to earn your trust, and maybe that'll make you want to earn mine in return."

"How can I trust a spy?"

Lainie chewed her lip a moment, then said, "I'm no spy, Simi. I'm a school teacher. Or at least, I will be soon."

Simi blinked at her.

"It's true," Lainie almost laughed out loud at how ludicrous it sounded even to her, here, now. "I have all my credits to graduate, Doctorate in Education. I'm just waiting to hear back from the committee about my doctoral thesis."

"Then how...?" Simi furrowed her brow.

For the first time since she had fled her apartment, Lainie told someone the whole story, the truth from beginning to end. When she described her telephone conversation with Brandt, Simi turned her face away from the moon, into shadow. The only things Lainie left out were secrets that were not hers to tell, such as the nature of the formula Simi's father

151

had developed and the bugs Steele put in Simi's apartment.

By the end of the story Lainie was sitting on the trunk of the Lexus, legs dangling. Simi hunkered down on the road's shoulder, shaking her head, picking up rocks and tossing them onto the tarmac. After prolonged silence, Lainie said softly, "Well? Say something."

"We have a saying in my language," Simi said, looking up at her. "Roughly translated it means that what you say is too unbelievable not to be true."

"We have the same saying," Lainie smiled.

Simi regarded her. "If it is true, then maybe I'm sorry that I tranquilized you, that I hit you."

"*Maybe?*"

"We will see," Simi said, standing and brushing her hands on her hips. "Do you trust him?"

Lainie knew Simi meant Steele. She glanced toward the amber lights, hoped he wasn't doing anything foolish. "Right now, even less than I trust you."

"Then why are you helping him?"

"Because with his help I've gotten this close to finding your father," Lainie said. "I don't care about the formula-slash-schematics, or Sayed or terrorists. Check that. I care. I do. But that's Steele's department. I'm no spy, I'm just a school teacher, I can't thwart a band of trained killers. What I want is to clear my name. Your father may have seen who killed Brandt. I need him to tell the police what he saw."

"If what you say is true, that Sean Brandt used fake papers to get my father into the country, then he is here illegally. Will they not deport my father for this?"

"They won't throw him back to these sharks," Lainie said. "Not with that formula in his head. If he gives them the formula and everything he knows about Sayed and the organization, they'll probably give him asylum here, hide him."

"You don't know that for certain," Simi shook her head.

"No," Lainie admitted. "I don't. But like I said, his chances are much better in the hands of the Americans than..."

Gunfire, distant but loud nonetheless, peppered the night and Lainie leapt off the trunk, looked in the direction of the dim lights and held her breath, listening for answering shots. None came. Had Steele been discovered? Captured? Shot?

Killed?

She glanced at Simi as the girl ran around the car and scaled the embankment. She paused at the top to turn back to Lainie and beckon. *Come on.*

"Where are you going?" Lainie called in a stage whisper.

Simi disappeared on the other side of the rise, in the direction of the lights, the way Steele had gone. Lainie hesitated, torn. Steele'd told her to wait here. Back-up was on the way. There was no need to risk their lives like this. What could they do to help Steele? Moreover, none of this would get Lainie any closer to finding Al-Sehremni, and might just get her killed.

On the other hand, who was Steele's back-up? More CIA agents? No, not on American soil. FBI, DHS, or both. What would they do when they discovered who Lainie was, that she was wanted for murder and arson in San Francisco, and for the murder of a NSA operative in Baltimore? More importantly, how likely would she be to find the scientist without Simi's help and trust, or if the girl got herself killed?

Lainie paced twice, pounding her thighs with her fists. Sighing, she turned and sprinted up the small hill.

"Wait up," she called quietly after Simi.

CHAPTER 29

"What are we doing?" Lainie asked for maybe the fiftieth time. She lay belly-down on a small dirt ridge between furrows in a field. Simi lay beside her squinting into the night. They lay maybe three hundred feet from a small cluster of buildings that looked like machinery storage for the farm on which they'd trespassed.

There was activity between the buildings, but almost complete silence. Four or five figures rushed back and forth between two elongated huts made of corrugated metal carrying loads indistinguishable in the dark, like ants carrying crumbs to the colony before going back for more.

"They are preparing to leave," Simi whispered.

The semi tractor and trailer that they'd followed here idled to one side of the compound, headlights dowsed but amber parking lights still dimly alight. Its burden remained hidden beneath the tarp, undisturbed. There was no sign of Sayed, unless he was one of those carrying things from one building to the next. There was also no sign of Cord Steele.

"Makes sense," Lainie said. "Sayed blew their cover when he took you and me hostage. I'd bug out, too. We should be so smart."

"We must stop them," Simi said.

"What? You and me? Why? How?"

Simi crawled forward on her stomach. With a sigh, Lainie followed.

Though furrowed for planting, the field must have been a fallow one, because only the occasional clump of grass or weeds grew here. They moved from furrow to furrow, watching the line of men for any sign that they'd been spotted before scrambling over the next rise. The ground smelled rich and loamy, fertile.

It wasn't long before Lainie saw what Simi's plan was, or at least part of it. The girl led Lainie around to the other side of the semi's trailer from the line of men. They stood now, blocked from being seen, and pressed themselves up against the passenger side of the cab.

Peering around the front Simi reached back. "Give me the gun."

"Why are you doing this?" Lainie demanded. "None of this will help you find your father. This isn't even your fight."

Simi turned intense, hate-filled eyes on Lainie. "I mean to kill Sayed for his part in my father's misery. I mean to kill as many of them as I can for taking advantage of his broken heart to make him do what he would never have done in his right mind."

Broken heart? Lainie wondered at the meaning of that, but said, "What if you get killed? How much help will you be to your father then?" The two women confronted each other, intent and unyielding. "I don't know how many bullets are in this gun, but I'm guessing it won't be enough. That's the problem with revenge, Simi. There are never enough bullets."

"Help me or don't," Simi said. She moved forward away from the truck and into the dim light.

Lainie rushed forward and pulled the girl back.

"Let go of me," Simi plucked at Lainie's fingers.

Sighing, Lainie drew the gun from behind her and offered it to the girl. "Here."

Simi took it. "Thank you," she said solemnly, then moved forward once more.

Again, Lainie pulled her back. "Geeze," she said in exasperation. "Get in."

"In?" Simi asked.

Lainie reached up and carefully opened the passenger door to the semi, then hoisted herself up and in. She looked back and said, again, "Get in," before sliding across to the driver's side. As Simi climbed in beside her Lainie studied the controls dubiously, especially the gear shift between the seats with it's splitter-switches.

She shrugged. "Fasten your seatbelt."

Simi looked around, found a shoulder strap and fastened it around herself. Lainie did the same. Huffing as if readying herself for a dive, Lainie grabbed the wheel with her left hand, floored the clutch with her foot, and grabbed the gear-shifter with her right. Forward left was reverse, that she remembered. She pulled the stick to the left and back, then gradually she let her foot off the clutch.

The engine promptly chugged once and died.

"Lainie," Simi said urgently, using Lainie's name, her real name, for the first time since Lainie had told it to her back on the road.

Lainie looked forward. One of the men in the line was looking their direction and slowing. Lainie cranked the ignition and the engine roared to life. More men stopped and looked.

Her rescuer, the trucker who'd picked her up after she'd escaped Simi and Ibrahim and collapsed in the middle of the highway, had given her pointers on how to drive one of these things. His voice came to her now, "Never start off in first gear. Unless you're carrying an extreme load, you won't get anywhere." Lainie fumbled with the shifter. Gears ground loudly as she forced them into what she was pretty sure was second gear.

"Lainie," Simi said again, her voice pleading for quick action.

Lainie let the clutch out. The truck lurched forward, throwing the two women back against the seat. By now several of the men were putting down their loads and coming toward the truck, hesitantly, craning their necks forward as if trying to see into the gloom of the cab.

"Lainie," Simi said a third time, hissing the word with venom. Lainie looked at Simi, who was looking past her at one of the buildings. Lainie looked that way. Sayed and a couple of other men were striding out of a door toward them, guns drawn.

"What are you waiting for?" Lainie asked, cranking the wheel in that direction.

Simi unfastened her seat belt, stood on the seat and leaned out of the window as the truck came around. Holding the window-frame with one hand and the gun in the other, Simi swung way out of the window and fired at Sayed. He and his companions dove for cover.

"Look out," Lainie yelled and Simi ducked back in. As the truck came around Lainie got the hang of shifting, though the engine strained at higher RPM's than sounded healthy for it. They picked up speed and Lainie steered directly for the buildings, straight at Sayed and the others that had come out of it.

Bullets rattled against the truck but none penetrated and the windows remained as yet unhit. Lainie closed her eyes tight and the truck plowed into the building at what must have been forty miles per hour. The impact threw her up against the wheel, forcing her breath out with a woof and making her eyes open again. She saw the building disintegrating around them and soon they were driving through the steel hut, crashing through rows of tables stacked with what looked like computers, guns, machinery, scrap metal and one with two coffee machines and six boxes of donuts.

Tied securely to a chair to one side, Steele's eyes were the size of hubcaps as they met Lainie's through the driver's side window when the truck breezed past him. She started to wave, then grabbed the wheel as it nearly tore from her grasp. She whipped her gaze forward once more. Had she seen blood trickling from the corner of his mouth?

The engine threatened to die and Lainie floored the

gas pedal, picking up speed in time to crash through several rows of bunks with rumpled bedding. The beds scattered and sprung apart. One top bunk was still occupied when the truck struck it, and a naked man bounced off the mattress and landed on his rump on the hood of the truck facing Lainie. They both screamed at each other, and then he was bounced off again, landing in a pile of mattresses and pillows.

Then the opposite wall of the building reared up before them, folded when they hit it, the truck bounding and jostling back out into the cleared and flattened area around the huts. Lainie spared a glance for Simi, who was sitting wide-eyed, clutching the gun with one hand and the strap above the door with the other, each with equal fear of letting either go.

Gunfire salted the outside of the truck again as Lainie fought the wheel, bringing the truck around for another pass. Simi jumped up and fired out of her window. As Lainie was aiming for another building, this time to broadside it, Simi ducked back in and cursed, dropping the magazine out of the gun's handle and throwing it on the floor.

She shouted an interjection in Arabic and pointed at the floor. An empty box with nine compartments lolled around at her feet. Beneath it, bouncing and rolling with the motion of the truck, were six palm-sized black spheres. Sayed hadn't stopped throwing grenades at the from the windows of the truck because he'd run out. He must've stopped throwing grenades at the Lexus because the crate had fallen off of the seat, Lainie guessed, and he didn't dare stop the truck to reach for them.

Simi bent and snatched up two, turning to Lainie with a grin of demolition on her face. As they crashed through the next structure, Lainie wrestling the wheel like a Brahma bull, Simi pulled two pins with her teeth and threw the two grenades out the window one after the other. The semi smashed through several SUV style cars parked in ranks inside the building. This was what the men were loading in preparation for leaving.

Lainie heard the explosions behind them as the truck

leveled off, once again on flat ground. The *whomp whomp* of the grenades were soon followed by several loud metallic *bangs* of gas tanks exploding. Someone was starting an engine somewhere in the distance as well, and there was a lot of shouting. Simi had two more grenades in her hands, peering out the window eagerly as if looking for more targets at which to throw them.

Lainie realized they couldn't go on smashing through the buildings forever. The push-grate at the front of the semi hung at a weird angle and steam was spraying from under the hood like a miniature geyser, and sooner or later someone was going to get a good clean shot at them. She needed one last good target to launch the truck at, to create enough destruction and chaos to give her a chance to slip into the first building, cut Steele loose, and for the three of them to get away.

On seeing Steele she had never questioned that she would make every attempt to rescue him, she owed him that much.

Continuing their arc to the right Lainie saw several men scatter out of the way. One man leapt up on the running board, pulling at the door handle on her side, but he couldn't maintain his grip and was thrown off to sprawl in the dirt. Lainie didn't know what she was looking for until she saw it, and she made for her target and revved the engine up to its highest pitch.

"Get ready to jump," she yelled at Simi, who had thrown her second battery of grenades and was chasing the remaining two around the floor. The girl came up with them and looked ahead. Her maniacal grin broadened as she saw what Lainie was aiming for and she stuffed the grenades into her pockets and reached for the door handle.

Lainie let her seatbelt loose and steered with one hand while fingering the handle of her door. Bullets rained down on them like hail. Lainie's window flashed milky white as a thousand miniature cracks spider-webbed across it, hit by a well-aimed shot. "Wait," she said slowly, "not yet...now!"

Lainie only hesitated long enough to be sure Simi got

out cleanly, then she leapt from the truck as it careened through the lot. The semi collided with a large propane tank shaped like an aspirin capsule and the size of a rhinoceros. At first there was only the sound of a large bell being rung. Lainie stared from where she sat in the dirt on her rump, heart singling.

Then the explosion came. The blast was so deafening it visibly rippled the air outward with heat and sound. Those not already on the ground were thrown there, and hard. For full seconds nothing moved.

Lainie struggled to her feet. Simi was already staggering nearby. Lainie stumbled over to her, grabbed her arm to lead her toward the building where she had seen Steele. They were picking up speed when Lainie saw Sayed running through the smoke and dust. At first she thought he was coming for them, but he veered the other way, toward the trailer, which had jackknifed and now lay on its side beside the hotly burning jets of gas shooting from ruptures in the propane tank. Sayed struggled with the tarp, which was smoldering in several places and would soon be in flame. He was desperate to reach something under that tarp.

Simi headed after her cousin with a growl of determination, breaking free of Lainie's grasp when Lainie tried to restrain her. Though Lainie wanted to rescue Steele, wanted to get away before Steele's backup arrived, wanted to find Simi's father and clear her name, she couldn't bring herself to leave the girl to fight Sayed alone. Besides, she owed the man a thing or two, herself.

Lainie turned and sprinted after Simi, toward Sayed. Whatever the killer wanted so badly that he'd risk burning alive to get it out of the wreckage was not likely to be something she wanted him to have. She wasn't sure how she could help Simi, but she was determined to try.

CHAPTER 30

It was hard to see anything through the sooty smoke. The other men fleeing looked like ghosts in the night behind a blanket of black satin. None of them came her way, they seemed too intent on making their own escapes to concern themselves with her or Simi.

Sayed was half under the tarp now, which he'd pulled free enough to expose a strange apparatus that could only be the weapon Steele had described to Lainie. It was shaped like a giant gun on a platform, with cylinders of various diameter connected to a large cockpit like a crane or a bulldozer. Twisted oddly on its side, it was cracked and smashed in many places by the fall, revealing that most of the outer casing was made of something porous like ceramic, as if it needed to be made of stuff capable of absorbing vast amounts of heat.

Sayed seemed to be struggling with something near the pilot's seat. As Simi came within ten feet of him he spun away, face twisted in fury. The roar of the burning gas drowned out their words, then Sayed drew a gun. Simi launched into her spinning-form of combat and the man's head snapped to the right, twice, hard, before he was bodily flung away and sprawled in the dirt.

Simi went after Sayed, pressing her advantage. Lainie couldn't help there, but she looked at where Sayed had been pulling at something on the shattered weapon. The heavy canvas tarp was burning in places now. A compartment in the cockpit was open and something stuck partially out. As Simi landed blow after blow on her cousin, driving him further and further away from his goal, Lainie ran to the wreckage of the weapon and examined what Sayed had been trying to do.

Smoke and heat cooked her face and toxic smoke burned her lungs. The thing Sayed had been trying to pull free was round, cylindrical and sticking out of a compartment that appeared made for it. The cylinder was wedged half out and wouldn't budge. Sayed had been tugging on this cylinder with all his strength and hadn't budged it, so instead of trying to force it as he had, Lainie examined it carefully.

She could hear the two cousins fighting behind her when she spotted a bent bracket that was trapping the cylinder against the lip of the compartment. Lainie cast about her and found a chunk of metal that had been thrown free of the crash. Placing this against the bent bracket, she levered and the cylinder came free and dropped to the ground.

Lainie picked it up. The canister was about the size of a quart of milk. It had a metal cap on each end, but the center was transparent glass or acrylic, and inside swirled a brackish liquid so darkly green it was nearly black.

HG3000, Steele had told her, *Horror Gas. New, nasty. It attacks the mucous membranes the way salt attacks a snail, only more violently. The eyes swell and pop like squeezed grapes, the tongue swells, blisters and cracks open in seconds, blood spurts out of the ears, the body reacts like a sack full of rats fighting.*

Horrified, Lainie nearly threw the thing into the fire, then hesitated. She couldn't risk releasing this toxin.

When Sayed's gun shouted its deadly report, Lainie spun around. Simi was on the ground and Sayed was throwing himself in Lainie's direction. Laine turned to run, but his sudden weight bore her to the ground. Face down, her cheek chafing painfully against the dirt, Lainie felt Sayed trying to reach around her to grab the canister. He grabbed her shoulder and turned her over. His face was puffy, blood coming from his mouth, one of his ears and one of his eyes.

He grabbed the canister and they struggled.

Simi's stern voice startled them both, "Sayed."

Still clinging to the canister, Lainie and Sayed turned their heads. Simi stood nearby with only a little new blood on her lips. She held one of her two remaining grenades, finger poised to pluck the pin out.

"Let it go," she bared her teeth at him, "or I will throw this and kill both you and that infidel American spy in one go."

Sayed cursed at her in their language.

Simi pulled the pin.

Sayed cursed again, but pushed himself up and away from Lainie. Lainie scrambled back from him before standing up. Sayed was looking from Simi to the canister Lainie still held, the conflict between his yearning for it and his fear of dying before accomplishing his mission clear on his face.

"Go," Simi said to Lainie.

Lainie started to protest.

"Go," Simi shouted at her, and threw the grenade.

Lainie turned and ran as fast as she could. When she heard the grenade explode she turned to look.

Diving forward when the grenade exploded, Sayed flew under most of the spraying chunks of burning magnesium, but now his clothing was aflame. Screaming, he got up to run, then threw himself down and rolled, then jumped up to run again.

Simi stood and watched him, not smiling but her eyes glittering. Lainie called to her twice before the girl looked her way.

"Come on," Lainie insisted.

Simi looked to the fleeing Sayed, his clothes a virtual fireball now.

"Simi," Lainie snapped, and the girl came.

Lainie looked at the canister in her hands. For lack of anything better to do with it, she stuffed the canister into her shirt before Simi came trotting up. The shirt, Steele's shirt, was big and baggy on her to begin with. The cylinder lay across her stomach. With any luck no one would notice it. Her skin crawled where it touched the hateful thing, and she tried to put it out of her mind.

"Are you okay?" Lainie asked.

Simi touched the back of her head and the hand came away drenched in blood. She showed the hand to Lainie. Lainie turned the girl and parted her hair gently. There was a furiously bleeding furrow in Simi's scalp, bone visible beneath, but no sign that the bullet that had plowed this wound had harmed the skull beneath.

"You'll need stitches," Lainie said, swallowing, "but you'll live. You were lucky."

Simi said something that sounded like "*hamdulah*" that Lainie took as meaning, "Thank God."

"Amen," Lainie agreed. "Let's go."

They ran side by side. Lainie took the most direct line she could recall to the building where she'd spotted Steele. Much of the smoke had cleared and she saw lone figures running off into the night across the field. She heard helicopters out there as the broad, bright beams of spotlights began picking them out one by one. The fleeing men refused to obey orders, blaring from loud speakers, that they stop and surrender, so sporadic gunshots rang out.

Beyond, out on the road she could see the frantic rotating lights of law enforcement speeding toward her. The cavalry had arrived. She needed to make herself real scarce. She just wanted to make sure Steele was all right, then make her escape, with Simi, her only link to the doctor.

She thought about the canister in her shirt. What would they do with it if she left it for them to find? Destroy it, or save it, use it? What this gas could do was just too horrible to contemplate, and she would never know if by leaving it she would be responsible for its use on other human beings.

They turned a corner and ahead was the first building they had smashed. All of the buildings had caught fire in a chain reaction beginning with the fountain of propane on the other side of the compound. This one, like the others, burned furiously.

"Wait here," Lainie said, and wasn't at all surprised that Simi ignored her and followed Lainie as she ran to the large opening the truck had smashed through this side of the building. In spite of this ventilation the building was filled with smoke.

Lainie picked her way through the wreckage, trying to get the lay of the place, recall where it was that she'd seen Steele tied to the chair. After several minutes of stumbling around, eyes stinging and throat burning, she heard a groan.

"Cord," she called, but there was no answer.

With Simi behind her, Lainie stumbled over shattered tables and other debris. When she came upon him she nearly pitched over his fallen body. He had knocked his chair over and had tried to use his bound legs to kick himself across the floor toward escape. Now he was almost completely unconscious, breath coming in ragged, pinched gasps.

"Help me," Lainie ordered and she and Simi struggled with the knots in the ropes. Lainie saw a bullet wound in Steele's left thigh about three inches above the kneecap and pointed it out to Simi so that they could be careful of it.

Lainie was feeling woozy, every cough ablaze like it was searing her lungs out of her chest, when they finally got the ropes free. Lainie took Steele's legs and Simi took his arms and they half-carried, half-dragged him out of the building and out into the relatively fresh air.

Once outside, Lainie used a piece of Steele's rope-bonds that she'd carried out with them to cinch a tourniquet at his hip joint, above the bullet wound. That done, the two women collapsed on either side of him, breathing the sweet air desperately. Lainie knew she needed to get up and move...but only one second more of rest...

She awoke to Steele shouting into his cell phone, which his captors had clearly not bothered to take from him, since he was tied up. He was standing a few steps away, and Simi was on her back, passed out from smoke inhalation. Lainie hadn't been completely out, but woozy enough to not remember how long they'd laid here. When he saw her, Steele smiled at her. He was pacing, limping, favoring his left leg, the tourniquet still in place. His pant leg was soaked in blood around the bullet hole.

"You okay?" he asked her, then resumed shouting into his phone again without waiting for an answer. Shouting not in anger but clearly so that those on the other end could hear him over the throb of the rotors on the helicopters overhead. He was coordinating their sweep from here, comparing the number of men he'd counted earlier with the number they'd picked up in flight so far.

Lainie leaned over and shook Simi until the girl's eyes came open, if bleary. "We need to split," Laine said. "Now."

Simi nodded. She was so unsteady that Lainie had to help her up, then support her. Lainie suspected Simi's unsteadiness was more than just the smoke, a concussion from the bullet wound was setting in. They started to back away from Steele, but he turned and spotted them. He gave Lainie a questioning look, walked over and latched himself onto Simi's other wrist.

Placing the phone against his shoulder, he demanded, "Where are you going?"

"I have to...to report in," Lainie stammered.

Steele nodded, but his eyes had gone to slits, a sure sign of suspicion with him. "Fine. Go ahead. I'll make sure Simi is taken care of."

Lainie had her arm around Simi's waist. "That's okay, I've got her."

Steele gave Simi's arm a tug. "You go on ahead. She's fine with me."

Lainie glared at him and tugged back. "You're busy here. We'll get out of your way."

Simi's head lolled on her shoulders, one eye open and the other eyelid drooping at half-mast.

Steele snapped his phone closed and slipped it into his pocket. "Amanda, give it up. She's in CIA custody now. The NSA will get their chance. I promise."

Simi was trying to look from one to the other with a furrowed brow as if she could focus, but fear and some anger was showing on her face. Her muscles were bunching and Lainie knew Simi was preparing to launch into her swirling routine. She also knew that if Simi tried she'd go down like a marionette with its strings cut.

"Lainie, don wanna go withim," Simi said, sounding drunk.

Steele seemed not to notice that Simi had called Lainie by a different name than Amanda. Lainie stepped toward Steele and fixed him in a cold stare. "Let go of her."

"Go, if you want," Steele said, not the least intimidated. "Simi stays."

"Don't do this," Lainie said. "I don't want to hurt you."

Steele smiled, seemed to be restraining himself from laughing out loud.

Lainie took a swing at him and he ducked her. But this brought her in close enough for her real attack. As she pretended to stumble past she grabbed his leg right by the bullet hole. She drove her thumb in as deep as she could. Steele cried out, into her ear, making her head ring. He shoved her away, but he went down as well. He tried to drag Simi down with him but Lainie held onto to her and tore the girl free of his grasp.

"I'm sorry," Lainie said, even as Steele tried to get up again and fell back down, cursing.

His captors may not have taken his phone away, but they'd been wise enough to disarm him. For this Lainie was grateful as she tried to hurry as much a possible, dragging and leading Simi beside her. Behind, she heard Steele yelling into his cell phone again.

CHAPTER 31

"Wake up," Lainie snapped, giving the back of Simi's arm another hard pinch. Simi cried out and tried to push Lainie's hand away, but her eyes opened again and she peered around her, blinking.

Laine was behind the wheel in a Jeep Cherokee driving down an unlit rural road, heading she thought maybe north, but couldn't be sure. When they left Steele behind, Lainie waited until she felt they were blocked from sight by the smoke enough to make a wide arc and double back. She mostly-carried Simi back to the quonset hut in which the lines of SUV's had been parked, the ones she'd smashed through with the semi. She found one someone had tried to drive away, then abandoned, the engine still running. She found why, the thing had high-centered on the edge of the concrete slab on which the building was built and the rear wheels were suspended...no traction.

Lainie had helped Simi inside through the open driver side door and to slide across to the other side, then she got in herself. The interior was still redolent of polymer and vinyl, that all too familiar new-car smell. She used the switch on the dashboard to engage the four-wheel-drive, clearly something the prior occupant hadn't thought of, and the SUV pulled itself off the slab with a lot of grinding of metal but no real effort.

Lainie kept the lights off and avoided areas where most of the spotlights and red and blue spinners were concentrated, on the other side of the compound, and cut deeper across the field away from the road. The fuel tank read full. Going slow, leaving the lights and commotion behind, Lainie eventually came to another road. Pushing slowly through the barbed wire fence until the fence stakes came up, Lainie drove over the wire and set out on the road.

They'd been driving for nearly an hour now, Lainie trying to maintain what she thought might be a northerly course. Simi had tried to doze off several times, but Lainie wouldn't let her, certain the girl would drop into a concussion-induced coma and never wake up. Simi's left pupil seemed larger than her right, but Lainie couldn't be sure because Simi couldn't seem to keep her eyes open, much less hold up her head.

"Need to find a main road back to New York," Lainie said out loud. "Need to get you some medical attention."

"No doctorsh," Simi mumbled. "Shteele find ush."

"We'll go somewhere they won't ask too many questions."

"Right," Simi said, the sarcasm coming through her muddled enunciation. "Shomewhere they won ass queshtons 'bout how I managed to get myshelf shot in the back of the head."

"It's just a flesh-wound," Lainie protested. "Doctors are required to notify police of inflicted wounds, but in some clinics, in neighborhoods where injuries are common, health care workers don't bother, and even when they do cops are slow to respond."

Simi closed her eyes again. Lainie pinched her arm and Simi cried out, opening her eyes. She rubbed her arm. "Find another plashe to pinzh, willee? Gettina bruce. D'yee know where to fine a hoshpital like 'at."

Lainie let her silence say no for her.

By the time she found what seemed like a major blacktop highway heading east again Simi was no longer dozing and was holding her own head up. They stopped once so that Simi could vomit out the open passenger door. Another hour and they were pulling into a town, and a few minutes after that Lainie saw the first sign pointing the way to the George Washington Bridge.

Once back on the Manhatten side of the bridge Simi directed Lainie to a drug store. Simi told Lainie what supplies to buy and gave her money, but Lainie only consented to leave the girl alone in the truck while she went in to buy them in exchange for a solemn promise that Simi would not go to sleep. As it was Lainie rushed through her purchases and returned in ten minutes, having added some cokes and packaged donuts to the grocery list.

Simi's head was lolling on her chest but her eyes were open. Sitting in the cab of the Cherokee with the dome light on, Simi faced away as Lainie cleaned the gunshot wound with alcohol and gauze, closed it with butterfly band aids, packed it with gauze and taped the gauze in place with medical adhesive. Simi remained stoic the entire time. Her shrapnel wounds were going to need professional attention to get the steel shards out – the heat had cauterized the wounds around them.

Lainie, struggling to keep her stomach down as she administered to Simi, admired the girl's grit. Black eye after broken nose after grenade blast after gunshot, the diminutive little coil of whipcord remained tough and unyielding, eyes dark with unrelenting determination.

They swapped roles and Simi dressed the cut on Lainie's forehead, commenting in her slur that it was deeper in places than in others but none of it so deep that it would leave a scar. Lainie tried to match her erstwhile companion's stoicism, but winced when the alcohol touched the wound.

After chasing aspirin with the ice cold Cokes the two sat looking at each other for a moment. Lainie imagined she looked about as beat-up as Simi, and that the two of them together must really look a sight. But the girl had powdered donut sugar on her upper lip and nose. Lainie began to laugh, a low chortle at first, but as Simi joined her they both laughed openly. Simi seemed surprised when Lainie leaned forward and gave her a brief hug, but she accepted it and even returned it.

But when they pulled apart Lainie was no longer laughing.

"What ishit?" Simi asked.

"Now I've made a fugitive out of you, too," Lainie said. "I should have let Steele take you. I didn't have any right to..."

"Shuddup." Simi caught a string of drool as it escaped the corner of her mouth and wiped it away. "I want to hep you caush you have been good to me. I think I trusht you now. Me and my fath...er will hep you firsht, then we will turn ourshelvesh in. K-o?"

"Okay," Lainie smiled. "You sound better, but you should stay awake for now."

Simi nodded, caught herself before she toppled into the dashboard.

"The question is what do we do? Where do we go until you feel better?"

Simi said something that was too muddled for Lainie to understand.

"What?" Lainie said.

"Shave Ibrahim," Simi said, concentrating on each word.

Lainie sucked in a breath. Simi wasn't actually suggesting they rid her brother of his beard, the facial hair that on his young face was still thin and scraggly. She meant that they should rescue him before Sayed's group got to him. But surely the FBI had apprehended them all at the farm, hadn't they?

Lainie knew she couldn't assume that, and even if so, there might be other cells, backup cells in case Sayed's cell failed in their mission. Having lost Simi, Ibrahim would be their only link to Dr. Al-Sehremni. As reluctant as she was to place herself in danger again, she couldn't deny that Simi was right.

They had to save Ibrahim.

*   *   *

Striated clouds on the Eastern horizon were ablaze with stunning, smog-enhanced orange and crimson in anticipation of the coming sunrise. Lainie drove the Cherokee through Friday pre-rush-hour traffic, back toward Greenwich Village and Washington Square. They were on their way to Simi's and Ibrahim's...and Sayed's...apartment.

What would they do if there were men already at the apartment waiting for them? What would they do if Ibrahim was gone, signs of a struggle, Simi's brother clearly taken hostage? Or, having gotten him safely away, what was their next step in finding the kids' father?

Simi's concussion clearly hindered her ability to form words, and it was a pretty good bet that she was not operating at peak efficiency, IQ wise. Lainie was afraid that making these decisions was left to her alone, and all she could think of was: A) go get Ibrahim, and B) run like the wind at any sign of trouble. It wasn't intricate, it wasn't clever, but it was a plan.

Lainie pulled into the parking garage and drove slowly past the slot that had Simi's apartment number stenciled on it, her assigned parking space. She didn't expect to see the van, of course. That piece of Detroit was shattered and smashed in an equipment storage yard somewhere in New Jersey. However, no one else had taken the spot in its place, either.

Lainie drove back out onto the street and took a spot at the curb a block away. Back to work, Lainie thought, as she gripped the wheel and breathed deep, bracing herself for what might be waiting for them up there on the seventh floor of that building.

She got out of the truck. As Simi climbed down Lainie heard her cry out. Lainie ran around the vehicle to find Simi sitting on her rump on the curb, holding her head and shaking it.

"Still a little foggy," she said.

Lainie helped the younger woman up and noted how she had to carry more of Simi's weight than Simi did as she helped the girl back into the passenger seat.

"I'll be all right," Simi said, putting her head between her knees. "Just give me a minute."

"You're going to need more than a minute," Lainie said. "You've got a concussion, girl."

Simi moaned, though whether in nausea or agreement, Lainie couldn't tell.

"You stay here," Lainie said. "I'll go alone."

"No." Simi snapped her head up, but her eyes rolled back in her head and she tilted toward the sidewalk again. She opened her eyes as Lainie caught and held her, pushed her back up into the cab of the truck. "Just give me a minute."

"We don't have a minute," Lainie hissed. "Every minute could mean Ibrahim's freedom. I'll go alone."

"But you're just a..." Simi started to say, then gave Lainie a sheepish look.

"Go ahead, say it." Lainie huffed. "Just a school teacher. But I'm all you've got right now. Wait here. That's an order."

Simi didn't nod, nor consent in any other way, she just sat and looked forward as Lainie took the apartment keys out of her hand. Before Lainie could shut the door on her, Simi reached out and grasped Lainie's lapel, pulling her close with surprising strength, given her condition, so that they were forehead to forehead.

"He is my younger brother," Simi said in a hiss harsh with intensity. "Papa did not want me to go away to school, but he charged me to look out for Ibrahim." Her eyes swam away for a moment, then came back again with even more piercing focus, if possible. The pupils had nearly returned to the same size once more, Lainie noted.

"If you would have me trust you," Simi went on, "protect him. Protect my little brother. Do this, and you will be a sister to me forever."

"I will," Lainie said, trying to match Simi's intensity.

Simi nodded and let her go. As an afterthought, Lainie checked on the canister of gas where she'd stashed it behind the passenger seat, all the more sinister, swirling, and gangrenous in the light of day. Simi was too out of it to notice and when Laine closed the car door Simi slumped against it.

Lainie watched for traffic, then crossed the street and headed into the building.

CHAPTER 32

Several rows of brass-fronted mailboxes covered the wall to the left of the entry vestibule, and on the one to the right was a bank of buttons corresponding to apartment numbers, and an intercom. Lainie let herself through the inner door with Simi's keys. The lobby was narrow, little more than a hallway and not much of a foyer. There was a bank of elevators straight ahead and a hallway going past them deeper into the building. A brushed-metal plaque hung by two chains from the ceiling over the threshold to the hallway, engraved with the words:

STAIRWAY
PARKING
LAUNDRY ROOM
WEIGHT ROOM
BASEMENT
(Tenant Storage, Utilities Access, Trash Compactor)

Next to the call buttons by the elevator was a similar but smaller plaque declaring that the superintendent's apartment was on the second floor, number 201. Once inside the elevator Lainie pressed the seventh floor button and felt herself lifted up into the bowels of the building. It struck her that the elevator had only one exit, that she'd be trapped if someone was waiting for her on the seventh floor. These are the things, she reflected, that probably would have been noticed by any real espionage professional *before* entering the elevator.

But no one was there when the doors slid open.

The hallway was narrow, papered in stripes and carpeted in maroon paisley. A plaque on the wall opposite the elevators told her that the odd numbered apartments were to the left, the even to the right. She turned right.

Apartment 736 was nine doors down and on the left. Lainie pressed her ear to the door. She heard nothing. She didn't dare knock in case someone had beaten them here, Sayed's people...or the FBI.

A door opened further down the hallway and Lainie saw a boy and a girl in jeans and sweaters, carrying backpacks and heading up the hall toward the elevators. Toward her. They looked at her oddly, as if about to ask her what she was doing loitering in the hall.

Lainie smiled at them, unlocked the door and stepped boldly into Simi's apartment, closing the door behind her. Glancing quickly around the darkened entry, she saw no movement. She listened again to the door, heard muffled conversation and laughter, the elevator chime, then silence.

The apartment was dim, but not dark. To the right of the small entry hall was a passage that led to a kitchen, to the left a coat closet. Further along and to the right a door opened on a guest restroom, and ahead was an open archway to the sitting room. The décor here was pedestrian, with furniture, wall-hangings and sculptures directly out of any Pier 1 or Pottery Barn catalog. On the TV was an eight-by-ten color photograph of Simi and Ibrahim and several other young people Lainie didn't recognize at some sort of outdoor festival or event.

She guessed the slightly stooped gentleman between the siblings with the more-salt-than-pepper beard was the enigmatic, elusive scientist Dr. Faisal Al-Sehremni. He had a sad cast to the nevertheless bright and intelligent eyes that peered from behind wire, half-lens reading glasses. One arm was crooked affectionately around Simi's neck and the other hand rested proudly on the narrow shoulder of Ibrahim.

To the right the kitchen once more, separated from the sitting room by a chest-high bar. Beyond the kitchen was a dining room and between them was a hallway leading back to the bedrooms. On the dining room table was a clutter of books and papers...and Lainie's laptop, propped open but not on. So this is where it'd gotten to after Simi and Ibrahim abducted her.

She wondered if they'd gotten past her password, then decided it didn't matter – there was nothing on her computer to interest a pair of siblings looking for their lost father. Nor, for that matter, Sayed and his cell of hardened terrorists.

Next to the laptop was her wallet, open with its contents spilled out including her driver's license, credit card, student ID, and the forty-three dollars she had left. She gathered this up and put it in her left hip pocket where it belonged. Then she bundled the laptop into its carrying case and took it with her on the rest of her search.

Lainie looked into the master bedroom, which according to Simi was shared by Ibrahim and Sayed. There was no sign of Simi's brother, although the made twin beds and uncluttered floor told her either he or his cousin was uncommonly neat for a college kid. The second bedroom, Simi's, was likewise vacant and not quite so neat, with magazines and clothes strewn about and a bowl and spoon on the bureau with the petrified dregs of what could be oatmeal. Lainie turned to go back to the dining room and kitchen when she heard a knock at the door.

Not again, she thought, her blood throbbing in her ears.

When she heard a key in the lock her heart only beat faster. Why would Ibrahim knock before entering his own apartment? If Sayed lived here too, wouldn't his fellow conspirators have a key of their own?

Holding the laptop case to her chest, she backed up the hallway and into Simi's bedroom as the apartment door opened. She heard whispered voices enter and the door close again.

"Ibrahim," a voice called.

It couldn't possibly be, but she knew she would never forget that voice. It played her spine like a harp in chilling minor tones, bringing memories of knives and grenades and bound wrists and feelings of utter, unrelenting hopelessness.

Sayed.

He should have been dead, should have burned to death after being hit by the white-hot magnesium-phosphate of the grenade Simi had lobbed at him. They'd watched his clothing burst into flame as he ran, screaming in panic. But here he was again, and once again he stood between Lainie and her only escape.

He called out something in Arabic, and of course received no answer. He and the others there with him began speaking in more casual tones and Lainie saw the glow of lights up the hall. She cast around Simi's room for a place to hide. Her choices were limited, the closet or under the bed, both hopeless clichés, the first places any hunter would look for prey.

She doubted that they would check Simi's room, but she wasn't going to take any chances. As the sounds of their chatter came muted down the hall Lainie knew they were settling in to wait for Ibrahim. Probably they didn't expect Simi to show her face here again, but they had clearly underestimated the depths of Lainie's own stupidity, she thought grimly.

Lainie chewed her thumbnail. She wished Cord Steele, Secret Agent, was here, and that made her feel like Lois Lane in a Superman comic, or Jane in an old black and white Tarzan movie. She didn't want to be Lois Lane or Jane, she wanted to be Lara Croft or, better yet, Cat Woman. In the end, she was just Lainie Parker, graduate student cum phone sex girl.

She didn't know how many were out there with Sayed, but she knew she had little chance going against them head on. She went to the window and looked out into the alley beyond and down seven floors, swallowing hard. There was no ledge for her to stand on even if she was to climb out, and there was no fire escape.

But there was a fire escape against the other building, across the alley. It was a pedestrian alley only, one of those narrow airshafts common amid some of the older buildings in New York, but it was still over ten feet away. There was no way she could make that leap.

She went to the bedroom door and, careful not to make a sound, closed it. She returned to the window. The laptop carrying case had a shoulder strap she never used, zipping it inside the case with the computer. She pulled it out now and used it to sling the case across her back.

When she opened the window the sounds of the city filled the room, the *shush* of traffic, horns, people, the distant rattle of a jackhammer. She waited and listened for the sound of someone coming up the hall to investigate, but none came. Stepping up onto the sill she balanced in a low crouch.

She held her breath and closed her eyes to steady herself. She nearly teetered over and off the edge and her eyes sprang wide as she grabbed the sides of the window and bit back a scream. Setting dramatics aside, she bunched her muscles, hesitated for a brief, doubt-filled second, then drove her legs straight and launched herself across the gulf.

The second she left the window sill she knew she wasn't going to make it. Both her breathing and her pulse came to a halt as she sailed across the alley, hard blacktop and concrete reeling far below her. She watched as her hands breezed past the rail she'd been aiming for...

...and cried out as they came in contact with the one below it. Her wrists and arms sreamed in protest, but she didn't let go until she'd swung under and was firmly over the iron-grate landing of the fire escape. When she did let go she landed on her rump hard. She grabbed her knees and sat trembling for a full minute.

When she opened her eyes and looked down, a man with shaggy beard, a ragged and stained duster and shoes that did not match was peering up at her, jaw slack and eyes wide. Lainie forced herself to stand and scramble down the rattling stairs as fast as she could make her feet go. The ladder descended the last twenty feet smoothly and then she was on the ground once more.

She looked back up the rickety structure and felt a sudden elation. "Take that, Cat Woman," she muttered.

Lainie rushed around to the street. She had hoped to have time to go to the truck, drop off the laptop and the gas canister and check on Simi before returning to watch for Ibrahim, but as she rounded the corner she saw him climbing out of a cab and ducking into the entrance to the building.

"Ibrahim." she cried.

She sprinted after him. She was flinging herself into the vestibule as he stepped into the elevator, and by the time she got the key out and used it to gain access to the lobby the elevator doors were sliding closed. She hit the button at a run and punched it repeatedly, but the car was already on its way up to the seventh floor.

Lainie charged the hallway to the door marked *Stairs*, flung it open and threw herself up the echoing stairwell. Wheezing like an asthmatic she pistoned her feet and drove herself against pain and fatigue up the tiled stairs, flight after flight, forgoing counting in favor of breathing as hard and as deeply as she could manage. Her lungs burned and still she tore up the stairs.

Fourth floor.

Fifth floor.

Sixth floor.

At the seventh floor she burst into the hallway and rebounded hard off the opposite wall. There he was, down the hall, on the far side of the elevators from her. His key was in the lock and he was opening the door when she called his name. Ibrahim stopped with the door ajar and turned to look at her, eyes wide with recognition and shock.

She ran toward him and he stepped away from the door to face her. He put up his hands defensively as she reached him and she stopped. He opened his mouth to say something and she put her finger to her lips. She pointed at the apartment door. He looked that way, then looked at her in confusion.

"Please," she whispered. "No time to explain. I'll take you to your father, but you have to come now." It was a lie, but the quickest way she could think to get him to come with her with a minimum of exposition.

He eyed her suspiciously. "What do you know about where my father hides?" he matched her whisper.

This was an odd thing for him to ask, Lainie thought. Just hours ago he and Simi were convinced Lainie knew where their father was, but now that Lainie claimed to know Ibrahim looked on the verge of calling her a liar. Just yesterday they had accused the government of holding Dr. Al-Sehremni prisoner, but now Ibrahim spoke of his father hiding. She would have expected him to ask another question instead, such as why she was whispering.

But she didn't have time to puzzled it out right now.

"Please," Lainie begged him, glancing nervously at the door. No sound came through the small gap. Sayed and his men had to have heard the key in the lock and must be wondering what the delay was. "I said no time to explain."

"I cannot go," Ibrahim protested. "Simi has disappeared, now, too. She did not return yesterday from classes. I just spent the night looking for her. I cannot find her."

"She's with me," Lainie hissed. "She's waiting for us down in the car."

"You lie," he said, almost out loud.

Lainie shushed him with a gesture again and winced. How could she make him trust her?

"Ibrahim? Is that you, cousin?" Sayed, calling from the apartment.

"Whether she is my friend or my prisoner," Lainie growled harshly under her breath, "you have to come. It's your duty, as her brother. Your father would expect nothing less."

At this Ibrahim's brow clouded, but this was language he understood, the sort of thing he expected from her, an American spy. "If you have harmed her in any way..."

"Shut up and come," Lainie hissed forcefully. "Now."

Ibrahim reached to take his keys out of the door handle.

"Leave them," Lainie snapped. "Come on, now."

Ibrahim squared his shoulders and nodded. Lainie led the way back up the hall at a trot. As they reached the elevator landing she heard the door of Ibrahim's apartment swing open.

"Cousin," Sayed called urgently.

Lainie grabbed Ibrahim's shirt and pulled him along as she picked up to a sprint toward the stairs. She didn't take three steps before the stairwell door opened and four men in black assault gear – vests, helmets, and guns like the one marked P-90 in Brandt's gun collection - stepped onto the floor, and somehow she just knew they were FBI. Steele's backup.

"Sayed?" Ibrahim strained to look back over his shoulder.

Lainie came to a halt and turned to look past Ibrahim toward Sayed. The killer wore a fleece pullover, the hood pulled up. He stood hunched as if in pain and his face was ablaze with rage. He, too, carried a naked weapon as three other men came out of the apartment to arrange themselves behind him.

"Get away from the woman, Ibrahim," Sayed shouted hoarsely.

Lainie looked from one group of men to the other, caught in the crossfire. Both were marching inexorably closer. This was not going to end well.

CHAPTER 33

Everyone froze as the elevator chime *dinged*, Sayed's men at one end of the hall, the strike force at the other, no one more nonplused than Lainie who crouched with Ibrahim between them. The doors slid open and Lainie found herself face to face with Cord Steele. He rocked back in surprise himself, standing before her with his leg wrapped in a makeshift white bandage, a tree branch in his left hand for a cane.

"S...Samantha..." he stammered.

Without thinking Lainie stepped forward and kicked out, aiming her foot at the direct center of the white bandage. Steele swept the branch-cane in front of him and smacked Lainie's foot aside at the ankle with an audible *crack*. Lainie cried out as she collapsed against the wall of the elevator.

"Not twice, kiddo," Steel said with cold humor.

Ibrahim stood, still in the hall, looking both ways as shouts and expletives volleyed between the two groups of men facing off. Steele reached out and grabbed the boy's lapel, yanking him into the elevator just as gunfire erupted in the hallway. Steele pushed the ground floor button with the heel of his homemade crutch and the door slid closed.

Lainie got to her feet as the elevator sank.

"Where's the girl?" Steele asked. He had a gun but

pointed it at the ceiling, as if, Lainie thought, he was presenting her with the decision to cooperate or not.

Lainie folded her arms stubbornly.

"You're tougher than I would have thought," Steele said to her appraisingly. "More resourceful, too. But you've made a total mess of things, and it's my neck on the line for not reigning you in much sooner."

"What do you mean?" she asked.

"How stupid do you think I am, Samantha?" Steele said. "Or should I say, Lainie Parker."

CHAPTER 34

"How long have you known?" Lainie asked. Oddly she didn't feel surprised or shocked. Though there was undeniable fear of what was going to happen to her now, her prevailing feeling was one of relief that the charade was over.

Steele smacked the emergency stop button with the back of his hand and the entire carriage slowed, shuddered, bounced, stopped.

"I knew within hours of our dinner together that first night," Steele said. "You left fingerprints on your wine glass that couldn't have been more perfect. Really, they were works of art. I commend you. Then it was confirmed later when an Agent Peck of the FBI field office in San Francisco called the hotline looking for you."

Ibrahim was looking from one to the other of them, clearly not following what was going on.

Lainie felt her temperature rising again. "Why the hell this whole game, then? Why let me keep thinking that I...that you..."

"Couple reasons," Steele said, leaning against the wall with a negligent air, still holding his roguish smile. "First, for what it's worth, I'm pretty convinced you're innocent of the crimes you're accused of back in San Francisco. You weren't fleeing from the law. Instead you were taking considerable risks to prove your alibi. Those aren't the actions of a guilty person.

"Second, Brandt's death came as a surprise to all of us. I never considered doubting you. It fit too well with the rest of your story, which I was already well on my way to believing. Seems you have a knack for getting into places you don't belong, finding out things you have no business knowing. I'm hooked, in spite of myself. You intrigue me. If you pushed this far to get the proof you needed, I was curious to see just how far you'd go. I thought you deserved the chance to get what you wanted. My superiors didn't agree, they wanted me to run you in. I didn't ignore them, exactly, just practiced delayed obedience."

But another, more pragmatic motive occurred to her. "The CIA is not allowed to operate within US borders. You were using me, your so-called pursuit of me on orders from your superiors, as an excuse to continue investigating this case."

Steele said nothing but the twinkle in his eye told her she was right.

"But you were going to take me in eventually," Lainie said between clenched teeth. "Jesus, I'm so stupid."

"On the contrary," Steele said. "You were magnificent. It was me, I was the stupid one. You were a loose cannon, a random variable. I was stupid to think I could ever control you. You flanked me, and you did it so easily, so elegantly, and right under my nose...it was dazzling."

Steele was grinning at her like a proud mentor.

"What in hell are you taking about?"

"While I was busy being a sneaky-son-of-a-bitch" – he said it this time with self-effacing sarcasm – "you stepped right in and stole Simi out from under me. You got her trust and got her to give you what you wanted, her cooperation."

"It wasn't like that," Lainie said to Ibrahim. "I swear. I'm not like them."

The young man glared at them, his face twisted in outrage.

"What makes us so different?" Steele asked, looking indignant. "We both want to find Dr. Al-Sehremni, and we both want to use Simi and Ibrahim, here, to do it."

Lainie looked at the floor. There was no escaping it, Steele was right. She was using Simi, just as he wanted to. She was no different than the spies and terrorists swooping like dark shadows all around them.

"I'll tell you the difference," Steele went on. "The difference is I have something to offer him and his family. Protection. Asylum. That offer is on the table, plain and clear, no catches, no hidden agendas. What are you peddling, Lainie? Friendship? Camaraderie? What good is that going to do them against a cadre of very, *very* determined killers?"

Lainie turned moist eyes up to Ibrahim. "I'm sorry," she said. "He's right. You're better off with him than with me. You and Simi, and eventually your father, will be safer. I was being selfish. Just like he says."

Ibrahim looked away, his lower jaw jutting petulantly.

Steele pulled the stop button back out and the elevator started moving again.

"Don't be too hard on yourself," Steele said to Lainie.

She wanted to slap him, but instead she continued to stare down at the floor.

Ibrahim lunged for Steele's gun, throwing Steele against the back wall of the elevator. Steele was not caught entirely off guard and clapped his hands over Ibrahim's, keeping him from gaining the weapon.

"Ibrahim, don't," Lainie yelled.

The two men struggled, each gripping the gun, grunting into one another's face. Steele's arm began to drop slowly, the muzzle coming down toward Ibrahim's head.

"I do not wish to go," Ibrahim said, his voice hoarse as he strained to break Steele's grip.

Ibrahim jerked forward, their foreheads came together with an audible crack, and the CIA agent blinked and shook his head. Curling his lip, Steele returned the favor, slamming his head into Ibrahim's. This time both men staggered as if dazed, but still neither relinquished his grip.

The elevator slowed, stopped, and the doors slid open.

Lainie slipped out and hit the top floor button as she went by. "Ibrahim, come on," she called.

Ibrahim butted Steele again and this time they both went down on one knee.

"Ibrahim," Lainie screamed.

Letting go, Ibrahim staggered back, and fell on his rump. Steele went down to his butt too, back against the wall, as Lainie grabbed Ibrahim's collar and helped him scramble backwards like a crab out of the carriage. Steele leveled his gun unsteadily and peered at Lainie blearily. Their eyes met, though Lainie couldn't be sure that his were focused.

"Don't shoot," Lainie said, facing him squarely. "There's nobody out here you want to shoot, Cord."

The doors began to close, and through the diminishing opening Lainie watched Steele.

"God damn it, Lainie," Steele cursed, dropping the gun into his lap. They didn't break eye contact until the doors broke it for them. Lainie looked up and saw the numbers had started advancing back up the floors again.

There was no one in the lobby. Ibrahim had gotten to his feet and they sprinted out of the building. On the street, sounds of sporadic gunfire filtered down to them from the seventh floor. Lainie led Ibrahim to the Cherokee and motioned for him to get in the back. As she climbed in the driver's seat she saw Simi had fallen asleep.

"Shit," Lainie cursed as she twisted the key in the ignition.

"Simi," Ibrahim cried out from the back seat. "What is wrong with her?"

"She has a concussion," Lainie said, pulling out into traffic. "Shake her, wake her up, do whatever it takes. Don't let her slip into a coma."

As she sped through the streets of the thickening morning rush-hour traffic Lainie hoped it wasn't already too late. She drove...well, really, nowhere...while Ibrahim lay over the console between the front seats shaking his sister and slapping her and calling her name repeatedly and loudly. Lainie saw no sign of pursuit. At one point Ibrahim addressed Lainie without turning away from this chore, "What have you done to her, you...American?" That he could think of no worse epithet to call her was supremely unfair, Lainie thought, as was the entire long history of misunderstood motives and misapprehended actions between their two cultures.

But she set her lips in a line, said nothing and drove. She wanted to weep in relief when she heard Simi murmur Ibrahim's name, saw the two siblings embrace each other. After a moment they began to speak in Arabic, rapidly and with many gestures and much inflection, exchanging their stories. Lainie was dying to ask what they were saying to each other, but she held her tongue.

"Lainie," Simi finally said to her. "Ibrahim has told me how bravely you saved him from Sayed - may Allah curse his name forever – and the CIA. Thank you."

Lainie blushed. "Yeah, well, it was a stupid move, trying to grab Steele's gun like that, Ibrahim. You could have gotten yourself killed."

"It doesn't matter," Ibrahim said. "I did not die."

"But you could have."

Ibrahim and Simi looked at each other, clearly perplexed by her anger. Ibrahim said again, "*Could have* does not matter. I did not die, that is what matters. It was not Allah's will." His tone had a finality to it, as if he expected no further discussion on the matter.

"But Steele was right," Lainie said. "You are endangering your family more because of me. Simi must have told you, I am not a spy. I don't have the training to..."

"That matters neither," Ibrahim said, his English much less fluent than Simi's. "For you have shown yourself to be our friend. We shall trust you. I do not wish to turn myself in to your government yet."

"But they have the resources to find your father," Lainie insisted.

"That counts even less," he said. "We no longer search for father."

"What do you mean?"

Ibrahim smiled at both Lainie and Simi. "While you were gone, I got a message, and now I know where Father is."

CHAPTER 35

Fatimah Guntherson lived in Fargo, North Dakota with the American defense contractor she had married, thereby disgracing her family. Though she had been disowned and cut off by their parents, Fatimah and her sister, Layali, stayed in secret correspondence throughout the years. Fatimah was also quite fond of her brother-in-law, Faisal, who helped her sneak out of the country to meet her fiancé and begin her new life as the wife of an American. So it was natural that Faisal would seek her out when he found himself in the United States.

Layali was Simi's and Ibrahim's mother, and Faisal their father. Fatimah was an aunt they had never met and knew so little about they had simply forgotten her. Until Faisal's telegram came last night.

Ibrahim assured Lainie that the telegram was sent anonymously, this time to the school in care of the Counseling Office. His father had written the telegram in a code that Ibrahim had made up as a child and he and his father played with frequently as a game. It gave only an address and nothing more. Lainie wondered if NSA analysts could break an Arabic code invented by a child and decided that they could, but hopefully she and the Al-Sehremni family would be long gone by the time they even thought to check the school for correspondence sent to either of the Al-Sehremni siblings.

The three of them drove the Cherokee, taking turns at the wheel and using what little cash they had between them for gas, tolls, and food. It was just over 1400 miles via Interstates 80 and 94, among others, and by only stopping long enough for gas and for the five daily prayers of Islam, not daring to speed for fear of drawing attention to themselves, they made the drive in just under 21 hours.

Ibrahim had a small compass, in conjunction with which a map and some quick calculations on a pad helped him locate the direction in which Mecca lay. A small, black-bound booklet full of what looked like printed timetables helped them to time their prayers accurately. Five times a day they stopped the truck, removed their shoes, laid out newspaper on which to kneel, and Lainie watched from the car, curious but respectful of their privacy. It reminded her of the paucity of religion in her own upbringing and she realized she respected people who could live by such faith. She knew she couldn't.

During the drive the three of them spent much of the time talking, mostly telling stories of their respective childhoods, happier times, studiously avoiding the horrors that had surrounded them in the last few days. Simi gave all signs of having recovered from her concussion permanently. She and Lainie cleaned and redressed each other's wounds, Lainie remarking that Simi's scalp-furrow would heal but leave a nasty scar it its wake.

While recounting her story in more detail for them it occurred to Lainie that she hadn't seen the killer who was stalking her, not since the airport. The man who'd actually shot Brandt, Mitch and Kim and firebombed the Capri offices. The mountain-sized man who repeated, "I always win," like a mantra. She had stopped using her credit card and so she guessed he had no way to track her. Would he vanish, fleeing to South America before she could get the proof she needed to set the authorities on his trail?

The prospect of living the rest of her life jumping at every odd noise, flinching from errant shadows, always looking over her shoulder filled her with horror. There was only one way to bring the murderer back within reach, and that was to use her credit card again, but she was loathe to try it without someone to back her up. Somehow she sensed that time was running out.

*   *   *

Lainie and Simi did speak briefly about Sayed, sitting in the back seat together while Ibrahim drove.

"I didn't get a good look at him at the apartment," Lainie said. "But if the burns he got from that grenade in New Jersey were serious, they didn't seem to slow him down much. Anyway, he and his men were cornered by the FBI last I saw them. I don't think we have to worry about them again."

Simi shook her head. "I won't underestimate my cousin again," she said. "He's still out there. He got away, somehow, and he's still looking for us."

Lainie saw the futility of arguing with her and so kept silent.

*   *   *

As it happened, Lainie was driving when they neared their destination. Simi sat beside her at the edge of her seat peering out past the lines of rain rushing toward them while Ibrahim lay among the blankets in the back. All Lainie knew about Fargo she learned from the movie of the same name, so she expected sparsely populated tracts of land blanketed in snow. She was not prepared for the heat. During the summer temperatures in Fargo averaged from the low 80's to the high 90's.

It was 82 degrees today, humid, and raining in sheets. It reminded her of some summers in San Francisco. The SUV hydroplaned rather sickeningly along the flooded streets of Fargo, but out of pity for Simi's excitement Lainie didn't slow down.

"We are almost there," Simi said again, glancing for the hundredth time at the map on her lap.

Lainie turned a corner in the pine-encrusted

neighborhood, upscale tract-houses set back from the road on manicured landscaping, a picture worthy of any Real Estate agent's wet dream. Not many people were out and about, but there were some, mostly children playing in puddles or catching raindrops on their tongues.

"There," Lainie pointed.

The house was indistinguishable from a thousand others except for the oversize numbers nailed to the garage. An older Caucasian man and three children, dressed snugly in rain gear, ran around the lawn, the man putting on a caricature impression of Frankenstein or some other monster, the children laughing and rushing past him just within reach. On the porch sat four other people, a nondescript younger couple and an older couple of clear Middle Eastern heritage.

As Lainie pulled to the curb the adults galvanized, uncertainty and fear showing clearly on their faces. The old Middle-Eastern gentleman stood with difficulty, his back bent, his head ringed with the same unruly white, wispy hair that obscured his face. When Lainie heard Simi gasp Lainie thought she knew who this might be.

"Father," Simi confirmed breathlessly.

The elusive scientist, Dr. Faisal Al-Sehremni.

"Ibrahim," Simi cried. "Wake up. It's father."

Then she was out of the car and running up the gentle slope toward him, getting drenched on the way. The older Caucasian man stepped in as if to intercept her, but even Lainie heard Al-Sehremni call out his daughter's name and the erstwhile Frankenstein stepped aside and let the two greet each other.

"Father?" Ibrahim said sleepily from behind Lainie.

"Yes," Lainie said as she watched Simi and her father embrace each other warmly. "It's your father."

Ibrahim launched himself out the back door and ran to join his sister and their father. Lainie stayed in the car, unwilling to impose herself on this moment of reunion. Besides, her vision was getting blurry and it was difficult for her to see the handle to open the door just now.

*　　　*　　　*

Simi and Ibrahim had a lot of catching up to do with a branch of the family tree with which they had never been acquainted before. Not only was there an aunt and her American husband, but three cousins, their spouses, and a grand total of ten nieces and nephews. One cousin, the oldest, was Layali, named after Simi's and Ibrahim's mother. It was her children that were playing with grandpa on the front lawn while she, her husband, a graphic artist named Rolph Pastori, and the children's grandmother and great-uncle watched from the porch.

During the tearful greetings Lainie stood aside and watched and listened. The family spoke English for the benefit of those who did not speak Arabic, which included just about everyone but Faisal, Fatimah, Simi and Ibrahim.

Lainie learned that Faisal had only sent the telegram on the insistence of his sister-in-law, the one Ibrahim retrieved from the university, in spite of his warning that it may bring danger to her doorstep. It seemed her husband, Stan Guntherson, still had many contacts from his days contracting for the State Department, and he was confident those connections would protect them from any excessive enthusiasm on the part of any agents who came calling. It was unlikely that those seeking al-Sehremni would be able to get hold of the telegram from the school without drawing attention to themselves.

Lainie watched al-Sehremni in fascination. After all, it was this one man around which so much pivoted. But she failed to note anything remarkable about him. He had a voice like tissue paper, thin and fragile, and eyes that seemed incapable of smiling. But he had a mild, self-effacing humor and she could tell from the way he looked at them that it was his children who gave him his only reason for going on in the face of the loss of his wife.

Later, the entire family sat down to dinner, some finding seats on couches, chairs, even stacks of newspaper while others stood. Lainie held back to the kitchen to sit at the rickety card table with the three children.

"No," Simi said, leading Lainie back into the living room. "You will sit with us. There is much to talk about tonight, and you have much to do with it."

Lainie found herself seated across from Al-Sehremni, Simi to his right and Fatimah to his left. Ibrahim sat next to his aunt. The rest of the family filled the large living and dining rooms, talking cheerfully, the feelings of clan and tradition rich and warm around Lainie. Fatimah announced that she had mastered a recipe that she had seen on the Cooking Channel and they all set to a saffron-encrusted roast chicken, almond wild rice, squash and store-bought reheated dinner rolls that were surprisingly tasty. All of her children had brought dishes to contribute upon being summoned to the impromptu reunion.

Overwhelmed by it all, Lainie remained reserved and let the family reassert their bonds. After dinner the women retired to the kitchen to do the dishes while the men moved to the living room to drink and talk. At some point a hookah appeared on the coffee table with many partaking. The smoke smelled fragrant and spicy.

It was late when the last of the extended family finally departed, leaving the house to Uncle Stan, Aunt Fatimah, Faisal, Ibrahim, Simi, and Lainie. The six of them now sat at the dining room table drinking tea. After they settled in, the stories began with Lainie. At Simi's urging she told them everything much the same way she had told it to Simi on the road waiting for Steele outside the encampment. Simi and Ibrahim interrupted with their parts, and Simi took over entirely when singing Lainie's praises on the use of the semi tractor-trailer to demolish the terrorist camp. Then Lainie continued with the rescue of Ibrahim, omitting much of hers and Steele's conversation in the elevator.

Early in the telling al-Sehremni stopped eating, set down his fork and stared at his plate. Lainie saw his face twitch cryptically when she spoke of overhearing the gunshot that had killed Brandt, and he flinched painfully on hearing about how

Sayed had broken Simi's nose, the gunshot that had nearly taken off her head. When it was done he wept openly.

"Father," Simi said, burying her face in his white hair and holding his shoulders. "Don't cry. Everything's going to be all right."

Finally and with difficulty the old scientist stood. He looked around the room at them and spoke in his wispy-thin voice, telling his side of the story.

CHAPTER 36

"I wish to tell it all, from the beginning, for even my beloved children do not know the entire story.

"I met my heavenly Layali in London, where I was attending Oxford. She was there with her father, a functionary in the Iraqi Diplomatic Corps. When I saw her I knew I must defy my family, who had selected for me another wife at home in Iraq, and marry Layali instead. My family was well placed in political circles and so we did well, we were wealthy, after a fashion, and so Layali's father was pleased to make the match.

"When we returned to Baghdad and were married, we lived well compared to others due to the political connections of both Layali's father and mine. This was before either American war. We lived well and were happy, until I fell out of favor with both of our families.

"Layali's sister, Fatimah who is with us now, worked at the American embassy in the cafeteria and confessed to us her love for an American whom she met there, the very Stan Guntherson who is our host this evening. Foolishly we urged her to confess her love to her father. Yes, he would be angry, but in the end how could he deny love? It was a mistake, for he beat her badly and forbade her from any further contact with any American. She was forced to quit her job and confined to the house. She was broken, talking to Layali of suicide.

"Layali came to me, begged me to intervene, which I tried, but their father would hear of no discussion on the matter. At Layali's pleading I arranged for Fatimah and Stan to meet, and at that meeting they begged me to help them elope. It was at the beginning of Ramadan, and so one night, during the family's revelry, when there was much celebration, many people and much activity, I spirited Fatimah away to meet Stan in secret. Even Layali did not know our plan, for we did not want to put her under suspicion. Stan snuck Fatimah across the border into Kuwait and from there to America.

"When my father-in-law discovered his daughter had run away he flew into a rage. Knowing that Fatimah would have confided in Layali he turned on his older daughter. He beat Layali so severely that when I returned I thought she was dead. I intervened and confessed to him my role in Fatimah's disappearance to save my Layali, and he banished me from his house. When my family found out what I had done they were as scandalized as was Layali's, and they too turned their backs to me.

"Layali and I moved to Kuwait to live out the rest of our lives. Though we should have been poor by Iraqi standards, we thrived there because of my work, and because of the more westernized economy. For years we lived happily, though Layali suffered continuing health problems, lingering from the beating her father had dealt her. Allah did not see fit to bless us with offspring, and many looked at us askance for that. I thought that too might be as result of the beating, but we were in love and we were happy.

"Simi was born the year of my fiftieth birthday, and though it was late in our lives we cherished her, even though she was a daughter and not a son. Soon Layali was pregnant with Ibrahim, and we looked forward to a house filled with the laughter and joy of children. But Layali's age and suffering health could not stand up to the stress of childbirth a second time, and Layali died in her maternity bed a week after giving birth to him. Though Ibrahim was born healthy he was never strong. I am sorry, my son, but it is true. Still, I thank Allah that my Layali had the chance to see her son before she was taken from us.

"At first I tried to raise the children as Layali would have me do, but a depression was growing deeper and deeper into my bones, for I had lost the only woman I had ever loved and would ever love. When the children were old enough they began to ask about her, and about their other family, grandparents and cousins, and this deepened my sadness, for how could I tell them that because of my foolish romanticism we had been outcast from their lineage?

"When Simi was twenty, Ibrahim was eighteen and I was seventy and feeling my age. Simi was attending college in Kuwait, but Ibrahim wanted to go to College in America. I wanted him to have that chance, but Ibrahim is a sensitive boy and I was afraid that the Americans would, how do you say, bite him up and spit him out? Simi was the strongest of us all, and so I sent her to America with her brother, to watch over him.

"It was then that I was offered a fellowship in an experimental lab in Paris. The lab was owned and operated by a Saudi man, though located in a western country. They were doing exciting things with particle acceleration and coding, things that my own research was leading me to. Without my children to live for I was truly despondent, and so I took the position in hopes of drowning myself in my research.

"It didn't take me long to learn that almost all of the research the lab was doing was military related, specifically weapon systems and chemical delivery systems. In my pride I tried to resign, and it was then that I was threatened with the lives of my children. Their own cousin on Layali's side, Sayed, whom none of us had ever met, was sharing an apartment with my children, with orders to kill them if I did not cooperate.

"I was trapped, and I was being watched, by days at the lab and at night by men in cars parked near my house. When Simi and Ibrahim came to see me at Ramadan they were in as much danger as they were in New York. I wanted to flee with them then, but I was weak and I was frightened and in the end I was a coward and did not.

"I met Jean-Pierre at the pub on my way home from the labs one night. I enjoyed coffee and pastries at the pub each morning and coffee and cucumber croissant sandwiches on the way home at night. I'd seen Jean-Pierre there before, regaling the company with ribald jokes and songs. He seemed well liked by everyone. Then he joined me at my table and began asking me questions about my life. They were simple questions, about my children, how my wife died, how we'd met, and so on. Then we hit on the mutual interest in chess. The next day, Jean-Pierre brought a chess board with him to the pub and we played several games.

"I am good at chess, having learned the game at Oxford, but Jean-Pierre was much, much better. I learned much about the game from him. We began playing every night, well into the evening. Jean-Pierre took to escorting me home at night, helping me step up curbs and cross busy intersections. Our friendship developed so naturally that I was hardly aware of it. It seemed easy, effortless like nothing else in my life had been for a very long time. Our visits became the highlight of each day, and I looked forward to them immensely.

"The next Fall, when Simi and Ibrahim came from America to celebrate Ramadan with me they were immediately suspicious of this gregarious Frenchman, but he won them over like he had won me over, effortlessly and with warmth and patience. He celebrated the month with us, spurning food during the daylight hours and helping with the preparation of each night's feast.

"I saw the spark between Jean-Pierre and my daughter even before Simi herself did. Jean-Pierre was not Muslim, but still I approved. Years before I had helped my sister-in-law-to-be to elope with her American fiancé because I believed that Allah loves love more than he does religion, and I felt no differently when it was my own daughter.

After Simi and Ibrahim returned to America, I could tell that something was troubling Jean-Pierre. I thought that the young man was struggling with his fear of seeking my approval of his feelings for Simi, but soon it became apparent that it was something much deeper, much darker and more grim than love that burned in this young man's breast.

"I thought I would make it easier for Jean-Pierre to get whatever was bothering him off his chest by telling him about how much I love my daughter. One night I told Jean-Pierre about how Layali and I had been told that we could not have children. When Simi was born, even though it was late in our lives, we considered her a gift from Allah, and Ibrahim doubly so.

"When Jean-Pierre finally broke down his confession was nothing that I expected. Who can say what crisis of conscience caused his break-down, but it was clearly a long time coming, perhaps even before our first encounter. Jean-Pierre told me that he had not planned it, but that he had developed a deep respect for me, had begun to think of me as a father. Jean-Pierre's own father had been killed in the first Persian Gulf war when he was just nine years old. When I asked him what his father was doing in an American war, Jean-Pierre confessed, letting go of his seamless, accent-less French, that he was, in fact, American.

"Jean-Pierre was really Sean Brandt, an American spy sent to kill me and take the research I had been forced to develop. I was both outraged and terrified, but Brandt promised that he would do nothing of the sort. He couldn't, not now, not after everything he had learned from me. He confessed that he knew about the men who held threat over Simi and Ibrahim, had seen them following my precious ones around while they were visiting during Ramadan. He vowed to help me escape them.

"Brandt convinced me that if I fled my children would be in no immediate danger, that they would be watched, instead, left unharmed as bait for me. He convinced me to flee to America with him, where we would find a way to take Simi and Ibrahim out of danger and disappear somewhere in Canada or South America. But I had one other stipulation. In fact the research was already complete, but I didn't report this success to the organizations funding my research. I hated the weapon and what it could do, found it an affront to Allah and to the memory of sweet Layali. I would only accept Brandt's help if Brandt would in turn promise that the plans for the weapon would not be turned over to American authorities, either.

"Brandt and I made a pact that no one should get the formulas, schematics, and blueprints. Brandt used his underground connections to get false identity documents for me and together we fled to Miami, in America. From Miami I tried to send my children a telegram, but when Brandt found out about it he immediately moved us to Colorado. He told me that he would go and get Simi and Ibrahim himself if I would promise not to try anything stupid like that again. Telegrams could be traced more easily than telephone calls, even more easily than regular mail.

"At the motel in Colorado, I walked to the canteen at the far end of the motel-strip to get some coffee after another late night of chess with Brandt. I heard the gunshot in the night, and I panicked and ran outside, ran into a nearby undeveloped plot of land and huddled in some dry brush, awaiting doom to descend upon me, waited all night. When it didn't come and the sun began to rise, I grew to assume that it was some unrelated altercation and, with some difficulty, went back to the room. There was no sign of Brandt, and no note or any indication of where he had gone. At first I thought that perhaps Brandt had gone to fetch Simi and Ibrahim as he had promised, but all of our luggage was gone, including the laptop on which Brandt had encoded my formula. I waited as long as I dared, but after two days went by I became convinced that Brandt would not have left me without giving me some instructions about what to do in his absence. No, something had happened to call Brandt away abruptly, and there had to be a good reason why he could not let me know he was leaving.

"So I fled the motel, unsure of where to go. I checked out, hoping that Brandt had left some message with the motel staff, but there was nothing. First, I took the very next bus out of Denver toward Utah, then I began to head East with an unformed plan in my head to retrieve my children myself. Finally, coming to my senses in a motel outside of Cleveland, Ohio, I realized how many different factions would be waiting for me to do just that. I needed to be smart about how I did it. I needed help.

"That was when I recalled Fatimah and her American husband. We'd been out of touch for more than thirty years. I thought they lived in some place with the word *South* in the name, and that their name was something like Gunmansan. These were details that had faded and become muddled over so many years. So I went to the library where I perused telephone books from South Dakota and South Carolina with no luck. Either they were not listed or I had gotten it wrong.

"I racked my brain, and finally checked phone books for North Dakota for no other reason than because it, too, had a compass direction it its name. There were no Gunmansans, but there were several Gunthersons, and this name rang a bell of recognition in my mind. I called the first one and reached Trey Guntherson, Stan and Fatimah's youngest son, who in turn put me in touch with the sister-in-law I hadn't seen nor spoken to for almost forty years.

"Stan and Fatimah bought me a plane ticket under the name on the false papers Brandt had gotten for me and within hours of our reunion they were encouraging me to send another telegram, this time coded, and to the school. I did so, and then we waited, not sure who was going to show up, Simi and Ibrahim, the US government, or gangs of machinegun toting extremists."

*   *   *

"So you see, young one," Dr. Faisal Al-Sehremni addressed Lainie directly for the first time, "though I am forever in your debt for the service you have done my family, I have no more clue as to who killed Sean Brandt than you do."

Lainie nodded at him and tried to smile. Finally, she lowered her head and let go a sob she'd tried to hold back.

Simi, Fatimah, and Layali all tried to rush to her side but she waved them away, eventually standing and rushing out of the room.

CHAPTER 37

Lainie was not a crier, but post-traumatic stress was a powerful thing. She surprised herself with her outburst and ran to the restroom to regain her composure. She'd taken more risks and seen more death in a week than in her entire life prior to this. So focused was she on a single goal in that week that the end of the road came with an emotional whiplash she hadn't expected.

A dead end, at that.

She'd stopped crying by the time the door closed behind her, so she took the opportunity to dry her eyes and splash her face with cold water. It was Sunday. Two o'clock this morning had come and gone, exactly seven days since Michael/Brandt had called Capri Entertainment, seven days since his death. After seven days, Lainie had nothing to show for her efforts to prove someone had murdered him nor to clear herself from suspicion of murdering Mitch and Kim and firebombing the Capri offices. Arguably, she had only made things worse for herself, becoming embroiled in a complex web of deceit. It was not enough that the San Francisco police were searching for her, now she had the NSA, the FBI, and a cell of very determined terrorists on her trail as well.

Lainie supposed that if anyone had a right to cry she did. But although depression loomed like an oppressive cloud pregnant with the storm that would be her destruction, no more tears came. She filled her lungs, let the air out slowly, squared her shoulders and opened the bathroom door. Simi stood at the threshold and reached up to brush a lock of hair out of Lainie's eyes.

"Are you all right?" she asked.

Lainie managed a weak smile and nodded.

Simi took her hand and led her into the dining room where the others waited with sympathetic smiles. Faisal stood with Ibrahim's help and walked toward her. He looked up at her with a smile belied only by the sadness behind his eyes. "You left before I could tell you something that might give you some relief."

"What?" Lainie asked.

"Let me show you," Faisal said. "Come, all three of you."

He led them out of the kitchen and up a short hallway that cut back toward the garage. Halfway along was a door. He opened it and motioned them all in ahead of him. Lainie went first, followed by Simi and Ibrahim.

The room appeared to be half den, half workshop. One side of the room had a desk, computer, bookshelves, and other office accoutrements. The other side bore a workbench, tools, clamps and other items. A plush leather couch under the window on the opposite wall was open to a sleeper bed. The man on the bed looked at Lainie with suspicion.

But when his eyes landed on Simi his face came completely alight with a smile of recognition. "Simi." His voice was cracked, nearly inaudible. For her part Simi stood very still next to Lainie, eyes wide and jaw slack. The man had a bandage around his throat. He looked as pale as a cadaver, drawn and weak, which is why Lainie supposed she didn't recognize him at first. That and a healthy crop of red-brown beard that covered the lower half of his face. But the greatest difference were his eyes, lively and spry with focus and emotion, unlike the dead ones that'd looked out at her from the photo on his NSA ID badge.

It was Sean Brandt.

*   *   *

Lainie felt no less stunned than Simi looked. Faisal was clearly trying to gauge their reaction, looking from them to Brandt and back again. The assassin in the bed sat up and swung his legs over the side, watching them in is own turn. When he tried to stand he teetered and Faisal rushed to his aid.

"Please, friend, you must sit," the scientist said.

Brandt nodded and sat back down on the bed. Then he tried to speak, his voice coming out in a squeak. But when Faisal tried to silence him he waved the old man away.

"Simi," he said, "I'm so sorry, I wanted to tell you..." The rest descended into a series of shallow coughs.

"Sean knew you were here all evening," Faisal said to his children, "and he kept insisting to come out and see you, but he has suffered greatly in the last few days and isn't fully recovered. I promised to bring you to him once things settled down."

"Father," Simi said, "he's an American spy, an assassin hired to kill you. How could you bring him into..."

"He's dead," Lainie said, sounding stupid even to her own ears. "I mean he's supposed to be dead."

Brandt was looking at her with a who-the-hell-are-you expression on his face.

"Sean," Faisal said, "I have a surprise for you. I wanted to wait until you saw her before I told you. This is Lainie, my children's savior."

Lainie felt herself blush. "Well I wouldn't go that far," she said. "But you would know me better as Samantha." When Brandt's face still didn't register recognition, she said, "You remember...phone sex..." She only mouthed the last two words, shielding her face with a hand from Simi's view, but they had a profound affect on Brandt.

It was as if his face tried to register several emotions all at once, only some of which Lainie was able to recognize before they were supplanted by others. There was dawning recognition, confusion, shame, confusion again. And then quite suddenly his eyes descended into that frighteningly dead mask that she'd seen before, in his photo. He was suspicious of her, and why wouldn't he be.

For her part Lainie was so stunned to see him alive, none the better for wear, that she wasn't surprised it took a few beats before she realized what this meant to her: Sean Brandt ne Michael Gaston was alive. He could himself support the voracity of her claim of the gunshot during their telephone conversation, which would go a long way toward supporting her story of the killer who came calling two nights later.

The question was, would he be willing to do so. Right now that hawk-like look he was leveling at her made her doubt that he would.

"Can I talk to Mr. Brandt in private," Lainie asked.

Faisal protested, "He needs his rest. He's really not well enough for a prolonged conversation, and his throat needs..." but Brandt's gentle hand on the old man's chest made him stop. He saw the look in Brandt's eyes now, too. "Come, Simi, Ibrahim, let's leave them to talk."

The old scientist and his two children stepped out of the room and closed the door. Brandt continued to stare at Lainie with a look she was certain you didn't want a trained government assassin looking at you with. She tried to smile at him, but the smirk died stillborn.

"I bet you didn't expect to see me," she tried. Still no smile from him. "Look, I know you have a thousand questions, and I can probably guess at some of them, so let me try before you start grilling me." Still he gave to sign of cutting her any slack.

"In a way," she said with a game air, "this is all really your fault. I mean if you hadn't called Capri Entertainment for phone sex – why the hell would you do that, by the way, with everything that was coming down on you...never mind – I would never have been attacked, and Mitchell and Kim might still be alive."

For the first time his face registered a shadow of

curiosity.

"Yeah," she said, emboldened, "your own damn fault. Wait, let me start at the beginning." She paced as she launched into her story for a second time, now filling in details she hadn't even shared with Faisal and his family. By the end she was sitting at the foot of the bed, feeling exhausted, amazed herself at all she'd been through in the last five or six days.

When she looked at him she saw a new expression on his face that she couldn't seem to read.

"So not to put too fine a point on it," she said to him, "what the fuck, Sean?"

Brandt tried to say something, coughed, then tried again, using only a whisper. "Faisal had stepped out of the hotel room," he said, "to find something for us to eat besides the fast food crap we'd been living on since crossing over stateside. Someone snuck in while I was on the phone with you. He must've been a stealthy mother-fucker, because I'm a professional, I should have heard him. Anyway, the bullet didn't kill me."

Here he paused to lean over and move the bandage to show her his wounds. "The bullet entered here, at the back of my neck, and exited here in the front. All the arteries, spinal cord and shit, I should be dead. Sheer luck that the bullet missed all of them. I woke up in the trunk of a car. I managed to unlatch it from inside. The car I was in was parked outside the loading docks of a dog food plant in Denver."

Lainie recalled that the killer, on the phone, implied that he'd disposed of Michael's/Brandt's body in such a place.

Brandt continued, showing the strain even from whispering. "I didn't see who shot me. I was injured and weak, but I made my way back to the motel. By the time I got there Faisal was gone. It didn't take me long to guess where he'd gone, the only place he knew of to go. I found the address through my own means and, fighting unconsciousness from loss of blood and pain, tending my own bandaging, I made my way here. They found me collapsed on the porch this morning."

"How are you now," Lainie asked in spite of other pressing questions that needed answers.

Brandt shrugged. "Can't seem to get enough sleep. Neck is stiff. Entry and exit holes burn like the devil, and it hurts to talk."

"Well you owe me an apology," Lainie said, trying to joke with him. "You've caused me one hell of a hard time."

He didn't laugh, but he did give her a rueful look.

"The least you can do is call a guy for me," she said. "A certain police Detective who thinks I'm either psycho or stupid enough to commit murder and arson just to prove a point."

"Phone calls require the use of your voice," he said.

"Right," Lainie said.

"I don't guess a letter, an affidavit would..."

Lainie shook her head. "They'd probably just add forgery to my list of charges. Say, why the hell did you call Capris Entertainment that night anyway?"

"Why do most guys call," he said.

"Bullshit," Lainie said. "I don't buy it. Don't get me wrong, the conversation we had seemed genuine enough. Why wouldn't it be, it was all trivial crap, and no reason for us to fake anything with each other. But I don't buy that you called just because you were lonely. There was some other reason."

He just looked at her.

"Look," she said, "I'm in this up to my neck. I already know more top secret shit than I'm supposed to. There's nothing you can tell me that could top what I've already seen. And you owe me an explanation."

"Yeah?"

"Yeah, damnit," she said.

"Okay," he said. "Faisal and I made a pact. We agreed the only thing to protect him was to be sure that neither side got the plans to the weapon. Not our side, and not their side. To ensure that, we had to put it someplace no one would ever think to look."

"No," Lainie said. "Not possible."

"While we talked, you and I," he pushed on past her protest, "I uploaded everything in a packed and encrypted cabinet file to your computer, then I permanently purged it from mine."

Orin had told her it was impossible for anyone to gain access to her computer through a VOIP connection. He'd assured all of the girls that using the website to connect to the clients in no way exposed them or any of their private files to the outside world. Likewise they were protected from virus uploads.

"I'm only glad that stuff is safe and sound back at your apartment in San Francisco," he said.

Lainie felt her face go cold from lack of blood as she turned wide eyes on him."

"No," he said.

She nodded.

"Not a laptop," he said. "Tell me you didn't bring it with you."

She said nothing, but bit her lip.

"Tell me they don't have it," he said, standing up.

She looked up at him. "No," she said, "they don't. But they did have it for several hours. I have no way of knowing if they got through my password or not."

He cursed so vehemently that he teetered and she helped him sit back down next to her on the edge of the bed. He sat hunched, bracing himself with his forearms on his knees and holding his head, as if trying to keep himself from passing out. It was a wonder he'd made it here from Colorado, weak as he was from blood loss.

Then he said, "Should have known."

"What?" she said.

"Of all the phone sex girls I could have gotten," he said, "I had to get one with that rare combination of smarts and real grit that make some women a genuine pain in the ass."

She thought there was a compliment in there somewhere. "I'm not a spy," she said.

He turned his head enough to look up at her from the

corner of his eye. "Don't fool yourself," he said.

CHAPTER 38

"It's not here," Brandt said in frustration.

He sat at the dining room table with Lainie's laptop in front of him. She stood behind him bent over having watched for the last hour as he searched every byte on her computer for any sign of the file he'd uploaded.

"I can't find it anywhere," he said, his whisper tight with frustration. "Not even signs of the file having been deleted. If they did that, they must've rewritten the sectors that held the file repeatedly to hide all traces that it had been there. But why?"

"To keep anyone else from getting it," Simi asked. She and the rest of her family sat around the table watching and waiting like Lainie.

"But they had the computer," Lainie said, "with no reason to expect they'd lose it again. Even if they did make a copy of the file anywhere else, why go to such pains to delete it from my computer?"

"Exactly," Brandt said. He shut the clamshell. "The file was hidden as a system file. Moreover, I set security on it to prevent copying. It wouldn't be impossible to someone truly motivated, but the encryption of the file is one of the NSA's finest. There's no way they can crack that in a century of Sundays."

"So what you're saying," Lainie said, "is that whether they found the file, copied it, and deleted it from my hard drive is immaterial, because they can't open it anyway."

"I'd still prefer they not even have it," Brandt said. "But you are right, and moreover, there's nothing we can really do about it now."

The room fell silent for a moment.

Then Lainie said, "So now what?"

"Now," Faisal said, "We complete Sean's plan. He, Simi, Ibrahim, and I disappear."

"But what about Lainie's problem," Simi said. "She cannot go home without some proof to clear her name. She has been nothing but brave and kind to us. Is there nothing we can for her? We owe her for more reasons than gratitude and sympathy for her own plight."

"Well said," said Stan.

"Thank you," Lainie said. "And don't think I haven't given it a lot of thought, but what can any of you do? Sean Brandt is alive, and he might be able to convince the authorities that it was he on the phone with me that night. But finding him alive doesn't change the fact that I thought he was dead. Detective Gillis is hanging his hat on the presumption that my motive for killing Mitchell and Kim and bombing the building was because they wouldn't believe my story. Does that change just because Sean turns up alive? Maybe. Is it enough for Sean to risk his career and his freedom over by turning himself in? I say no, it isn't."

"What will you do?" Simi asked.

"Go home," Lainie said, resigned to her fate.

"But what about the police," Simi asked. "Won't they arrest you and take you to jail."

"Most likely," Lainie said, "and if the federal government doesn't have a few Obstruction of Justice charges they want to level I'll be surprised."

Then Lainie said to Faisal, "I'm sure the US government will still grant you asylum, even though we gave them the slip. You need not run and hide for the rest of your life."

"No," Simi said, more as if she were telling her father than Lainie. "They will most certainly separate us and use father to get his formula and schematics, much as the others did. Now that I know all that father has gone through, I will not allow us to be separated again, nor will I allow anyone to lay a finger on him ever again."

Faisal smiled at his daughter. "I have a boat prepared," Faisal said. "Sean and I will take Simi and Ibrahim and we will go to Canada. That was Sean's plan, and he already has papers forged through his contacts in the underground for the four of us. I see no reason not to continue with that.

"You should come with us," Faisal continued, turning to Lainie. "The boat is big enough, and you are more than welcome. We owe you more than one life debt."

Lainie gave them all a grateful smile but shook her head. "No, I really have nothing I want to do in Canada. My life is here. I'll go back to San Francisco, get a lawyer, face the music, hope against hope that they find some evidence to show it couldn't possibly have been me that did those horrible things. Or hope for a jury that's collectively deaf, dumb and blind."

She meant for that to be a joke but no one laughed.

*   *   *

Lainie's eyes snapped open and she sat up in bed. Was the scream that had awakened her from a dream, or from out here in the real night?

"I heard it, too," Simi confirmed.

At Aunt Fatimah's insistence everyone agreed to spend one night before setting out in the morning, but no more in spite of Brandt's continuing need of recuperation. They dared not risk it. Faisal slept on the couch and Ibrahim on the floor in the living room while Lainie and Simi shared the bed in the guest bedroom.

Now Simi rolled out of the bed and crouched nearby. There were unmistakable sounds of a struggle outside the bedroom door, a grunt, a spate of unintelligible stage-whispers. Someone turned the doorknob to their room. Simi launched across the bed, grabbed great fists-full of Lainie's clothing, pinching her in the process, and dragged her off the bed to the floor, placing the bed between them and the door as it opened.

Lainie bit back a cry of protest and pain.

Someone moved about the room. Lainie breathed as quietly as she could under Simi's slight weight. The beam of a flashlight blinked on, scanned the far wall briefly, then shut off again. The floorboards creaked under the intruder's feet ominously.

"Be ready to run," Simi said in the slightest of whispers.

With the door open the sounds of struggling in the hall were more distinct. Another scream, unmistakably Aunt Fatimah's, was silenced suddenly as if sliced off with a razor. Simi cursed softly in her language and Lainie felt the diminutive girl's corded muscles tighten with readiness.

The flashlight beam appeared again, scanned the floor beyond them. Another loose floorboard, closer, creaked and the light brushed their heads. A man gasped something in Arabic.

"Run," Simi screamed as she launched herself from Lainie's back.

Lainie rolled over to see her little friend performing the same sort of whirling, spinning, kicking, and punching ballet she had used before in the parking garage in New York. She had fought to win Lainie's freedom then as now. A man dressed all in black was staggering backward off balance. Simi's fist slapped a gun from his hand, sending it flying. Her foot hooked the flashlight and sent it shattering against the wall, darkening it.

Lainie stumbled to her feet, ducked past the melee and dashed into the hallway. She flicked a light switch as she passed meant to illuminate the hall but nothing happened. Maybe that was best, because her eyes didn't have to adjust to the darkness where they would most certainly have had to adjust to the sudden light.

There was movement in the house proper and she stepped up to the archway and looked out into the darkened family room. Figures were struggling, and beyond them the front door stood open, rain pattering the tile entryway. Intruders dressed in black were dragging two other struggling, shrouded figures out into the night, and another was being carried. By the sudden cessation of her scream earlier Lainie guessed the one being carried was Aunt Fatimah, and Lainie hoped the cheerful old woman was still alive. One of the other prisoners would be Uncle Stan. The remaining one would be Ibrahim because shrouded as he was by a blanket she could still tell he was too tall to be Faisal.

Lainie dropped to her knees and scampered out into the family room, pausing between the couch and the coffee table just as another stranger turned from the living room toward the hall and bedrooms, presumably to see what was holding up the man who'd been sent to gather she and Simi up. Faisal was not on the couch, and Lainie assumed he had already been taken out the door.

Then Simi was there, scrambling up beside her in her hiding place, breathing hard. "When I go, follow me."

"Where?" Lainie asked.

When the kidnappers left the room, five to take Fatimah, Stan, and Ibrahim outside and one to go to the guest room, Simi jumped up and ran to the study. Lainie didn't follow her but waited to see if Simi was spotted, planning a diversion if more men appeared and went after her. But the intruders had their hands full as they slipped with their burdens out the front door.

Lainie got to her feet and sprinted to the den as well. The door was closed. She flung it open. Slipped in and closed it as quickly but as quietly as she could.

She turned, expecting to find Simi there with Brandt, but Faisal was here as well.   Though stooped himself, he was trying to help Simi support Brandt, who's bandage was stained with blood. The erstwhile assassin, drawn and obviously weak, a mere shadow of what he most certainly once had been, held a gun and seemed ready to fight.

"Who is it," Brandt whispered.

Simi hushed him sternly, and Lainie shrugged.

Faisal wrested the revolver from Brandt's weakened grip, left them and walked over to Lainie. He said, looking at the weapon as if he'd picked up a cobra, "I've never actually fired one of these things before." He offered it to her. "Have you?"

"Yes," she said, pushing the gun away. "Unfortunately."

"Faisal." The call came from outside the room. Lainie recognized a voice she would probably hear in her nightmares for years to come.

Sayed.

"I have your family, Faisal," he called to them. "Throw out any weapons and come out with your hands in front of you."

Faisal looked at Lainie and she nodded to him. "They took Stan and Fatimah and Ibrahim," she whispered.

"How did you find me?" Faisal called out.

Lainie noticed he was looking at his gun, adjusting his grip as if considering fighting his way out.

"Don't," she said. "You'll be killed. Or they'll kill the others."

"Your daughter and the American woman," Sayed answered from beyond the door. "They drove one of our own SUV's here, too stupid to think that we had GPS tracking devices on our own property. How else do you think we coordinated our actions?"

Lainie mentally slapped her forehead. Of course. "I'm so sorry," she whispered to Faisal. "We didn't even think. We led them right to you."

Faisal dropped the gun to his side and looked defeated. He said, "Never mind. It was worth it to see my family one last time."

He took a few steps toward the door.

"No, Faisal," Brandt hissed. "Not giving up. Not yet."

Simi put soft fingers over Brandt's lips and looked at her father. "There's still a chance."

She motioned for them to open the window. As Lainie rushed over to do so, Faisal turned to yell out the door again:

"How do I know my family will be safe when I go with you?"

Lainie climbed out the window into the rain, her bare toes squishing into the mud of the shrubbery below the sill, Simi close behind.

"I do not control the safety of your family," Sayed went on. "You do. They will never be safe. They will always live under a cloud of danger. But I can assure you, that danger will never descend upon them as long as you cooperate with us. You will never see them again, but you can be assured they will be kept safe."

"Sean," Simi hissed up through the window. "Come."

Brandt waited. "Faisal," he said.

Faisal looked at them and hesitated.

"Dr. Al-Serehmni," Lainie whispered. "Faisal. They won't hurt Ibrahim and Fatimah and Stan before they get you. But if you go to them now, what's to keep them from killing all of us."

Faisal's face twisted in the agony of his dilemma.

"Father, please," Simi pleaded.

"We still have a chance to end this our own way," Brandt added in his damaged voice, "on our own terms. Come. Now. Before it's too late."

Faisal turned, helped Brandt mount the windowsill and the two young women helped the assassin lower himself to the ground. He leaned against the wall as they then helped the bent and aged scientist climb out as well. Faisal did not relinquish his grip on the gun. Supporting Brandt between them Lainie and Simi followed Faisal as he squelched across the back lawn to the gate and out into an alleyway.

"Why don't they have the house surrounded?" Lainie asked.

"Neighbors," Faisal huffed.

"Witnesses," Brandt expanded. "They would have drawn too much attention. They counted on Faisal to give himself up."

Simi shushed him yet again, clearly concerned lest he damage his vocal cords further.

They were hurrying as fast as Brandt could up the alley toward a side street. The rain was a deluge, and all four of them were soaked quite through in mere moments. It was a cold rain, but not a freezing one. Still, Simi complained that they should get Brandt out of the weather as soon as possible.

"Where to now?" Lainie asked as they reached the street and peered left and right at nothing but more mini-mansions on tract after tract of residential zoning.

"I don't know," Faisal answered miserably, his breath coming hard and wheezing.

Lainie looked to Simi, who said, "Me either."

Taking the lead, Lainie chose a direction away from the Guntherson residence and they hurried as fast as the equally frail Faisal and Sean Brandt could go in the cold night rain. Lainie had no idea where she was leading them, nor how she ended up in the lead in the first place.

All she knew was the nightmare wasn't over. It'd taken an intermission, but it was back again as deadly as ever.

CHAPTER 39

"It's my fault," Lainie groaned. "I should have guessed they'd have a GPS device on their own vehicles."

"No, it's my fault," Simi said. "I should have insisted that we ditch the car and ride the bus. I know better, but I was so anxious to see Father."

"If it is anyone's fault," Faisal said, "it is mine. I brought these vultures down upon the heads of my family. I should never have come here. I should never have left Paris with Sean. Good though his intentions were, we have seen nothing but misery and misfortune since."

They sat in a coffee shop they'd managed to walk to, dripping with rain and not wearing any coats. The waitress eyed them suspiciously, even more so when they ordered nothing.

"Okay," Lainie said firmly while keeping her voice down. "So there's enough blame to go around for everyone to have a piece of humble pie. It's time we decide what to do next. We're in over our heads. Lets call Cord Steele – I still have his number – and let the authorities handle this."

Simi's face turned hard, showing her disappointment.

"No," Faisal shook his head so firmly that a nimbus of rain sprung from his beard in all directions. "They will not take to heart the safe rescue of those I've put in danger, my son, my sister-in-law, and her husband. All they will want are the plans for the weapon, and everything else would be secondary."

"I'm afraid he's right," Brandt whispered, touching his bandage and wincing with pain.

"Then we promise them the formula and stuff in exchange for the rescue of Ibrahim and the others," Simi said.

"But we don't have it," Lainie said.

"Sayed does."

"We don't know that."

"In fact," Sean whispered, "if they did they would not have come for Faisal tonight. This is an act of desperation. If they have the file, they cannot crack the encryption."

"Even so," Faisal said, "that research is a blight on my honor, my family's honor. I will give it to no one, not even the Americans."

Lainie said, "Maybe our government can find ways to counter that ray or beam or whatever it is, in case Sayed and his group do crack the encryption on the file. The US would probably hire you, Faisal, to help them. I'm sure they'd give you, Simi, and Ibrahim citizenship in exchange for your help."

"What about Sean," Faisal said. "He defied his orders and betrayed your government. They would not care why. His freedom would be sacrificed."

"So far all he's done is failed to kill you," Lainie argued.

Brandt shook his head. He mimed writing, and Simi nodded. She called the waitress and asked the woman for a pen and paper. The waitress was surly about it, but the woman returned with the items.

"No," Brandt wrote, Simi, sitting beside him, read aloud, "I've disobeyed direct orders. I've obstructed federal officers in the lawful pursuit of their duties. They could probably even make a case for High Treason. I wouldn't put it past them to try."

"All of this is moot," Faisal said. "None of it matters. Sayed and his men have Fatimah, Stan, and my son. They will surely kill them if we do not do something."

"We must use the formula as bait," Simi said, "to get them to release our loved ones."

"But you don't have the formula," Lainie said.

"Yes we do," Faisal said, "just not in written form."

"So what you mean is you," Lainie said. "You want to use yourself as bait."

"No father," Simi said, "out of the question."

"There is no other way," he said, "and it must be soon. They will kill all three if they think we will not negotiate for them."

"Bait is not enough," Brandt wrote, Simi read. "We need leverage of our own."

"What sort of leverage?" Lainie asked.

Sean looked up from his pad with a smile. Not a pleasant smile, but one that seemed to revive the same dead, predator look Lainie originally saw in the photos on those fake IDs back at his apartment.

The cold, deadly, calculating smile of the soulless killer.

CHAPTER 40

Uncle Stan was an avid ice-fisherman, but this time of year was not the season for such things. Safely before Spring thaw the fishing shacks were towed in off the lake and gathered in an enclosed compound, a sort of slum on the shore nearby, a storage area guarded by a man called Old George. George was a fixture so ancient that few remembered when Old George's father, Crazy George, used to man the same post. There was a small trailer, an office, with a phone, but during this season Old George ran a boat rental miles up the shore from the shack compound and really only had time to check on the place once every few days or so. The rest of the time the place was deserted. The shacks were largely devoid of valuables anyway, so short of vagrancy or senseless vandalism the compound was in very little need of oversight.

It was from here that Faisal planned to launch the escape boat to take he and his offspring to Canada, and it was to this place that the four conspirators came to prepare for a daring rescue of their loved ones held hostage by a cell of terrorists bent on taking Faisal back with them to complete his work.

Lainie didn't like the plan, no, not one bit, and she protested vociferously and repeatedly, so much so that the sound of her voice was becoming tiresome, even to her. Much of the plan was sound, or seemed so to a special ed. teacher from San Francisco, California with no military background, not even a stint in Girl Scouts.

It was the culmination of it that disturbed her, seemed like suicide for Faisal and damned dangerous for the rest of them. These were terrorists they were dealing with, after all. Against what? Three young people, Simi, Ibrahim, and Lainie, herself, with more education than real-world experience, and three elderly people, Faisal, Stan, and Fatimah, who, lets face it, weren't as spry as once they might have been. The only one of them with any real training was Sean Brandt, and he was still suffering from a gunshot to the throat and severe blood loss.

Faisal frowned, shaking his head. "Ms. Parker, I fully expected you to offer your help, brave as you are. Of course we cannot accept. This is not your fight."

Whether the plan was good or bad, as afraid as she was, she was not going to just walk away. "Not my fight? That creep who killed Kim and Mitch has put a serious crimp in my plans for the summer. That bastard Sayed did this." She held up her hair to show the healing cut on her forehead. "I owe someone some payback. This is just as much my fight as it is yours, now. Besides, all I have waiting for me at home is jail. Sure would like to see how this turns out before I spend the next twenty-five-to-life in a five-by-nine cell."

Simi smiled, nodding approvingly, and looked to her father.

After a moment Faisal nodded. "Very well."

It'd been an easy thing for Sean to pick the lock on the rolling chain-link gate, easier still to slip the lock on the door to the caretaker's trailer just inside. The compound was well off the road around a shoulder of bluff hidden from the county route, quite secluded. Now they all sat inside the trailer drinking coffee and stamping their feet to stay warm.

Brandt's plan relied on drawing both Sayed's terrorist cell and the feds to this compound at the same time. "The compound is ideal," he told them in his whisper, "because of its location, clear from any risk of collateral civilian damage.

Timing will be critical. We want the FBI to be here to arrest Sayed and the terrorists, but not before we can manage to rescue the hostages and get the four of us – Faisal, Simi, Ibrahim, and I – on that boat and out of here. Lainie, you'll handle calling in the cavalry through your contact with the CIA."

He paused and sighed. "The trick is how to lure Sayed to the battlefield. Simi, you have his cell phone number, don't you?"

Simi took out her own phone and eyed it. "Do you think he'll pick up?"

Sean chortled. "Oh, he'll answer. They're expecting our call, and we better call soon or they might decide their hostages aren't the leverage they thought they were. So let's get a move on."

Earlier that morning they'd rented a car using the credit cards and ID's Brandt had forged for their escape, which Faisal still carried in his pockets. Their first stop was to a sporting goods store, their second to a home improvement chain, their third to a grocery store for supplies. Except for the groceries, which were inside the trailer, everything they bought was currently laid out on a pair of picnic tables under an awning outside.

Brandt sat in a nearby lawn chair they set up on a stack of crates so he could oversee operations and give explicit instructions on what was to be done. "Listen to each of my instructions completely," he told them, "then repeat it back to me and wait for me to confirm that you got it right before you perform the action. Ask questions if anything is unclear. There is no room for error here, especially in the later stages. Keep your masks on at all times – even though we are doing this outside, the fumes are still quite deadly."

During a lull in activity while they waited for chemicals to drain, leaving volatile solids on top of filters, Lainie sat on the crates at Brandt's feet. Faisal and Simi were inside making more coffee.

"So Sean Brandt," Lainie murmured, "freelance NSA

Analyst and CIA Assassin, kept a credit card account in another man's name. Michael Gaston. For personal use when he didn't want his activities traced by the government, a ruse he learned from them. A kind old scientist he'd been hired to assassinate brought all of his doubts about his current career to a head, and rather than kill him he vows to help that neo-paternal figure extricate himself from the entanglements of both terrorists and spies."

Sean said nothing, but she could hear him listening to her.

"He helps his new friend escape Paris and come to the states, evading pursuit the whole time. While in a motel in Commerce City, Colorado planning how to rescue Faisal's son and daughter from the danger they are in, our man Brandt decides to use his personal stolen identity to call a phone sex service and transfers the file containing a formula to hide it, in case he and Faisal need it later. A formula he was hired to get for our side."

"Yes," Brandt whispered. "The plan was to track you down and retrieve it later. For future leverage, should we ever need it."

"Faisal, unable to find you, makes his way to Aunt Fatimah's house here in Fargo," Lainie continued. "Unaware that you survived the gunshot and, knowing where Faisal would go, were trailing him here as well. Meanwhile, the shooter who tried to kill you is now after me."

Brandt grunted, finally seeming to understand her.

"Lainie," he whispered, "I'm sorry for what I did to you by sending you that file. I do remember what we talked about on the phone that night. It was...nice. Thank you. I know I owe you, no less for getting Simi and Ibrahim out of New York City. By rescuing them from Sayed you managed to do what Faisal and I couldn't."

"Maybe," Lainie said, "but I also managed to lead Sayed right to you and Faisal and get three other people kidnapped in the process."

"Don't," Brandt said. "What you did was brave...it was

incredible, for a civilian. Don't sell what you've done short. It was nothing short of heroic. Joining us on this suicide mission just shows your grit. I have to say, I'm impressed.

"I owe you a debt I can never repay," Brandt said. "But I plan to make an installment, at least. After all this, if we live through it, I plan to send Faisal, Simi, and Ibrahim off on the boat alone."

"What?" Lainie said.

"I'm going back to San Francisco with you," he said. "I'm going to turn myself in."

"Why," Lainie asked.

"For a lot of reasons," Brandt said. "Faisal and his family will be in the clear, which is what this has all been about anyway. I might be able to further put the government off their trail, if I can lie convincingly in debrief.

"But most of all for you, to help you clear your name. We all owe you that much, but I do more than the others. I put you in danger and you've done nothing but step up for all of us over and over again. It's the least I can do."

"Simi's not going to go for that," Lainie said.

"Who are we fooling," Brandt said. "Her culture, mine, and I'm at least ten years older than her. It wouldn't have lasted. In the end, I am what they made me. Crisis of faith or not, I'll never be anything better than a weapon, an extreme solution to other people's problems."

Lainie didn't know what to say to that, so she said nothing. Later, as everyone retired, She watched Simi and Brandt climb into the rental car parked outside the compound. Soon the windows steamed up in the rain. Both Simi's religion and Brandt's injuries made Lainie doubt that anything more was going on than simple, quiet intimacy between long separated lovers.

For some reason she thought of Cord Steele. She felt as if she could really use his cocky self-assuredness right about now. As much as it annoyed her, it did convey a certain sense of confidence and comfort, as if he always had everything under control. She felt bad for sticking her thumb in his bullet wound, for leaving him on the floor of that elevator.

But mostly, she envied Simi for someone to hold her on this, the eve of what might certainly be their last day on Earth.

CHAPTER 41

Lainie, Simi and Brandt crouched in a sleek speedboat that was beached by a pier, beneath an evil-smelling tarp. They peered out through grommet-holes at the compound. Getting Brandt to consent to play only a minor role in the plan was a battle and in the end it was Simi's assertion, that he would not only be of no help in his weakened state but would be more likely to get one of them killed if he tried, that finally made him acquiesce.

It was mid morning, but a silver mist cloaked the shore of the lake and combined with the low-hanging, black, overcast sky the shacks looked like ghosts standing hooded and slouching in a cluster like a congregation of druids praying to their gods. Up on the dock above them stood the frail, bent form of Dr. Faisal Al-Serehmni, clutching his buckskin coat around him against the chill like a straightjacket.

"I don't like this," Lainie cursed again.

"We have no choice," Simi said. She looked very proud of her father.

"He could be killed," Lainie protested.

"Then that would be one sort of end to this," Simi said. "Allah willing."

"How can you be so casual about your father's life," Lainie asked.

"Casual," Simi said. "No. But there can be no greater sacrifice before Allah than to die for a just cause."

Lainie felt a chill. No matter how much she may respect Simi's devotion to her religion, there were still aspects of her new friend's culture Lainie would never understand. Westerners were raised on heroes such as Bruce Willis' John McClane or Harrison Ford's Indiana Jones – the point was to win the day, but to survive doing it. Death was no glorious sacrifice, it was just another kind of failure.

After their preparations under Brandt's critical supervision the day before, Faisal spent the rest of the night in prayer and meditation. Lainie used a pay phone at a bait shop up the road, dialed collect to Baltimore and spoke to Steele via his cell phone.

"Where the hell are you?"

"North Dakota," she said.

A beat while he decided whether to believe her or not.

"Trace the call if you don't believe me," she said.

"I already am. What the heck are you doing there?"

"Running from you," she said, "and terrorists. Not very successfully, I might add, at least on the latter count."

"They're there?" he asked.

"More or less," Lainie said. "Sayed's here with some men. I don't know if it's every terrorist in the country, or even in his cell, but they are here."

"Why North Dakota?"

"Dr. Al-Sehremni," she said.

"You found him."

"Say, Cord," she said. "We're in a bit of a fix over here. Wondered if you could come bail us out."

"What's going on?"

She filled him in, leaving out any reference to Sean Brandt being alive.

"No, Lainie," he said flatly. "It's suicide for all of you. If you think they'll let al-Serhemni's family live after they get their hands on him you're not as smart as I thought you were. Just stay put there and we'll bring you in."

"I'm not the only one who has a say in this," Lainie said. "Faisal and Simi have their minds set. You'll just have to go where I told you. But hurry, because you're right, they'll kill us all if you aren't on time."

"Lainie, wait..." he protested.

She hung up.

She'd directed him to the Guntherson house. The next call would be to give him their exact location, but it had to wait until this morning, because they had no idea how quickly Sayed and his men might be able to reach the compound, and they couldn't have Cord and the FBI interfering until after the al-Serehmni family got away. Timing was critical.

Simi called Sayed's cell phone to invite he and his men to the compound to trade Ibrahim, Aunt Fatimah, and Uncle Stan for her father. As it turned out, they were still holed up at the Guntherson's home. She had the phone on speaker mode so everyone could hear the exchange.

"Do you expect me to believe that you would sacrifice your father," Sayed demanded.

"It isn't my choice," she said. "It's his."

"And you and your brother will come back with me to New York," Sayed said.

"We will negotiate when you get here," Simi said.

"How do I know that the FBI won't be there as well," Sayed asked. "Where will the American woman be?"

"The Americans are no friends of ours," Simi told him. "They would exploit my father just as you would. The difference is they do not have innocent family members as hostage. The American woman is tied up in the trunk of a car in town somewhere. Perhaps they will find her before she suffocates, perhaps they will not, but she is out of our hair either way."

There was silence on the other end.

Finally, "We will come, as you say. But do not try to betray me again, dear cousin. There will be consequences. Oh yes, consequences."

Simi hung up the line, then dashed the telephone

against the wall. It shattered and she growled her rage out much like an angry bull.

"Not much time now," Brandt said. "Let's roll."

No doubt Sayed would leave some men at the house in case this was a ruse, and wouldn't they be surprised when the FBI showed up on their doorstep?

Lainie's group had enough guns and ammunition from the sporting goods store for the seven of them, including the three others should they successfully negotiate a release. These they lay at the bottom of the boat, on plastic tarps to keep them dry, except for the ones Lainie, Simi, Brandt, and Faisal armed themselves with. Lainie held her gun awkwardly, feeling pretentious carrying it. Could she be a better shot this time around than she'd proven to be up to this point? Could she bring herself to fire it at all?

The next item of preparation was the thing put together from purchases both at the sports store and the hardware outlet, and it was that thing that truly needed to be handled like it was full of rocks and eggs. As Simi and Brandt helped Faisal put the vest on Lainie stood back and stared in unblinking horror.

"Ironic, isn't it" Lainie said, "a suicide bomber's vest."

It consisted of a leather duck-hunting vest covered in pockets. Having spent most of the prior day following instructions from Brandt, working outside under threat of asphyxiation by extreme fumes, wearing overalls, goggles, gloves and surgical masks, Lainie, Simi and Faisal purified copious amounts of generic brand aspirin with sulfuric acid. Combining other household chemicals, they finally backed carefully away hours later from a picnic table laid out with twelve bricks of homemade C4 the size of decks of cards.

Brandt told them it was relatively stable, really only set off by an ignition source. Still, the three others handled the bricks like they were made of fine crystal. They placed these blocks of volatile explosive into the twelve pockets of the vest, front and back, and Brandt himself sewed the pockets closed. Brandt and Faisal worked on the vest together, adding detonators and a firing mechanism. The trigger was a simple hand-held button on a cord. It was rigged as what Brandt told them was called a Dead Man's Switch - pressing the button armed the detonator.

Releasing the button would detonate the vest.

*   *   *

Now, huddled in a speedboat under a tarp beached by the shore of the mountain lake, Lainie, Simi, and Brandt peered at the frail-looking but deadly old man through a lingering mist and awaited the arrival of the extremists. The rain had lost most of its original enthusiasm and now just fell straight down, as if bored with theatrics and simply dropping limply to the ground.

In the weird acoustics of foggy weather, they heard the engines of the coming vehicles whole minutes before the first black SUV loomed out of the gray curtain. It leapt up over the low ridge surrounding the lake and came to rest, headlights leering down at them out of the mist like menace. Others leapt up around it and stopped as well, five in all. Lainie felt her clammy skin turn to ice.

As if by silent command, all but the lead vehicle descended the hump and arranged themselves in a semicircle outside the compound fence, then the lead vehicle came last and took it's place in the center as the silhouettes of armed men climbed out of the SUV's and took up positions along the chain link. Sayed got out of the passenger side of the lead vehicle, Lainie recognized the arrogant, cocky way he carried himself as he moved.

She also recognized Ibrahim and Uncle Stan, supporting an obviously shaken Aunt Fatimah between them. Lainie heard Simi issue a sigh of relief that they were alive and silently concurred. The three looked uncertain and frightened, cowed by the many guns around them, but otherwise uninjured.

Lainie counted almost twenty of the enemy. So many, she thought, and shook her head. Clearly they were taking no chances against possible ambush.

Finding the gate open, the thugs lead their captives among them and entered the compound. They were cautious, checking corners before they crossed gaps between the shacks and keeping the prisoners in their midst as protection. They had spotted Faisal at the foot of the dock and were making toward him.

When they were close enough for Lainie to make out the expressions on their faces, Faisal opened his coat and the mob froze. Each of them recognized the vest for what it was. They evinced no fear, just normal, human caution in the face of immanent threat. Several guns had already been leveled at Faisal, and none wavered now.

Sayed stepped forward with a sneer on his face that was a curious combination of wry irritation. His head and neck were wrapped in bandages, and where his face showed there were signs of angry first- and second-degree burns. His beard had been partially singed away.

"Hello, Uncle," he said. "You've been away far too long. You've been missed. You've had your little adventure. Time to come home, now."

"Keep your distance," Faisal said, his ancient voice sounding frail and timid above the patter of the rain.

"Where are Simi and that American – " The last word Sayed used to indicate Lainie was said in Arabic, but said with venom. "What was that," Lainie whispered, "what did he call me?"

Simi refused to answer, and when Lainie looked at Brandt all he would say was, "It's not a term of endearment."

"This is no place for women," Faisal said.

Sayed nodded. "There's no need for these dramatics," he said. "I'm a man of my word. You come with us, peacefully, and we release your family."

"Let them go now," Faisal said. "Let them get into the boat."

Sayed looked at the boat as if seeing it for the first time. "Shall I have it searched first?"

"Quit wasting time," Faisal rasped. The rasp broke off into a coughing fit that wracked the old man's entire body. Sayed took a step forward and, still coughing, Faisal raised the trigger for the vest high over his head. Lainie noticed that he had pressed the button, arming the vest. Sayed backed away a step and they waited until the coughing fit receded.

"Shit," Lainie said. "He's armed the vest. That wasn't part of the plan. He was only supposed to threaten them with it."

Again neither of her companions would answer her, and she realized that her understanding of the plan had been a naïve one. Faisal was, indeed, prepared to blow himself and the terrorists up to save his family.

"You see, Uncle," Sayed cooed. "This damp weather is not good for your health. You must come with us. You'll be safe, well looked after."

"You need me alive," Faisal said when he recovered. "Let them get into the boat, or we all meet Allah today."

"Then we meet Allah," Sayed said, opening his arms expansively. "My soul is prepared, old man. Is yours?"

"Fine, then," Faisal said. "Let it be so. Then no one shall have the plans. Let your last act on Earth be to fail your so-called holy calling."

Sayed's sneer faded to a scowl. Finally, he nodded to the men over his shoulder. Ibrahim and his Aunt and Uncle moved forward, tentatively at first, then with more alacrity. Brandt emerged from hiding, as planned, to go meet them and lead them back to the boat. Sayed and his men watched Brandt without surprise, but also without much recognition. Lainie realized it was entirely possible none of them had ever seen him, that their cell was based here in the US, that it was a whole other cell in Paris that had been watching Faisal there.

Ibrahim, Fatimah, and Stan crossed toward where Faisal stood.

"Don't get between me and them," Lainie heard Faisal say to his relatives as they neared him. "Are you fine? No, don't touch me. There will be time for reunions later. Get into the boat. Follow Sean, he will show you."

Brandt led them up the pier to the boat. Stan got in first, then he and Ibrahim helped Fatimah down.

"Are you there?" Ibrahim whispered.

"Yes," Simi answered from under the tarp.

Lainie and Simi slid the guns that they had bought out from under the tarp. As hoped, the terrorists' attention were on Faisal as Stan and Ibrahim armed themselves. Brandt remained on the dock. "Start the boat," he said.

"Get in," Simi said.

Brandt bent and tried to pull the cord on the outboard. The engine whined but didn't start. It was rather cold.

"The choke," Stan said, leaning over to pull the plunger out. "Try again."

"Get in," Simi said, no longer whispering. Lainie tried and failed to hold the girl from rising up and revealing herself to Sayed.

Brandt tried again. Nothing. He stopped, breathing hard and blinking as if in pain.

"What are they doing?" Sayed demanded. "Who else is in the boat?"

"They are starting the engine," Faisal said. "They are preparing it to leave. You see, I am not going with you, Sayed."

Sayed and his men started forward and Faisal raised the trigger over his head again to stop them.

"That was not our agreement," Sayed protested angrily.

"Please," Faisal wheezed sarcastically. "Spare me your injured feelings, as if you would have kept your end. You would have shot my family dead as soon as I turned myself over to you."

"What's to stop me from doing so now?" Sayed pointed at the boat.

The barrels of seventeen guns all swiveled to the boat and the three visible occupants looked back, eyes wide in shock and fear, there own weapons still kept hidden.

"Is this a detonator I have in my hand," Faisal said, "or is it a desert flower?"

Lainie knew that the critical part of their plan had come, but Faisal had kept them all out of this part of it. He had no intention of coming with them. He had every intention of detonating the vest after his family was well away on the boat.

"Don't let him do this," she said to Brandt. "He can still join you on the boat and you can all speed away to the far side of the lake."

Brandt looked at her and she saw the realization dawn on his face as well. He spun to look at the old man. "Uh oh," he said.

"What?" Simi asked.

Brandt was now standing and watching the proceedings, his professional eyes darting from the group of terrorists to Faisal and back. "We got a problem," he said.

"Yes," Simi agreed, "I know. Rain may have gotten into the fuel line."

"Not just that," Lainie said. "Look." She pointed and Simi looked.

Sayed had his own gun raised and he was advancing on Faisal, shouting now. "All of you will die, here and now."

"Sean," Simi shouted, rising up out of the tarp into full view. "Don't."

Lainie saw that Brandt had abandoned trying to start the boat. Instead, he'd drawn his gun and was advancing on Sayed as fast as the terrorist captain was advancing on Faisal.

Sayed stopped within five paces of Faisal and leveled his gun at the old scientist's head. "You are traitors to Allah," he shouted, enraged. "All of you."

The blast of his gun was magnified by the rain and the flash cut blindingly through the fog.

CHAPTER 42

For a moment the tableau froze. Seventeen killers stood with their guns trained on four people in the boat, two of which had only just appeared from under a greasy tarp. Those four in the boat stood in horror, staring at the eighteenth killer, their captain, whose gun even now steamed from the rain that landed on the hot steal of the weapon. An old man, the firearm's erstwhile target, crouched at the foot of the dock with a hand thrown over his face for protection, the other hand clutching the button that could detonate his vest if he released it, killing them all.

In front of him stood the old man's friend where he had leapt the moment the terrorist captain's gun was fired, his own gun falling from a grasp gone suddenly limp, his face turning up to the deluging sky as if in supplication to the heavens. His knees buckled and he fell back against the old man, who struggled to catch him, but eventually fell back himself under the weight of the dead man.

"Sean, no," Simi screamed from next to Lainie. Lainie could see that Faisal was screaming something as well, but she couldn't hear him, because suddenly Simi was firing over and over again, leaping up onto the dock and charging down on her cousin.

At first, Sayed didn't move, as if mortified himself by

what he'd done, then turned to look at Simi as if she were a ghost emerging from out of the eldritch fog to damn him for the murder of her inchoate love. The terrorists around him were firing now, too, but also retreating in momentary shock at the sight of the beautiful, bereft girl running at them and shooting.

"C'mon," Uncle Stan shouted, jumping to the dock and firing his own gun to back Simi up, only glancing back briefly to be sure that Aunt Fatimah got down into the boat and took cover.

Lainie followed suit, just half a beat behind him. Her own gun jumped in her hands as she fired it over and over again, at first counting her shots but then eventually losing count. She saw some of the terrorists go down under Simi's and Uncle Stan's sudden onslaught, not fooling herself into thinking any of her bullets had landed yet. She also knew they were outnumbered, that the terrorists would rally very soon now and lay waste to them all.

It was gratifying, however, to see Sayed turn tail and sprint away from Simi as if she held his own death in her hands.

"Kill them," she heard the cell captain shout as he ran past his band. "Kill them all."

The terrorists began to return fire in earnest just as Uncle Stan reached Simi and tackled her, bringing her to the ground and probably saving her life. Ibrahim knelt on the dock firing, covering his aunt who hid in the boat.

Lainie went down on her belly on the drenched dock right next to where Faisal had fallen under the weight of his dead friend. Crawling over, Lainie helped pull the corpse of the assassin Sean Brandt off the old man, who still clung to the trigger button desperately.

Faisal was crying, clawing at the body of his friend, saying something in Arabic that Lainie didn't understand. He cast about him and Lainie followed his gaze. Stan and Simi had reached cover behind one of the first of the fishing shacks, but were pinned down now. For the moment the terrorists were dealing with that immediate threat, ignoring Lainie and Faisal.

Sayed was nowhere to be seen.

"I cannot go on," Faisal said. "My leg."

Lainie looked at the elderly scientist's right leg and saw that it was twisted at an impossible angle, broken at the knee when Brandt's body had been thrown against him by the gunshot.

"Stay here," she said. "Better yet, try to make it to the boat if you can. Fatimah's there. Try to start the boat. We're going to need a fast way out of here."

"Where are you going?"

"You're kidding, right?" She nodded forward.

"You're a brave American, Lainie," Faisal managed through his tears. "Allah will bless. Thank you."

"We're not on Allah's doorstep just yet, Faisal," she said. "Now go."

In a crouch, Lainie rushed forward. As an afterthought she skidded to a stop and landed on her rump before crab-walking backwards to Faisal once again.

"Give me the vest," she ordered.

"What?"

"Give it to me," she said again, struggling with the buckles herself to release it from his chest. Faisal managed to squirm out of the thing and Lainie slipped her gun-hand through the sleeve holes, holding it one-armed, like a purse.

"I can't..." Faisal proffered the hand holding the detonation button on its cord. If he released it...*kaboom*.

Lainie took his hand to steady it. "Carefully, now," she said, trembling herself. The gunfight raged around them as Lainie carefully used her thumb to slide Faisal's aside, replacing his with hers, so that now she was holding the trigger instead of him.

"What are you going to do with it?" he asked her.

"I don't know," she said. "Yet. Now go."

She crouched and crept forward again, vest draped over her right arm, the hand of which also held her gun, left hand gripping the cord, thumb white as it compressed the button as hard as she could manage. She made her way toward the shacks where the terrorists were working their way around to surround Simi and Uncle Stan.

She stopped for a moment and glanced back to make sure Faisal was making progress toward the boat. He had only dragged himself two feet, and he had made such little progress because in spite of his broken leg he was dragging the corpse of Sean Brandt behind him along the wet planks of the dock.

"Oh, Faisal," Lainie murmured miserably to herself. "Leave him, he's dead."

Shaking her head, she moved forward again.

Simi and Stan were pinned down and slowly getting boxed in. Lainie needed to draw fire away from them. Instead of running to them, she veered to the right along the perimeter of the compound just inside the fence, keeping the cluster of shacks between her and Sayed's men.

Having made almost a quarter of the circuit around, she then ventured into the makeshift little shanty town. Each shack was made of wood and sat on runners like a sled. Some were larger than others, some quite elaborate with shingles and vinyl siding and generators mounted to the outside while others were very plain, just a frame and wooden slats. At least a couple were little more than rafts, with no walls.

Lainie picked a shack somewhere near the center, trying to move quickly. She picked it because as nondescript as it was, the door was painted with a beautiful scene, turned on its side, of ducks flying over a mountain lake with reeds and sword grass and Lilly pads, and the words Donaldson Whiskey over the top. She tried the door, which had clearly once been the lid to a large shipping crate, and found it unlocked, held closed by a rather stiff hydraulic mechanism like a screen door. Inside were benches, shelves, some discarded refuse. She propped the vest just inside the door, then backed out.

She didn't know if the hydraulic cylinder at the top of the door held firm enough to keep the button compressed, and no time to find out. This was the best thing she could think of, and if she was wrong, it would all be over now. She lay the trigger so that it rested on the threshold and was trapped in the jamb. Pushing the door hard, nearly crushing her thumb, she slipped the digit out and winced.

Nothing.

She slowly let go of the door.

It held.

Breathing again, she turned away from the shack and fired her gun into the air. She heard a minor change in the timber of the shouts that came from the direction of the dock and hoped it meant they were coming for her, toward her makeshift booby-trap. She advanced toward them and fired a few more shots into the air. The shouts came again. They were definitely coming her direction. How many, she couldn't tell, but they were coming. Hopefully enough to take the pressure off of Simi and Stan and give them time to escape.

She ducked into another shack between the oncoming terrorists and the one she had booby-trapped. Propping the door open just a crack with her toe, she waited for one of them to show themselves. The rain rapped on the roof of the shack like native drums. A single drop drizzled down her nose, hanging from the tip precariously.

Then just like that, one of the terrorists stood within view. He was being cautious, but hadn't spotted her. From the way he looked back occasionally she knew there were others behind him. Aiming carefully down the sight of the gun she held, Lainie pulled the trigger slowly. When the gun went off the recoil bounced off her nose and she cried out.

She'd missed the man and he had sprung back, but there was shouting and she knew they were alert to her now. Counting to five, she popped out of the shack, making sure they saw her do so, and fired several shots at them without aiming. Shots were returned as she ducked around the shack and headed back the way she had come.

With more of the shacks between them, Lainie didn't doubt they were in pursuit of her now. As she passed, she opened and slammed the door of the shack just to the right of the one with the vest in it, then she ran on. It was her hope that, on hearing the door slam, they would begin searching the shacks for her, that they would eventually open the booby-trapped one.

Now she needed to put as much distance between herself and that shack as she could. She had no idea what the blast radius of C4 was, much less homemade plastique, but she didn't intend to cut it close by any margin whatsoever. Reaching the perimeter again she paused, deciding on her next course of action.

She could make her way back to the boat where Fatimah, Ibrahim, and, hopefully, Faisal huddled, waiting for it all to be over, one way or the other. However, if spotted, she could draw the attention of the terrorists that way, and right now they were being kept busy elsewhere.

Then her memory gave her a jolt. There was one last element to the plan that had yet to be triggered. She pulled out the prepaid cell phone Brandt had given her for just this purpose and dialed carefully.

"Steele," the answer came.

This call was to have been made from the boat, just after leaving the terrorists at the doc, after which she was to have thrown the phone onto the shore to be traced.

"Lainie," came Steele's angry voice over the phone. "Where the hell are you? I have a hundred men staged at this house with helicopters on standby at the airport, like you said. You better have a destination for us."

"Hi," she said. "Can't talk long. The plan has fallen apart. I'll leave this line open. Triangulate on it and come guns blazing. We're getting killed out here."

"Do you have any idea how long it will take us to set up and triangulate..." Steele started.

"Who are you fooling," she snapped. "You started that as soon as this call went through. I'm not playing around, Cord, listen..."

She held the phone up so that he could hear the gunshots. When she put it back to her ear he was demanding, "...Christ, Lainie, are you all right?"

"I am," she said, "but I don't know how much longer the others will stand up. You have to get here, soon."

"Where..."

"Just come," she said, then pushed the phone under the raised floor of the shack she leaned against without hanging up, to keep it out of the rain.

"I give the plan a one in four chance," Brandt had said last night before they'd all retired. "Let's not fool ourselves. There's a three in four chance it'll just come down to a shootout. In which case we'll all die, sooner or later."

He'd been right, Lainie reflected. But no one had been deterred then, and she, at least, was not prepared to give up yet.

Her new plan was to make her way to where the vehicles were parked. There might be spare guns, ammo, grenades like at the compound in New Jersey. Failing all else there was gasoline in the gas tanks.

She ran along the fence in the opposite direction of the shore, around toward the gate in the fence and the makeshift parking lot beyond it. It was strange for her to think that Sean Brandt was dead. She'd thought so once before but he'd turned up alive, and somehow she'd begun to think of him as indestructible, too good a spy to be caught much less killed. Yet killed he had been, throwing himself in front of a bullet to save Faisal's life.

"There's your redemption," she thought. "Maybe it isn't enough to get forgiveness for everyone you, yourself, killed, but it ought to count for something."

Would Sayed have placed a sentry at the compound entrance? She hefted her gun and wondered how many shots were left in the magazine. She had a spare magazine in the pocket of her jeans but decided to wait to reload and hoped she was right to do so.

Having run a good distance she paused to listen, determine how the fight was going. She was upset that she hadn't heard the expected explosion. Could they have been so stupid as to have missed the shack with the vest in it? Had

Brandt's recipe for homemade C4 been a dud? Maybe they had the shack surrounded, thinking she was inside, and were awaiting further instructions from Sayed. Which reminded her, where had the terrorist captain fled to when the shooting started?

There was ongoing gunfire, sporadic now, and shouted communication between hidden factions. Shooting was good, it meant that Simi and Stan hadn't been taken yet. She hoped Faisal, Ibrahim, and Fatimah were keeping their heads down, as well. Lainie vacillated between going on toward the vehicles and going back to the shack with the ducks on the door to see why no one had tripped the bomb yet.

She resumed running toward the SUVs, which were just in view ahead. Reaching the breach in the fence, she slipped through, glancing back to be sure no one was watching. Gunfire peppered the fog, but none in her direction. She ran to the lead vehicle, the door of which still hung open, the engine running.

She stiffened. Now was no time to doubt one's instincts. Lainie was certain she'd heard the briefest hiss of static, cut short, behind her. Someone with a radio was standing behind one of the other vehicles nearby. She thought she might know who it was. Without turning, she listened closely and heard the squash of boots in mud. Someone was creeping up on her from behind.

She jumped into the truck and slammed the door. Out of the corner of her eye, in the side view mirror, Sayed was sidling up along the sleek black flank of the SUV toward her door. Casting around, she spotted a cell phone in a holder mounted to the center console, picked it up and pretended to dial.

"Agent Steele," she said out loud to dead air. Not looking directly at the mirror, her peripheral vision told her that Sayed had stopped, listening. She didn't have to fake the quaver of terror in her voice. But now, for the first time in this affair, this ruse called for a skill Lainie had perfected over many years – she was one of Capri Entertainment's top telephone actresses.

"I need your help. I'm in Fargo, North Dakota and Sayed is here with his men. I've found Dr. Al-Sehremni. No, he's safe for now. I know you're all the way in Maryland, damn it, do you think I'm an idiot? Don't you have someone out here you can call? Yes, I've hidden the doctor where no one will find him. Well, if you must know, he's in an ice-fishing shack, under the trap door. Even if they search it they'll never think to look for him down there, but there's more room to hide down there than it seems. Why do you need to know that? Okay, it's the one with a painting of ducks flying over a lake on the door. Yes."

Lainie thought Sayed might run off right then, thinking to take Faisal and blow himself up instead, but unexpectedly the truck door popped open and he grabbed her arm and wrenched her out of the seat, sending her sprawling into the sandy mud. She maintained the presence of mind to throw the cell phone away as she fell, but Sayed followed-up with a well swung boot and the hand holding her gun stung with the impact, letting the gun fly, as well.

He came down on her chest with his knee, letting his full weight crush her into the mud. Rain blurred her vision and tried to get into her mouth and nose even as she struggled to regain her breath. She was gagging and coughing and bright spots were dancing in front of her eyes.

Someone was saying something urgently from a great distance, behind the roaring in her ears. She realized it was Sayed, not that far away after all, shouting directions into a two-way in his native tongue. He was telling them where to find Faisal, she was certain, about the shack with the ducks painted on the door.

Quite suddenly the weight was gone. Something else was happening, angry grunts and commotion. Someone trod cruelly on her thigh and Lainie cried out, sitting up, struggling to clear her eyes of rain and tears. Someone was attacking Sayed, spinning and swirling like a dervish, kicking and punching him repeatedly, hammering him relentlessly. She only knew one person to use that pirouetting style of combat.

Lainie shook her vision clear and watched Sayed go down in a splash of muddy rainwater, panting and grunting in pain. Simi stood over him, one boot planted in his chest, screaming at him in her own language. Lainie didn't understand what was being said, but she heard Sean Brandt's name more than once. Simi's dark hair hung down from her beautiful face in ropey strands and splashed water down onto his prone form as she screamed at him.

Suddenly she stepped off of him, turned her back and took a step away. Sayed gasped for breath, then raised the gun he still held and tried to level it at his young cousin. Lainie would have cried out a warning, but something made her stop.

Simi had turned her back but her head was down and light glinted from one visible eye. She was watching Sayed from under that curtain of drenched hair, over her shoulder. She deliberately waited for him to act first. As he lifted his gun to shoot her she spun one last time, simultaneously dropping into a crouch, her own gun raised and steady.

The shot from Sayed's gun flew harmlessly into the mist, but it was echoed by the single shot from Simi's gun, the bullet of which drove his skull back forcefully into the mud once again. A single hole in his forehead just above his right eye drizzled blackish blood. He didn't move again.

CHAPTER 43

"Come," Simi said. "We must save father." Without a second glance at what she'd done, Simi ran off into the fog.

Lainie sidled away from Sayed's corpse before standing. She cast about for her own gun and couldn't spot it. Pausing only briefly, she reached down and tugged Sayed's gun out of his dead grasp. Only then did it register on her what Simi had said.

If Simi'd overheard Sayed speaking into his radio, giving his men directions to where to find Faisal...

"Simi," she called. "Wait, Simi. He isn't there. It's a trap."

Lainie ran into the fog after Simi. The rain was beginning to let up, but if anything the fog was deepening. Huddled shacks of various size and shape sprung up around her as if from nowhere, like a forest of stumpy trees, and very quickly Lainie was lost. She didn't dare call out to Simi again for fear of drawing the wrong sort of attention.

The gunfire only reverberated through the mist occasionally now. Simi had been alone. Did that mean Stan was dead? Lainie shook her head to clear the thought. She knew her only hope was to find Simi before the girl stumbled upon the booby-trapped shack. She turned in place, utterly lost. Cursing to herself, Lainie picked a direction and moved forward at a crouch, trying to look all directions at once.

Weaving randomly among the shacks as they loomed up in front of her, Lainie literally stumbled upon Uncle Stan. Her toe hooked something that she thought at first was a root or something sticking up out of the mud and she fell forward. A man cried out and she spun on him, her gun leveled at his head, as his was leveled at hers.

"Lainie," Stan said in relief, lowering his gun again.

"Uncle Stan," she whispered, crouching next to where he sat. "What the hell are you doing here? You should be on the boat."

"Got shot," he croaked, "lost Simi in the rain." He looked pale and drawn, his eyes sunk into darkened sockets. He was breathing hard and clutching his abdomen.

"It's my side," Stan said, indicating the large bloodstain in the khaki of his shirt on the right side. She strained her eyes in the dimness and saw the wad of blood-soaked cloth he held there to staunch the bleeding. It was his outstretched leg that she'd tripped over. "Simi didn't see me get hit, ran on without me. Have you seen her? Is she all right?"

"She's fine. She killed Sayed."

"Good for her," Stan said, then winced at the pain of his bullet wound. "And the rest?"

"Brandt's dead. Faisal, Ibrahim, and Fatimah were hiding in the boat last I saw. Can you move?"

Stan slammed his arm into Lainie's chest, knocking her rudely against the wall of the shack against which he'd propped himself. His gun barked. A dark-clad figure toppled stiffly, face-first into the mud nearby like a felled tree. Lainie hadn't even seen him.

"Nice shot," she said, rubbing her chest.

"Thanks," he said without a hint of irony. "Haven't fired a gun in twenty years. Nice to know I still have the chops. To answer your question, I can try to move. Why?"

"Try to make it to the boat, if you can. It's our only escape. As soon as I find Simi that's where we're headed."

"I'll try," he huffed. "But don't wait. If you get there before me, go."

Lainie decided not to argue, only nodded. "Be careful."

"You too," Stan said, hoisting himself to stand against the wall with his free hand, moaning miserably.

Lainie left the older man and ventured out into the fog once more. She tried to follow the direction of the occasional gunshots she heard, but it was impossible to tell in the strangeness of this mist which direction any sound came from.

She heard murmuring from somewhere. Stopping, she strained her ears, picked the direction it seemed to be coming from, then went the opposite direction. She needed to find Simi, not stumble headfirst into the terrorists. But in the inexplicable acoustics of fog she found the same murmurs began to grow ahead of her as she went. Stopping, she sighed, exasperated.

She crept forward more. There was a group of them. She could barely see them in the mist. They were gathered around one of the shacks. On the door, dimly in the fog she could just make out the mural of ducks soaring over a mountain lake. The words Donaldson Whiskey were even more visible. They had surrounded the shack, guns trained. One of them was calling into his radio.

They wanted to know where the hell Sayed was, Lainie was certain. Why wasn't he answering their calls to him on the radio, they were wondering. Were they to wait for him to come or move in and take Faisal themselves?

A movement to her left caught Lainie's eye and she looked. Simi, crouched in the dim light, was a distance away and making her way toward the group of men gathered around the booby-trapped ice-fishing shack. Where Lainie could only guess at what they were saying, Simi would hear it quite clearly and know that this was the shack in which they thought Faisal hid, thanks to Lainie's ruse.

Lainie couldn't call out a warning to her friend without drawing attention. Once more, she reminded herself that she did not know what the blast radius would be, but she knew that the closer Simi got the more danger she was in. Lainie looked from the gathered terrorists to Simi and back again.

Lainie dropped to the mud, on her belly. Propping her elbows into the rain-sodden ground, she peered down the barrel of Sayed's gun. She'd fired more guns since this entire ordeal had begun than ever before in her entire life. Once in Ibrahim's and Simi's van, what had only been meant as a warning shot, again from Cord's convertible pursued by motorcycle-mounted terrorists, where she had failed to hit a single target at which she had pointed the weapon, and once this morning, another critical miss. But she put such thoughts out of her mind and took careful aim.

Trying to ignore the urgency, the sheer panic that made her heart hammer in her chest like the striker of a fire bell, she closed one eye, held her breath and slowly pulled the trigger. Several things could potentially go wrong with this shot, not the least of which her poor marksmanship. She may misjudge just where inside the shack that the vest was propped, the bullet may fail to penetrate the plank-wall of the shack, or the bullet may penetrate through the lumber, strike the vest and still pass through the fabric without hitting any of the twelve bricks of explosives sewn into the pockets.

The hammer fell.

A blast lifted Lainie up off her belly and flopped her onto her back and into a hollow filled with muddy rain. She sputtered and screamed, her own cries sounding muffled in her ringing ears. The explosion stunned her. It didn't rumble like thunder or boom like such explosions in the movies. It had been sudden...and sharp...like the world's largest door slammed as hard as possible. She didn't even remember the sound of her gun as it fired.

She looked around her, at first afraid that she was blind before she realized it was her own hair plastered to her face. Shaking her head she peered forward. The mist swirled violently, backlit by an angry reddish-orange glow, and from a break in the fog a black plume of smoke rolled toward her.

Scrambling to her feet, she ran to where she'd last seen Simi, carelessly calling out the other woman's name. Simi wasn't where she'd last crouched, but nearby one of the shacks lay on its side, one wall splintered inward. Lainie spotted Simi struggling to extricate herself from the wreckage, having been thrown through the clapboard wall by the blast. Lainie ran to Simi and helped her out of the rubble.

"Father," Simi sobbed openly, peering back in the direction of the explosion.

"He's safe," Lainie said, scanning Simi for serious injury.

"But he was in..."

A shard of wood the size of an ice pick protruded from Simi's left bicep.

"No he wasn't," Lainie said. She grabbed the splinter and, refusing to stop long enough to flinch away from what she was doing, yanked it free.

"But the explosion, his vest..." Simi hadn't felt a thing, nor did she react as Lainie tore the girl's sleeve and wrapped it around her arm, tying it into a tourniquet.

"He's safely in the boat with Fatimah," Lainie said as she worked. "I'll explain later. Which way to the boat?" Lainie trusted someone else's sense of direction, anyone else's, to her own.

"That way," Simi said confidently, "down the slope."

As she pointed the air around them began to thrum rhythmically, the mist took to swirling violently around them and a growing downdraft threatened to press them back into the ground.

"What now?" Lainie shot angrily.

"Helicopters," Simi said, blinking up into the overcast sky. "You managed to call Agent Steele, didn't you?"

In the distance they watched three or four lines etch themselves out of nowhere in mid air, and shortly bulky shapes slid down them, men dressed in riot gear, wearing helmets and goggles, armed with submachine guns.

"Cord," Lainie breathed in relief, "of course. We have

to get to the boat. You and your father and your brother have to get away."

Holding hands the two women sprinted, Lainie following Simi's lead. Gunshots resounded around them again as the fog began to blend with smoke and the crackling of flame could be heard between the staccato blast of bullets. They dodged away when the conflict seemed to draw near, but Simi kept them confidently on track back toward the dock.

At one point Simi nearly steered them away again as another shape loomed out of the mist to their right, but something about the figure made Lainie pull back. One man shambled blindly, alone, gibbering to himself, headed in the wrong direction.

"Uncle Stan," Simi cried out. Simi and Lainie each took one of the injured man's arms, supporting him as the two women hurried as fast as the man could go.

The three stumbled into the shallow surf at the shore of the lake, but Lainie pulled them up short before pitching headlong into the water.

"This way," Simi said, steering them to the left.

The dock loomed out of the smoke and mist, and beside it bobbed the speedboat. Faisal, Ibrahim, and Fatimah sat upright, each holding guns out before them in two-handed grips. All three guns came to bear briefly on the stumbling group, then Fatimah called out her husband's name and the woman ran to help her niece and Lainie carry him forward.

"Get in," Ibrahim said, pushing Simi toward the boat.

Simi did as she was told. She knelt by Brandt's body on the floor of the boat and briefly brushed his face with her hand. Clearly Faisal had managed to drag the body all of the way back to the boat with him. Lainie saw that the bottom of the boot was a-swamp with blood and Brandt's skin was already taking on a bluish hue, his eyes glassy and lifeless.

"You too, Lainie," Simi called, turning back to the shore. "Get in the boat."

Lainie shook her head and broke free of Ibrahim, who was trying to draw her toward the boat. "I'm done running."

"We can't stay," Faisal said.

"Go," Lainie said. "Send me a postcard."

Simi jumped from the boat, rushed forward and clenched Lainie in an embrace that nearly winded her, but Lainie tolerated it and laughed, though her eyes were burning, becoming moist. She returned the hug.

"Go with Allah," Simi said. "We will meet again, Lainie Parker. I promise."

"Take care of your father," Lainie said.

Simi let go, peered earnestly into Lainie's eyes, then turned and leapt back onto the boat.

To her surprise, Faisal reached out from the bow of the boat and took her hand. She could hear his breath wheezing as he fought back tears. He whispered, "You are the bravest women I have ever met, Lainie Parker. No exceptions. I am sorry we had to meet under such circumstances. I'm sorry, and also not sorry. You saved my Simi's life, and my son and the others, too. We will never forget you."

Then the old scientist let her go and turned abruptly, lowering himself into the boat gingerly. Ibrahim bent to start the outboard engine, and again it merely puffed and did nothing.

"Let me," Lainie said. She pulled hard on the engine cord and the motor burped and turned over, roared to life. Ibrahim kept it alive by turning the throttle-handle briefly. The rattle of the motor could barely be heard over the incessant *thwop-thwop-thwop* of rotors overhead, the gunshots still ringing out in the compound behind, and men shouting.

Three remained on shore, Lainie and Stan who leaned heavily on his wife, while the boat slid quickly into the fog and was gone. Simi, under Faisal's arm as much to support him as to gain comfort from his presence, continued to wave until they were beyond sight, and for all Lainie knew she continued to wave well after that.

"Lainie Parker."

Lainie turned. Cord Steele stumped down the slope of the sandy shore toward her. In place of a makeshift crutch now he supported himself on the right side with a cane, but he still hobbled badly. He came so quickly toward her Lainie thought he'd pitch forward at her feet. He surprised her by bowling into her and clasping her into a hard and urgent embrace.

She hugged him back, if a bit uncertainly.

When he pulled back his striking blue eyes pierced the mist as he scanned her up and down. "Are you all right?"

"None the worse for wear," she said ruefully.

His expression turned from concern to anger without transition. "Goddamnit girl." He looked as if he wanted to take her over his knee and spank her good. "I ought to lock you away for the rest of your life."

"I expect nothing less," Lainie said.

He sighed angrily. "Where's Dr. Al-Sehremni?" he demanded, eyeing Uncle Stan doubtfully. "Where are Simi and Ibrahim? Where is Dr. Al Serhemni?"

"I won't tell you," Lainie said, "and in just a few hours, by the time you could get me to an interrogation room or torture chamber or whatever, I won't even know. They'll be long gone."

Steele peered past her out over the fog-shrouded lake. "I could have the area zoned and searched."

"Sayed's dead," Lainie said. "The formula's nowhere to be found, and Dr. Al-Sehremni has sworn to die before he reveals it to either side, theirs or yours."

"Ours," he corrected her.

"Yours," she affirmed pointedly.

"And what about you?" Steele asked, barely concealing his frustration. "What about murder and arson?"

She didn't bother to answer. "I'm tired, Cord, and bruised and sick and tired."

He eyed her and his mouth worked spastically, as if trying on and discarding several curses. Finally, he took off his windbreaker with the letters CIA emblazoned on the back and draped it over Lainie's shoulders. The rain had stopped.

"Come on," he said. "All three of you. We'll get you looked after, then you're going to have a lot of questions to answer."

He put an arm around Lainie's shoulders protectively and led them up the slope toward one of many parked and idling helicopters.

CHAPTER 44

Lainie's keys rattled with comforting familiarity against her palm as she unlocked the door and stepped into her apartment. Knowing what to expect didn't prepare her for actually seeing it when she turned the lights on. The place had been ransacked after she had left in order to find information to track her with, credit card statements and the like.

But it was good to be home. So good in fact that she just stood in the entry way and looked around her for quite some time. Then she set her luggage down and set to straightening the place up.

Lainie never saw Cord Steele again after he dropped Stan, Fatimah, and her at the local FBI offices. He remained taciturn and resentful during the ride. The three had been questioned separately and at length. They had already agreed not to hold anything back. They each told the truth, fully and without reservation, and because of that their stories meshed too perfectly to be lies, and the men from the DHS and the NSA and the FBI all knew it. The facts, that none of them could possibly know where Simi, Ibrahim and their father intended to go next, and that the authorities still believed Sean Brandt dead and had no reason to ask them about him, protected them from any further duress. After forty-eight hours they were released.

Lainie returned to the Guntherson residence where the SUV she and Simi had stolen from the terrorists still sat parked in front. She retrieved her things from the vehicle but declined to drive it back to San Francisco. Lainie used her credit card to rent a car and drive from North Dakota to San Francisco. She had missed her flight when Simi and Ibrahim kidnapped her, but her luggage had been checked and made the flight just as if she'd gone with it. It waited for her in the unclaimed baggage office at the airport.

It took her two hours to get her apartment ship-shape once again, and in that time she already felt herself falling back into routine, feeling the warmth and comfort of home once more. When she checked her voicemail it made her chuckle.

"You have ninety-nine messages. Your mailbox is full. Please delete existing messages in order to make room for new ones."

The first six messages were from Detective Gillis, each more strident than the last, demanding to know where she was and what she was up to. After that she stopped listening and just resorted to deleting. Then she dialed the police station.

"Detective Gillis, please," Lainie said.

"He's not in right now, can I help you?" Another detective, male, younger.

It was two o'clock in the afternoon. Gillis must be working the night shift again.

"Tell him Lainie Parker called. Tell him I'll be turning myself in tomorrow morning, around ten. Thanks."

She hung up and turned to the copious stack of mail that had clogged her mailbox when she arrived. There was only one thing out of the ordinary bills and junk mail. A telegram. She opened it.

It read simply, "Thank you. S, I & F."

*   *   *

Lainie had shrouded herself in her favorite oversized T-shirt and now curled up on the couch with her laptop, checking her email. On a whim she opened a browser and entered the URL for Capri Entertainment, Inc. Unexpectedly, the site responded. It was different, slightly, but it was there. Some stockholders or board of directors had rebounded from the firebombing of the original offices and had the company up and running again in less than two weeks. It was as if nothing had ever happened.

Lainie was hauntingly tempted to call the old number, half expecting to hear Kim's cheerful voice, or Mitch's gruff one. She resisted the urge, knowing that when she didn't hear those voices it would be depressing to her, and she didn't want to be depressed. There was plenty of that on the horizon for her, once she turned herself in, why ask for it sooner than necessary?

She moaned when a knock came at the door. Rising to answer it, she called out angrily, "I'm not going in until tomorrow morning, Gillis. I've earned at least one night's R&R."

"Who's Gillis and how jealous should I be?" came the muffled answer.

"Cord," Lainie cried, struggling with the chain and the locks and flinging the door opened. There he stood in his rakish brown bomber's jacket and sandy hair, crooked smile and disturbingly blue eyes. He held flowers in one hand and a bottle of red wine in the other, but Lainie only had eyes for him.

She threw herself into his arms and held tight, not wanting to let go.

"Gee, happy to see me?" he laughed. "Can I come in?"

"Of course," she said, pulling him in by the hand.

He stumbled a little. "Easy, easy."

"Oh, I'm sorry," she cried. "Your leg. How is it?"

"Not a hundred percent just yet, but I'll recover."

She led him to the couch, apologizing again, took the flowers and wine and carried them into the kitchen.

"Nice place," he said. "Decorate yourself?"

She looked at him as he fingered a spot on the wall

above the couch that she hadn't noticed before. "What's that?"

"Looks like a bullet lodged in the drywall."

The stray bullet that had ricocheted off of the pot when the killer shot at her what seemed like an eternity ago. If Gillis had done more than turn in place in the middle of the room he may have found it back then, at the beginning of it all.

Lainie laughed. She couldn't help herself. She felt giddy and, to be honest, more than a little close to hysteria, a post traumatic stress reaction, she knew.

She placed a vase with the flowers on the bar, then carried two glasses to the living room and sat on the coffee table opposite him. She handed one to him.

"To you," he said.

"To Dr. Al-Sehremni and Simi and Ibrahim, wherever they are," she amended.

His smile faltered.

"I'm sorry," she said again. "That was insensitive of me. You must be really angry with me for helping them disappear."

He shook his head and reasserted his smile. "Forget it. I forgive you. To them." He sipped.

She shot hers down and eyed him challengingly.

He laughed and shot his, too.

"We searched for them, of course," he said as she went to refill the glasses. "Don't worry, we didn't find them. Found the boat, looked in on a cabin that reported a break-in where only food was taken, and a hundred dollar bill was left behind. Checked on another report further up the road of a stolen vehicle, found the vehicle just across the Canadian border. That was it. End of the trail."

Lainie plopped down next to him on the couch this time and handed him his glass. "I'm sorry for you. Glad for them." She wondered what they did with Brandt's body. Her guess was they dropped it in the lake. Burial at sea, she reflected.

She found her hand on his knee, not sure how it got there, not sure she cared. She moved it slowly up, felt the muscles tense, his eyes on her face hot and smoldering. Looking into his eyes, she let her roaming hand find the tip of his growing erection and she scraped a fingernail across the head, the rough fabric vibrating, felt the organ surge in response.

He groaned.

Then they were kissing, his lips strong and powerful against hers, his tongue both intrusive and welcome. At first she couldn't breathe, and then breath came in a series of rapid huffs and gasps that seemed unable to bring enough oxygen to her lungs. They were pawing at each other's clothes.

Naked, intertwined on the couch, she teased him at first, allowing him a mere half-inch of penetration before moving her pelvis away from his. When she finally permitted the full intrusion, he was alternately grunting like an animal and gasping like a man dying of thirst and given his first drink. She let him slake his thirst at will for a while, then forced him on his back and worked at slaking her own.

She came twice, once on top, then again simultaneously with him as he took top position once more. They collapsed together amid the tatters of their own clothing. Gulls screed outside, but no other sound penetrated the silence once Lainie's and Steele's own ragged breathing subsided.

"I had this whole seduction scene planned," he said breathlessly. "Steaks by candlelight, red wine, back here for some crème Brule...and desert. You ruined it."

"Sorry," she said.

"Do you make it a habit to have sex with strange men?"

"The stranger the better."

"Seriously."

"No," she conceded. "It just seemed...I don't know...I mean I wanted to and I couldn't think of a single reason why not to."

"How about now?"

"Still no reason."

"Good," he said, then rolled over and serviced her

again at a much more luxurious pace.

*   *   *

Somewhere between the third and fourth times, they made their way to the bedroom and her bed. The bedclothes got rearranged, entangled, then discarded entirely. Now they lay amongst the wreckage of their lovemaking, and he dozed softly in nothing but boxers while she looked down at his ruggedly handsome face. She'd gotten up long enough to put her robe back on.

Aside from a brief infatuation with Bruce Willis when she was a young girl, Lainie had always fancied herself attracted to more cerebral men, honest, thoughtful men, ethical and philosophical. Cord Steele was gleefully sneaky, obstinately secretive, and coolly violent, everything she despised and detested. So why did she feel such elementary school butterflies when she was with him, even now? Why did she feel an urge to jump him, rip his clothes off, and ravish him? The attraction was entirely physical, and yet how wonderful to just give in and not over-think things as she was usually wont to do.

"How cozy."

The low, rumbling, sarcastic voice froze Lainie's blood in her veins and she leapt from the bed, turning to the door and struggling to pull a sheet up from the floor to cover herself. In the threshold stood the hulking man, Brandt's shooter, Mitch's and Kim's murderer, murderer of an unnamed NSA agent in the VIP lounge at the airport in Baltimore, arsonist of the offices of Capri Entertainment, Inc.

"How did you..."

"I misplaced you for a while," he said. "You stopped using your credit card. So I came back here to wait."

"You've been here the whole time..." she stammered.

"Watching the place," he said.

She looked down at Steele, who slept dreamily on,

completely unaware of the danger. Visions of fire and knives and gushing arterial blood jumbled her thoughts and prevented her from formulating a coherent warning, much less voicing it.

The murderer stepped out of the doorway. He held a shotgun at his side, and it clicked as his large thumb released the safety.

"I waited, patiently. I knew you'd come. Eventually. And you did. You see, I always win."

He came forward to the opposite side of the bed and grinned down at her, his eyes gleaming wetly with lust for the kill. Lainie had fought terrorists, unprincipled murderers every last one of them, but somehow this apparition struck her dumb in ways neither Sayed nor any of his men ever did. The terrorists killed with passion. Granted it was mad, unreasoning hate, but it was emotion. She'd seen this man kill once, and he did it coldly, without emotion, efficiently. Somehow that impressed her as more terrible.

When Steele moved it was so quick Lainie nearly missed it. As it was, his arm was nothing but a blur as it whipped out and gripped the gun just in front of the trigger guard. Using that as leverage he hoisted himself up and planted a fist directly into the center of the murderer's face.

If Steele expected this to knock the giant backward, he was disappointed. The black man's head snapped back briefly, but then came forward again and centered his hungry gaze on Steele. Steele wasn't waiting for a reaction, but was already ducking under the gun-arm, twisting it around behind, trying to force the murderer to release the weapon.

The intruder grunted, then pulled, muscles bulging through a light blue button-down shirt, and, through sheer force alone, brought the arm back down and around, flinging Steele bodily back onto the bed once more. Lainie saw Steele's eyes widen in shock as he was flung around like a rag-doll. When the giant's sledge-hammer fist connected with Steele's face the agent's entire body was flung over the bed and landed at Lainie's feet.

She bent to help Steele up, but he sprang to his feet again without her aid. He threw himself into Lainie and carried them both down to the floor as the murderer raised the shotgun and fired. The roar was deafening and fluff flew into the air like snow as part of the blast caught the edge of the mattress where they had been standing, atomizing it.

Steele rolled off of Lainie as soon as they landed. Still in his boxers, Steele launched himself at the intruder and they grappled. Steele had his left forearm across his opponent's throat and his hand clamped around the back of his neck, squeezing, choking.

The murderer locked his arms around Steele's torso, his massive left hand clamped on his right wrist, the equally as massive right hand still gripped the shotgun, and he was intermittently squeezing Steele, bringing wheezes and whimpers from Steele's lungs. The murderer's eyes were bulging, and sweat had broken out on his face, attesting to the strain Steele was putting him to.

Meanwhile, Lainie wasn't idle. She ran to Steele's clothing and rummaged for his gun. She didn't find one, but from a small pouch just inside the cuff of his suit jacket she discovered a spring-loaded spool of thin, nearly invisible wire, the snare she'd seen him use so effectively before.

Pulling out a length of the wire, Lainie ran up behind the big man and looped it around his neck above Steele's arm.

"No," Steele protested in a strained, almost inaudible voice.

Lainie pulled on both ends of the wire...and cried out in pain, dropping them. She looked down at her hands where the meat of her fingers had been cut deeply, nearly to the bone. So cleanly and neatly cut that blood had not even begun to appear, yet.

But she had also made the brute drop Steele and twist away from the agent's hold on his throat. The wire left the smallest of weals across his neck from earlobe to earlobe, but certainly not a life threatening wound. He brought the gun up to aim it at Lainie and she dove out of the bedroom door as the blast splintered part of her doorjamb. He chased her, filling the doorway. Steele sprung to the man's back, encircling massive shoulders with arms more ropey than bulging.

"Call the police," Steele croaked.

Lainie dove for her telephone.

"Not here," Steele said, chucking his head toward the apartment door.

The intruder's chest expanded as his lungs filled like a giant bellows. Finally, Steele was forced to let go. Lainie paused halfway to the door when she saw the brute turn on Steele and fling him against the wall. Steele threw himself forward again and his jaw met the butt of the shotgun. Steele staggered, and to his credit shook it off, but the second connection with the hard wooden stock of the gun dropped him summarily.

Lainie screamed and threw herself to the floor as the monster turned and trained the shotgun on her. He pulled the trigger and the hammer clicked on a dry chamber. Cursing, he breached the chamber, empty shells bouncing off his face as they leapt free, and fished in his pocket for more shells. Lainie knew it was her chance, perhaps her only one.

She rose, hoisting one of her oak barstools over her head and threw it at him. He dodged it and batted it aside almost negligently, like King Kong swatting at a biplane, and returned his attention to reloading. Lainie lifted another barstool over her shoulder, holding it by the legs with cut hands coated in her own blood, and charged him, roaring her rage.

She swung the stool and he raised an arm to protect himself. Throwing all her strength and weight into it, the stool struck him a splintering blow, forcing a cry from his lips, knocking him back. He stumbled over Steele's supine form and fell. The shotgun tumbled from his grasp as he fell on his back. Lainie tried to swing the stool again but it slipped free of her bloody grasp, so she dove for the gun.

As the murderer scrambled to his feet Lainie brought the gun up and pointed it at his chest. He froze, looking at her, then smiled and held his hand up, letting two red plastic cartridges fall from his fist to bounce and roll on the carpet. Gritting her teeth in anger Lainie pulled the trigger and nothing happened.

The intruder lunged at her and she turned to run. Her foot came down on something hard and cylindrical that rolled under her step and pitched her forward to the floor, banging her knees and elbows cruelly. She rolled over to see him looming over her, a humorless grin of triumph dominating his face.

"I told you," he said. "I always win."

"Win what," she demanded angrily. "What is there to win? Sayed's dead, his cell are all either dead or in prison, Dr. al-Sehremni has vanished and with him any hope of completing the weapon. You've already lost, don't you get it?"

He was cocking his head at her strangely and he looked for all the world to her like a Rottweiler trying to think up a multiplication table. "What in hell are you talking about?"

"Sayed," she said again. "The terrorists?" Prompting his slow intellect. "Faisal al-Sehremni?"

His face darkened, "Don't talk to me like I'm stupid," he growled. "I'm a damn sight more intelligent than you. I'll bet you haven't won a serious game of chess in your life. I don't know any of those people. I don't know what the fuck you're talking about."

In spite of the danger, Lainie was nonplused. Surely he was toying with her. "You shot Sean Brandt."

"Probably," he said. "Who's that?"

"Michael," she said, using the alias with which Brandt had called Capri Entertainment.

"Ah, yes," he nodded. "The guy in Colorado. The one talking to you on the phone when I put a hole in the back of his neck."

Lainie swallowed. "Yes. You shot him to get the plans."

"What plans?"

"The blueprint," she snapped, growing impatient with his obstinate refusal to make sense. "The schematics. The laser beam...or particle beam, whatever. You shot him to get it."

"Once more, bitch," he growled, "I'll thank you not to talk to me like I'm stupid. Like I said, I don't know what the fuck you're talking about. I killed the mother fucker because I always win."

"What the hell does that even mean," Lainie screeched in terror and frustration.

"It means, no one beats me," he said. "Unless they cheat. I may not spot how they cheated, but if they win, then they had to cheat. I track the mother fuckers down and I blow their mother fuckin' asses away."

"Win what?" Lainie insisted. "You aren't making any sense."

He brought a hand down backwards across her face, hitting her so hard she stumbled, only remaining on her feet by sheer force of will. "I warned you," he said. "I'm talking about chess. No one beats me. I'm the best. So when I play other people online, and they win, I know they cheated."

"Online," she asked, tasting blood. "You mean over the Internet?"

"Yes," he said. "I wrote me a nifty little chess program of my own. It traces their connection and lets me track mother fuckers down anywhere they are. So if they win...if they cheat...I can find them, and kill them. This mother fucker, Michael or whatever, he been beating me online for months, but he's in Paris, and for certain reasons I can't get me a passport - picture, fingerprints. John Q. Law be on my ass before I take another step. The Michael guy pissing me off. Every time we play he wins. Every time we play he cheats."

"How can someone cheat at chess?" Lainie asked, "and in a program you wrote?"

For a moment he seemed confused. "I don't know how they do it." Then his former self-confidence reasserted itself and he leaned down into her face. "But if they win, then they gotta cheat. Because I..."

"You always win," Lainie said. "Yeah, I heard."

"You want another smack?"

She flinched away, but didn't answer.

"Anyway, suddenly, he's in Colorado. I got my chance. I track him down to that motel and I do him. He was the biggest cheater of them all. I never won against him, and I always win."

"But the room was clean when the FBI checked it," she said.

"To win, you can't get caught," he said. "I cover my tracks well."

"But what did you do with his things," she asked.

"I tossed it all into the incinerator at the dog food manufactory."

"His luggage. His computer?"

"Luggage, yes," he said. "But I never waste a good computer. Thing is, he wiped it."

"What?"

"Nothing on it," he said. "Some companies are so protective of their secrets that they put a kind of security on their computers, you don't use the right password to open it, it wipes itself. All data, programs, everything, gone. He must have worked for a company like that."

"So let me get this straight," Lainie said. "You don't have anything to do with the terrorists? With Sayed, or Faisal al-Sehremni? None of it? All this started over a goddamn game of Internet chess? Jesus Christ."

He slapped her again. "I'll thank you not to take the lord our God's name in vain. It may be nothing to you, but it's my self esteem, winning chess. It's all I got." He drew a large knife out of the inside of his jacket and hefted it.

"Now, I have to remove the last witness."

Desperately Lainie looked down at what she'd stumbled over a moment ago and saw her empty laptop carrying case. Her laptop still sat on the end table where she'd left it when Steel came to the door. Even as she wondered what would be still inside the case to trip her up she remembered what it was. She lunged for the case, but he was too quick for her. He snatched a fistful of her hair and lifted her by it, bringing a cry of pain from her as he flung her back to where Steele lay.

"What do we have here?" he asked, bending down and coming up with the case and re-sheathing his knife. He reached inside and drew out the gas canister that had been inside the weapon prototype at the terrorist's encampment. The one Sayed had tried to retrieve after Lainie had wrecked the semi and trailer carrying that prototype into a propane storage tank. The one she had carried with her since and nearly forgotten.

HR3000, Horror Gas.

The brackish, green clouds moved fluidly and sickeningly inside the transparent portion.

His brow furrowed as he looked at it. "What is it?"

He looked at Lainie for an explanation. She was standing now, bringing the shotgun to bear on him once more. At first he seemed unconcerned, the weapon was still unloaded, after all, but as Lainie raised the thing over her head with both hands like a club his eyes widened and he stumbled backward against the windowsill, unable to duck away. He winced and turned his face, raising the canister defensively, but it wasn't his head she was aiming for.

Lainie brought the solid steel barrel of the shotgun down onto the glass center of the canister.

The cylinder cracked and hissed as he was thrown bodily back against her front window. The glass shattered and he teetered over the edge. Green tendrils of gas encircled his head as he see-sawed, legs flailing to regain his balance. But then he clenched his eyes shut tight and bellowed. The lids bulged and blood began to trickle from under them, and from his ears, now, too. Lainie flung herself to the ground by Steele's body and pulled a couch cushion down over them.

She heard a loud snap, presumably the cylinder bursting once and for all, because the murderer's bellow became one of abject agony and faded as he fell out the window. His screaming only stopped with a final thud as he obviously met the pavement.

Lainie rose to her knees and checked Steele's pulse. He was still alive.

She approached the window cautiously. The green tendrils of gas seemed to have dissipated. Looking down, she saw the huge man laying on the sidewalk below, having missed the shrubbery and the lawn. A fall of a mere two stories would not have normally killed him, but a cloud of green gas was even now shredding and fading around him. His body moved as if alive, vibrating and rumbling, bumps and nodules appearing through his flesh, moving and disappearing again. Orange foam bubbled out of his lips and ears and his eyelids hung limp over now empty sockets.

Lainie looked away in disgust.

CHAPTER 45

"So," Detective Gillis said, "mysteriously missing bullet in the wall over there. Perpetrator on the pavement outside looking like maggots been at him for a week. A witness, and from the CIA no less, vouching for you and pulling rank on me, something about the National Secrets Act or some such bullshit. That about cover it, Ms. Parker?"

"I think so," Lainie said.

She sat next to Cord Steele on the couch, holding his hand. They were both dressed, and he was holding an ice pack against a more than respectable shiner beginning to swell almost the entire left side of his face. A paramedic was just finishing wrapping Lainie's hands in gauze. She met Gillis' gaze firmly over the EMT's shoulder.

FBI Special Agent Peck was there, as well, hands clasped behind him, looking around the room with a bored expression. "The bureau's been tracking a serial killer for the last two years, seems to pick his victims from Internet chess games."

"No shit," Gillis observed.

"Huh-uh," Peck responded.

Gillis shrugged and snapped his notepad closed. "No harm no foul," he said.

Lainie's jaw dropped.

"Come on, fellas. Nothing else to see here."

Gillis headed to the door, the three officers that had come with him to inspect the place filing out ahead of him. He left the door open behind him without a backward glance.

"What an asshole," Steele said.

"Say it loud," Lainie agreed.

The EMT and his partner hoisted their gear. "You want to get those wounds looked at by a doctor," he said, and they brushed past Peck on their way out.

"I'm glad everything seems to have worked out for you, Ms. Parker," Peck said. "You're one tough phone-sex girl. I never doubted that it would."

"Thanks," Lainie nodded.

Peck left, following the emergency techs and closed the door.

Lainie leaned over to kiss Steele, but as their lips met he hissed and pulled back.

"I'm sorry," she said.

"So he shot Brandt over a stupid game of chess?" he said. "It had nothing to do with any of the shit that came down last week?"

Lainie nodded and stared off into space.

"Hey," he said.

She snatched her attention back from far away and looked at him. "Hey yourself."

"Want to come work for the CIA?"

Lainie burst into peels of laughter. "No, I don't think so." She was still laughing as he pushed her back, got on top of her and pawed at her clothes.

EPILOGUE

John Ross scanned the files on Lainie Parker's hard drive. The girl was beautiful, he'd give her that, but she sure didn't know how to treat a computer. She'd dropped her laptop last night and shattered the LED screen but good. He'd been able to talk her into an upgrade and now he was transferring all of her data from the old computer to the new one, which she expected to pick up the following day.

But John loved his job, and he thought of the computers his customers brought to him as his patients. Patients whose owners were constantly exposing them to viruses and spyware and all sorts of hazards. So while he transferred data from one computer to the next, John also scanned for anything that didn't belong.

So far he was able to identify all of the bad things Lainie Parker had allowed on her computer, but there was one file he couldn't figure. It appeared to be encrypted. He traced its source and it had come through a channel most viruses didn't come through. He knew Lainie used VOIP, or Voice Over Internet Prototcol, to make telephone connections via the Internet, though he didn't know exactly what she used it for. It appeared as if this strange file had come through there, which was supposed to be technically impossible.

He'd used every tool at his disposal to crack this file and it just wouldn't crack. It was a large file, but data or program, he couldn't tell which. In the end, he was relatively certain it had been put there without her knowledge, and that it didn't belong there. So finally, failing any way to identify it...

...he simply deleted it.

ABOUT THE AUTHOR

Having first been published as a teen, Kevin Paul Tracy has publish countless fiction and non-fiction pieces over the years. He has travelled extensively spanning half the globe and and both sides of the equator, and has held just about every odd job you can think of, from cave spelunking guide to interstate courier. He currently lives in Vail, Colorado with two very charismatic St. Bernards.

You can follow Kevin at:

http://www.KevinPaulTracy.com   http://KevinPaulTracy.Blogspot.com

http://www.Twitter.com/KevinPaulTracy   http://www.Facebook.com/KevinPaulTracyWriter

www.ingramcontent.com/pod-product-compliance
Lightning Source LLC
Chambersburg PA
CBHW070320260626
47160CB00003B/895